THERE
IS A
RIVER

PATRICIA SWEET

DEFIANCE PRESS
& PUBLISHING

THERE IS A RIVER

Copyright © 2024 Patricia Sweet

First Edition: 2024

DEFIANCE PRESS
& PUBLISHING

ISBN-13: 978-1-963102-38-3 (Paperback)
ISBN-13: 978-1-963102-44-4 (eBook)

Published by Defiance Press & Publishing, LLC

Bulk orders of this book may be obtained by contacting Defiance Press & Publishing, LLC. www.defiancepress.com.

Public Relations Dept. – Defiance Press & Publishing, LLC
281-581-9300
pr@defiancepress.com

Defiance Press & Publishing, LLC
281-581-9300
info@defiancepress.com

"There is a river whose streams make glad the city of God."

Psalm 46

PART ONE

POINT OF NO RETURN

CHAPTER ONE

Everyone clapped except for Carly as her husband lowered the pretty divorcée into the river. The elders' wives on the beach joined hands to pray for their newest sister, but Carly stood apart, studying the girl's face. As far as she could tell, the joy there was genuine, no secrets clouding her big blue eyes.

Rick's expression, however, was far more complicated. He took the hand of his first new convert in ages, leading her to shore as if she were a princess and he a prince. While the congregation sang "Amazing Grace," Carly held out her hand to the tall blonde, shivering in the June breeze. If she could only talk to the girl, get to know her a little, the tightness in her chest might release.

Too late. Rick drew her away from the crowd, the two of them locked in private conversation.

The brethren were all smiles as they waited to be dismissed. A few had already drifted from the little patch of sand to the backyard of Carly and Rick's riverfront home. Rick's secretary stood on the patio with a tray of food. From the water's edge, Carly called, "Wait, Keri Ann, I can do that!"

"No need, kid. I've got it. Relax. You look tired."

Carly was tired, but the last time she'd zoned out, she lost track of her five-year-old. Ten minutes later she found him up shore at the state marina, watching a yachter backing his trailer onto the launch pad. Now, the boy had just slipped out of view again. The rest of the church kids were digging moats in the sand, but as usual, little Benny wasn't among them. Carly ran along the waterfront calling his name, her voice raw.

"Carly, if you're looking for Benny, he's inside."

Her heartbeat slowing, Carly thanked her husband's secretary as well as the angel she was convinced had been assigned to protect her little boy.

"No problem. Take it easy—you don't look so good."

Carly tugged at her stained sweatshirt. No, she did not. If there was one person who looked fantastic on that chilly spring day, it was their brand-new sister. She'd come to the event in a tailored pink blouse and tight white jeans, both now dripping wet. *Oh, yeah. Towels.* Something else Carly had forgotten.

Rick lifted the new sister's hand high. "Now, everyone, please make Serena feel welcome!"

The faithful of New Wine Fellowship shouted "Alleluia!" and "Praise the Lord!" in response, but when their backs were turned, he caught this Serena up in a bear hug that lasted a little too long. No—*way* too long.

Those remaining on the beach high-fived each other, celebrating one more soul entering the Kingdom of God. Apparently, none of them had noticed the affection her husband had just lavished on the attractive young woman. Or perhaps, like Carly, they simply wished they hadn't.

Carly looked at the sky. Geese heading toward Canada formed an imperfect *V. What was that psalm about wanting wings to fly?* Twenty years ago, when the idea of living like the Christians in the Book of Acts was new and exciting, Rick hugging some girl who'd thanked him gratuitously for a sermon he'd preached or a word of encouragement he'd given her would have seemed normal. Those days were long gone.

Carly's reminiscence was interrupted when Rick announced to the stragglers on the beach that it was time to eat.

From the patio, where she'd laid out a spread of fancy sandwiches and pie, Keri Ann shouted for Rick. "Pastor, we're waiting for you to say the blessing!"

Rick shot Carly a look. "Are you coming?"

"Maybe later."

"I want you to join us."

"I will—in a minute."

Honestly, Carly just wished they'd all go home. Hanging out with church people had become exhausting. For years, the group of aging Jesus freaks who'd formed the New Wine Fellowship had been growing further and further apart. Rick, of course, attributed this to her overactive imagination. Perhaps. But one thing she had not imagined was all the lost time and money that her husband could never explain.

Rick's movie-star features registered saintly tolerance as he turned his attention from his wife to the elders. Last year, a few of these men had taken him aside to mention that they felt Carly had been acting strangely—detached, depressed. They suggested that she might benefit from professional help.

Her husband had chosen to lay these concerns on her last December, right before Christmas, just as she had finally gotten in the mood to decorate the house.

"I wanted to wait until after the holidays to tell you, but there's been talk."

Carly heard her favorite ornament crunch underneath her as she collapsed on the couch. "About what?"

"That you might need a shrink."

The broken bulb pierced her skin, causing her to jolt upright. "Why?"

He shrugged. "You avoid people. They think you're depressed."

"Do you think so?" She dabbed the cut.

It had taken him a minute to answer. "Well, I do think you get all worked up over nothing sometimes. And as far as your 'I want to be alone' act, I assume you're a different person at work."

He had been wrong on both accounts. The missing money was not "nothing"—and neither was the way he failed to show up at places he said he'd be. And Carly acted no differently at the hospital than she did anywhere else, even though she'd taken a hit for it. As a pastor's wife, she'd been excluded from jokes and happy hours. That hadn't done much for her social life, but at least at the hospital she'd felt like part of a team.

When she failed to respond that day, he added, "I know what you do can be stressful."

"Maybe I should quit," she murmured, so low that he might not have heard. If she quit nursing, they'd never be able to pay their bills.

He'd heard her, alright. "Be serious, Carly. Anyway, I smoothed it over, but I thought you should know. People are talking."

As if she hadn't known. She'd stopped going to Wednesday night meetings when the prayers began sounding too much like gossip. And if anyone ever heard her most fervent prayer that her husband would come clean about a few things in his life that weren't adding up, it just might jeopardize his ministry.

But the elders were right about her avoiding people. To keep the peace, she'd agreed to see a doctor, and he'd lost no time diagnosing her with anxiety and mild depression. As she'd anticipated, the most the drugs he'd prescribed did was help her pack on ten extra pounds.

After the baptism, Carly wandered to the end of the dock, shook off her sandals, and sat, dangling her feet over the water. Her toes tapped the surface of the freezing river, which had just reached the high-water mark. Weeks ago, the mighty Niagara had been clogged with ice. When she was a kid, she and her sisters dared each other to stand barefoot in the slush until, one at a time, the older two wimped out. Her father had said, "That's my Carly, never knowing when to . . ."

What, Pop, quit? Maybe he had been right.

If she quit nursing or even went part-time, she'd at least have more time for her sons. After moving to Grand Island, Nathan hadn't adjusted well in the new school; he needed her just as much as little Benny did. But the church's income barely covered the mortgage on their building. For a congregation of loyal tithers, this shouldn't have been a problem, but recently Rick had begun seriously neglecting his books. The last time Carly had snuck a look, the ledger hadn't been written in for months.

He'd defended himself. "You try heating the place, fixing the pipes, printing programs, and all that after paying the note every month."

"But didn't we hire Keri Ann to keep track of that stuff?"

"There you go again, blaming Keri Ann. I told you not to involve her! She's got enough to deal with." Whatever that meant—and it still didn't explain the missing money.

High-pitched laughter blew out to Carly at the end of the dock. She'd shared the purest joy possible with a few of these happy women after assisting them in childbirth. She'd praised God while handing them their newborn babies. Even after thirteen years of waiting for her second child, Carly had done her best to rejoice each time her sisters had their next. But her efforts to maintain these relationships evidently hadn't been enough. The women had drifted so far away from her that Carly couldn't imagine calling one of them to chat or even just to ask for prayer.

Her toes, all blue and stiff, were now officially numb. The right thing for the pastor's wife to do right now was to get up and help Keri Ann serve lunch, but a memory held her in place.

When Nathan had been Benny's age, a sister from church whose home birth Carly had attended took her out to lunch to let her know she was once again pregnant.

"Carly, I didn't want you to hear it from anyone else."

Throat tight, Carly squeaked out a response. "So, how far along are you?"

"About ten weeks. Enough about me—how are you doing? It must be great with Nate in kindergarten. All that free time! I'd die for some."

"Sure. Free time."

Every woman in the fellowship knew how desperately Carly had wanted another child. But at least this sister had taken the time to share her news in person—truly an act of kindness.

As they chatted, the door of the Spot Café swung open and two more young mothers from church breezed in, one with a newborn strapped to her chest. "Looks like we all had the same idea!" They hugged and kissed their pregnant friend, confessing that they'd already heard she was expecting. The conversation immediately shifted to maternity clothes, jolly jumpers, and highchairs. When Carly said goodbye and slipped away, the others barely noticed. That was the first of her many vanishing acts.

From the end of the dock, Carly looked across the river to Buffalo, the city where she'd spent most of her married life. Out of habit, she avoided the sight of the Huntly Plant, an abandoned factory that had been crumbling to dust since she could remember. Its windows were like eyes, its boarded-up door like an angry mouth. This monstrous building had fascinated her as a child. She'd sit where she was now and imagine herself perched atop its ancient smokestack, far away from family, friends, everyone. It had seemed like the loneliest place in the universe. Almost as lonely as she'd felt at that moment.

Looking instead at a patch of sunbeams twinkling on the waves, she noticed something floating among them— a rowboat? *Funny. That wasn't there a second ago.*

Inside the boat sat a person peering straight at her, a

man, she thought. Whoever it was seemed to recognize her. But while shielding her eyes to get a better look, the boat, the man, the whole thing disappeared. *How could a man in a boat be here one minute and gone the next?* Was this another product of her imagination? If so, she was farther gone than she realized.

No. She was sure she'd seen a boat with someone inside, watching her. His eyes had met hers. Her legs wobbling, she ran back to the house.

Whatever had just happened, she'd wait until they were alone to mention it to Rick. There was an outside chance he'd take her seriously. More likely, he'd dismiss it as the result of too many nightshifts and remind her that their vacation was just weeks away.

As if this annual campout at Allegany State Park was any kind of break for Carly. If Rick had a minute to listen—*really* listen to her in between consoling newly divorced women, writing sermons, and conducting church business—she'd set him straight. What he called "a time of refreshment in the Lord" was more stressful to her than a baby coming out feet first. In fact, she'd take work any day over camp. At least at the hospital, she didn't feel invisible.

Camp had gotten even tougher since she had Benny. Last year, a mother had taken her aside. "I'm telling you, Carly, if you ignore the boy's odd behavior, you're going to end up with a real problem on your hands."

Why? Because he didn't say "please" and "thank you" when she handed out the crayons? Carly might have confessed that Benny was still working on calling her "Mommy," but she'd deferred to the sister, hoping to cut the conversation short. Alas, no such luck.

"And he's so much younger than Nate that he might as well be an only child, so I'm sure he spends too much time in his own little world."

"Yes. That's why we bring him to camp."

"It doesn't seem to be working."

When Benny was a toddler, Carly had tried setting up playdates with other mothers, but after getting together once or twice, the others failed to accept her invitations. Their excuses were sincere, as most were busy running their older kids to soccer and ballet.

She no longer had much in common with these women. As far as getting together as couples, unless Rick was there, forget it. With all of that in mind, the last place she wanted to spend this precious week off from work was with a bunch of happy parents and their normally developing children. If there'd been one person there she considered a true friend, it would have changed everything. She'd hoped to make a connection with one of the survivors of a local church split who'd been attending New Wine, but the new people tended to stick together. She didn't blame them. Being new at their church was almost as tough as being old and disregarded.

With the post-baptism picnic finally over, the last family packed up their minivan and took off. Carly perched anxiously on a lawn chair, deciding whether to tell Rick what she'd seen out on the river. If he wrote it off as her being mentally unbalanced, she'd be in no worse shape than she was now, she supposed. And who knew? If he thought it had to do with the spiritual realm, it might lead to an actual adult conversation—their first in ages.

Keri Ann marched outside, her sunglasses pushed up on her head. She handed Rick a plate of sandwiches, warning him no leftovers were allowed. Carly joined him at the table. When their secretary went back inside, she took a deep breath and spoke. "Rick, I saw something out in the river today, and I don't know if it was real or ..."

"Or what? Your imagination?"

"Well, yeah. I saw a man in a boat."

"Big deal." Rick pointed to her sandwich. "Are you going to eat that?"

"Take it." Carly leaned close, her voice a whisper. "But then it all disappeared."

He washed down the sandwich with some punch. "Maybe you need your prescriptions filled."

"No." Not a lie. She had plenty of pills. She'd just stopped taking them.

"Maybe you should go back to that doctor—what was his name?"

"Dolittle." She waited for him to chuckle, but instead he grabbed the last sandwich. Either he was no longer listening or he hadn't gotten the joke.

So much for an adult conversation ... forget him. Forget all of them. Whatever had happened out in the river was something she'd need to deal with on her own.

She reached over to pluck a dying blossom from the rickety old trellis. "When I think of how my mother used to baby these roses ... she'd spend a whole afternoon picking out each little bug."

"What?"

"This bush. Look, it's infested." Carly turned over the leaf, revealing a cluster of tiny insects.

"To tell the truth, I've never even noticed the thing."

Rick never noticed a lot of things. If he'd been out on the dock with her earlier, he might have looked right past that man in the boat. He wouldn't even have even seen it. Maybe the vision, if that's what it was, had been just for her.

Since her parents had given her the house on the river, her husband had never once gotten up early to watch the sun rise over Strawberry Island or remarked on how perfectly the water reflected an overcast sky, the kind of details Carly had always loved about this place. She plucked another fading blossom and laid it between them. "You used to love to bring me flowers."

"Tell you what, I'll buy some bug spray next time I'm at True Value."

Petals scattered when Keri Ann kicked open the screen door. She set a half-eaten pie in front of Rick. "Remember what I said? No leftovers allowed." Tilting her head, she asked, "Carly, is something the matter?"

"Why do you ask?"

"You look ... stressed." She patted Carly's hand and smiled. "Ricky, Ben's watching cartoons on cable. Is that OK?"

"No. Put in a tape—*Veggie Tales* or something."

Keri Ann rushed back inside, and Rick cut a slice of pie. "The kid's going to have to get used to no TV at all in a few weeks."

Right. Family camp. Carly hadn't planned on bringing this up, but this was as good a time as any. She brushed the remains of the rose off the table. "Listen, Rick, I might have to skip camp this year."

"Oh? How come?"

"A midwife I know asked me to help her deliver a set of twins, and her due date falls on the Fourth of July. Of course, no one knows exactly when they'll arrive, but I'll need to be on call." At least part of this was true.

Between bites of tart rhubarb, Rick said, "OK, if that's the deal ... whatever works."

That sure was easy. Apparently, not having her around worked fine for him. Whatever. She was glad to be off the hook.

Camping with the church had not always been such an ordeal. Spending a week at Allegany over the Fourth of July was the first thing she and Rick had done with the gang of new believers they'd met while on the road nearly twenty years ago. Back then every day had been a celebration, all of them praying, dancing, and worshipping the Lord.

Allegany was where Carly had received the vision to finish her nurse's training and Rick had firmed up his plan to go into ministry. The brethren pooled their meager funds, rented a storefront, and before they knew it, The House of Light was the hottest thing going on the Elmwood Strip. On any given night, fifty or sixty people would crowd inside to hang out and hear Rick preach.

A core group formed, and Rick was voted head elder. Soon, most of them paired off, got married, and started having babies. Carly herself became pregnant with Nate. All the women were close at first, but as their husbands found better jobs and moved to the suburbs, things changed. As the working mother of one who still lived in the city, Carly no longer fit in. It was proclaimed a miracle thirteen years later when she gave birth to Benny, but by then the women at the fellowship were planning high school graduations, and then there was Carly, still hauling around a diaper bag.

No matter. Having Benny had been a huge blessing,

though at five, he'd been reaching his developmental milestones very late. Carly wasn't sure what to do. Take him to a doctor? Fast and pray? Nothing at all? Her husband had made it clear he'd picked option three.

The day before the Fourth of July, Carly lifted Benny's pail out of his sandbox and out wiggled a tiny snake. She jumped. The poor little critter must have been sunning himself. Still, it shocked her. Her older son, Nathan, honked the horn. "Come on, Mom! I don't want to be late."

Late? Really? The best thing about camping was not having to worry about time. Most women would be ecstatic that their seventeen-year-old couldn't wait to get to family camp while his friends were celebrating the holiday by drinking and getting high. Carly did consider Nate's loyalty to the family a gift. Especially this year, since he'd promised to help watch Benny. She'd offered to keep the boy home with her, but Rick insisted on showing up with both of his sons.

In truth, the three messages on their answering machine from the newest member of the congregation, Serena Petrick, complaining about spending a whole week without plumbing or central air had unsettled Carly more than the snake. After the last message, Carly pressed the call-back button and almost told Miss Serena if she wanted to steal her husband, fine, but so much for her new life in Christ. It was one or the other—Jesus or Rick. But that was crazy talk. She put down the phone and reset the machine.

"Mom, it doesn't feel right leaving you behind like this" Her son squeezed her hand through the driver's seat window. "Are you sure you're going to be OK?"

"Of course, sweetheart. I'm fine, and I'll be there before

you know it. Take good care of Benny."

While Nathan tried to get his brother to wave goodbye, Carly envisioned unfastening the car seat, grabbing her little boy, and just taking off.

"I love you, Mom. I bet you're lonely without us."

"If the delivery is simple, I'll be down soon."

Nathan looked away. Apparently, her smile was not doing the trick. He'd always been insightful, and his eyes had a way of betraying his heart. Right now, they were telling Carly that he knew she was lying. There would be no delivery, she would not be down soon, and she'd failed him—again.

"Goodbye, Mom. Take care of yourself."

Gravel crunched beneath the tires, and the two loves of her life were gone. The migraine she'd been trying to pray away stabbed her behind the eyes. If she could only explain why she needed to stay home, Nate might have understood. But the kid already had enough to worry about, and he might have let their secret slip.

She swallowed two Ibuprofen and cleared off the papers on her bed. Since all her husband had had to offer about what she'd seen in the river was a reminder to take her meds, she'd set her mind to learn all she could about visions, apparitions, and people popping up out of nowhere.

The day before, Carley had scoured the resources at the Grand Island Library, but nothing turned up that she hadn't already read in the Bible or accessed online. Most of the non-biblical texts blamed such experiences on hoaxes, drugs, or tricks of the mind. A hoax was out of the question, and it had been almost twenty years since she'd ingested anything stronger than communion wine. That left tricks of the mind—in other words, seeing things that weren't there.

In nursing school she'd studied mental illnesses, and this one, commonly known as schizophrenia, was not her problem. She'd been diagnosed as mildly depressed, but since she always managed to get herself off to work and home again—at that point, at least—she'd been successfully holding things together. And since her days as a student, she had enjoyed conducting research. Chasing down an explanation for what she'd witnessed in the river had proved an intriguing diversion. At least it had been something to do besides worry.

Though yesterday's deep dive had been disappointing, the time had not been wasted. She'd literally bumped into an old friend on the sidewalk outside the town hall. Late for her last day of work, she'd run smack into Janine Spinner.

"Carly La Nova, no way!" The woman took her hand and put the other one on Carly's no-longer-twenty-four-inch waist.

"Janine?"

"What are you doing on the island?"

"We live here now. My parents moved to Florida and gave us the house. How about you? Last I knew, you were in Texas."

"A few of us come back every year for an unofficial reunion. I suppose you're still married to ... ?"

"Rick? Yes."

"And you still go to that ... ?"

"New Wine Fellowship, yes." Carly's lips began to quiver. She tried to speak but instead moaned, "Oh, Janine, I've been so lonely."

CHAPTER TWO

After the ministry meeting, Rick couldn't wait to get to camp. Driving shotgun with his new associate pastor, Malcolm Xavier Worthy, Rick had been trying to keep the chitchat on the light side, but it was clear Malcolm had different expectations.

They'd been on the road for over an hour and had aired out every item on the Urban Christian Ministries agenda, from parking lot issues to whether or not to lock their buildings during the day, but Malcolm always brought the discussion back to Rick.

"Rick, one thing I want to know is why you don't speak up more at those meetings. I mean, you obviously have opinions."

Rick hooted. "You should have heard me when I was new. They couldn't shut me up."

"What happened?"

"Nothing."

"What do you mean?"

"I mean nothing happened. We have the same problems we've always had. People moving out of the city in droves, and those still there not willing to mix it up with churches on the other side of Main Street. But most of all ..." He stopped short. He'd intended to keep things light, and once again Malcolm was pulling him off his game.

"What?"

"Nothing. Really. All water under the bridge." If he didn't come up with a safe topic soon, Malcolm would zero in on his childhood—or worse, his marriage. "How about those Bills? Are we going to make it to the Super Bowl this year?"

Rick had already gathered that Malcolm wasn't much of a fan, but apparently even he'd heard of the infamous "wide right" controversy.

"Haven't watched one since they played the Giants back in ninety-one. Clearly, that was one they weren't supposed to win."

"You mean you think it was rigged?"

"Rick, the NFL is rife with fraud. It's almost as bad as the government."

Letting Malcolm talk politics was almost as deadly as getting too personal. "If you ask me, Washington is just one big soap opera. The less I know about what happens there, the happier I am. Come on, we all know they're on the take, but guys like us can't do anything about it. I mean, they're about as useless as that bunch of Urban Christian ministers we waste half a day with every month." Rick opened the passenger window and stuck out his head.

"Then why don't you speak up more at the meetings?"

"Malcolm, I told you. I used to go out of my way, I mean *really* go out of my way to work with those guys, but from the start they took me for a rookie. Still do. Don't tell me you haven't noticed. But then you walk in and they treat you like a king."

"Do you think it's a race thing?"

"No. Not race." But rather than get into how Malcolm had been raised in a better family, that he was smarter than Rick, way more sophisticated, and never gave a hoot about proving himself to anybody ever, once again, Rick changed the subject. "It must be great to have daughters."

"Don't tell Anya, but before she was born I was hoping Pauline, our second, was going to be a boy."

"God spared you."

"I don't know, Rick. It looks to me like a man couldn't ask for a better son than Nathan. Anyway, he really impressed Anya and me at his graduation party. What are his plans?"

"He's got some wild ideas about acting."

"Oh no."

"I might have let it play out if he'd shown a little raw talent."

"Has he starred in many plays in school?"

"He was in the drama club but never even tried out for a part."

"I can see why you're concerned." Malcolm slowed down as they pulled off the Southern Tier Expressway and into the park.

"That's not the half of it. I'm not crazy about the friends he makes in these clubs. Kind of effeminate, if you know what I mean."

Malcolm slowed down further. "You know my opinion on that subject."

Malcolm had firsthand knowledge that some of the less physical boys on the street were straight and some of the toughest were not. In his neighborhood, one gang leader was out of the closet. According to Malcolm, he'd never even been in one. But it wasn't Malcolm's son they were talking about.

"I've been hoping Nate will get a grip and do something sensible, like join the army."

Malcolm stopped at a booth and a woman poked her head out of the window. "Eight dollars, please."

"We're staying for the week. Here's our registration." Malcolm showed her the form, and she waved them through.

Rick leaned even farther out of the window. "I've always regretted not enlisting ... but enough of that. Here we are, Malcolm! Two city boys in the great outdoors."

He was right about him and Malcolm both being city boys. Although the chances of them ever meeting as kids had been slim, as they'd grown up on opposite sides of town. But that was another touchy topic. "Malcolm, the part of this I love best is driving up behind the lodge and hanging out with the brothers. All of us unpacking, setting up tents, getting in the groove. Reminds me so much of the old days."

Minding the ten miles per hour speed limit, Malcolm stopped completely to let a chipmunk pass. "As a kid I thought it would be cool. You know, the hippie, get-back-to-nature experience."

"You mean to say your folks never took you camping?"

"That's where Black Muslims drew the line. Anyway,

Mother never could tolerate bugs."

"Mine never took us, either. My old man was too busy bribing his way into the Lackawanna Fire Department."

"You never talk about him."

"What do you want to know? He spent half his life buying drinks for councilmen. When he finally did get hired by the city, we never saw him. Just as well—he was a mean old dude. Today, they'd call him abusive. Threw my mother around, beat the heck out of us kids. But I got it the worst. He really hated me. Said I'd never amount to anything. When I couldn't take it anymore, he pretty much packed my bags and pushed me out the door. That enough for you?"

"Where you able to forgive him?"

"Too late. He's dead." Rick smiled and smacked the dashboard. "I don't mean to make light of it, Malcolm. I'm just telling it like it is. Hey, here's our trail." Rick sighed in relief as they turned off the main road toward Group Camp Twelve. He directed Malcolm to turn left at a fork in the dirt road. Pulling up behind the lodge, he looked for the guys. Cars were parked everywhere, but where was his welcoming committee?

Rick's face fell. He'd been hoping for a big greeting from his home team. He could use a few pats on the back at the moment; those meetings always heavied him out.

It was a good thing Keri Ann hadn't been there. She'd have asked a bunch of tough questions and kicked Rick's shins under the table if she thought he wasn't holding up his end of the conversation. But she'd had something else to do that morning—a doctor's appointment, some-thing about cancer, something she shouldn't have had to do alone. A better man would have skipped the ministry meeting and gone with her. A guy with more class like Malcolm, whose parents had raised him right.

His sons should have been around somewhere. He'd hoped to spend some real time with Nate this week. Carly coddled him. Always had. The boy was almost eighteen and still hadn't gone on a date with a girl. Then there was his quiet little Benny. As if Rick didn't have enough on his plate.

Not a soul in the lodge. Malcolm excused himself to go look for his wife just as Rick heard the crack of a bat and cheers coming from the direction of the base-ball diamond. *All the guys must be over at the game.* The only one around was Serena Petrick, sitting all alone in a shelter hovered over her Bible.

"Pastor Rick!"

"Hey there, young lady. What are you doing here all by yourself?"

"Reading the book of Acts, and I have some questions. Did those early believers really sell all their stuff and move in together? How did they manage? I mean, some-thing like that sounds too good to be true."

"Interesting observation, Serena. And I promise to ad-dress it, just not right this minute. Catch me later, OK? And remember, this week is supposed to be fun. God isn't against us lightening up sometimes."

She flashed him that thousand-watt smile. "I know, but it's awkward for me, as a new person, breaking into a group of people who've known each other for so long."

"Maybe you need to push yourself a little." He winced, knowing he said the same thing to his wife all the time.

"But everyone here seems so perfect."

"None of us are perfect, Serena. Trust me."

"You would know. I mean, they all come to you for guidance."

"For a while. Until they get better at figuring things out for themselves. And that's pretty much everyone at this point."

"Ouch!" She pulled a handful of golden hair out of a rubber band and let it her spill over her narrow shoulders. "I don't know if that will ever happen in my case."

He cleared his throat. "Nothing to worry about, Serena. Some of the brethren still like to get together to talk. It all depends. And now with Pastor Malcolm's group joining us, things are bound to change. But don't worry, it'll all work out. Always does."

"Hey, where's your wife?"

Sudden cheering. The game must have taken a turn. "Carly? Oh. She couldn't make it this year. She's on call to deliver a set of twins."

"Coming out here isn't that important to her, I guess."

He slapped a mosquito. "What do you mean?"

"Well, if Mrs. Green needs someone to talk to or pray with, you're always there for her. I have to make an appointment."

Rick rubbed his forehead. How does a guy follow up a comment like that? Fortunately, Malcolm was heading toward them. "Serena, this is Malcolm Xavier Worthy, my new associate."

"Xavier, that's Spanish for savior, right?" She held out her hand.

"Yes. However, my parents were thinking more about the Marxist radical Malcolm X when they named me."

Rick stepped in when Serena's lovely eyebrows turned up in confusion. "Serena, you and me and Malcolm have something in common—we all came to know Jesus as adults."

Malcolm interjected, "However, my grandfather was a preacher. Let's hope faith in Christ doesn't always skip a generation. Speaking of children, here come mine."

"Daddy, Daddy, you're here!" Malcolm's twelve- and eight-year-old daughters ran up the hill, plowing into him and almost knocking him over. When he wrapped his arms around them, they squealed, "Not so tight! Mommy put up the tent. Come and see!"

"Pauline, Grace, where are your manners?"

"Sorry, Daddy. Hello, Pastor Rick. Hello ..."

"Mrs. Petrick," said Serena with a quick wave.

"Hi, girls," said Rick. "Have many of your friends come camping with you?"

"No. They don't like camping. Too many—"

Grace elbowed her little sister. "But we're making new friends."

"Good for you."

"We gotta go. Mommy says we better put on boots if we want to catch crayfish in the creek."

As soon as his daughters were out of earshot, Malcolm asked, "Is this creek safe?"

"It depends on the water level. Let's go see."

Serena touched Rick's arm. "Leaving already? I have so much to ask."

"Serena, remember what I said. It's OK with God if you have a little fun once in a while."

"I will, but maybe I'll see you later?"

"Of course."

Rick and Malcolm walked across a stone bridge and down a path. Finally, Malcolm spoke. "Rick, do you know why my old boss at Midtown Bible Chapel had to leave the ministry?"

"Sure. He ran away with the organist." Rick burst into laughter. "Sorry, Malcolm, but you know as well as I do, people are just waiting for us to pull off stunts like that."

"I agree. But cliché or not, it ruined him. His wife kicked him out, and his kids can't stand him."

"I know all about that, Malcolm. Why bring it up now? Like I said to Serena, camp is supposed to be fun."

"Serena, huh?"

"Mrs. Petrick. I baptized her last month. I believe you were there."

"Yes. I saw ... everything. Just be careful, brother."

"Are you trying to say there's something going on between me and Serena?"

"All I'm trying to say is, be careful."

Rick put his hand on Malcom's shoulder. "Let me set your mind at ease, brother. I am not having an affair with Serena Petrick. She's been hurt. Badly. When I spend time with her, I'm only trying to build her up in faith. And even if I did have, shall we say, an occasional inappropriate thought, tell me one guy who hasn't. But thoughts and actions are two different things, right?"

"Yes, for the most part. It's just that I've seen a lot of good men fall." They jogged down the grass to the edge of the creek. "Looks a little fast. Maybe the kids shouldn't be playing down here."

"I say let them. Risk is good. It's how we learn." Rick sent a stone skipping downstream. The final bounce pierced the reflection of his older son, Nathan, half hidden in brush across the creek, shoulder to shoulder with another boy.

CHAPTER THREE

Grand Island had only one diner, a greasy spoon called Open House whose coffee, with its distinctive oily finish, had been keeping Janine Spinner awake while Carly spilled her guts about Rick. "He's seeing another woman, I'm sure of it."

"Of course he is. That's what men do." Janine rolled her eyes.

The bear claw Carly had ordered sat on her plate, untouched. Janine reached over and stabbed it with a fork. Though she'd been married twice, the only advice that her old friend had come up with for Carly was to go out and have some fun for a change. What had she expected? As far as Carly knew, none of their old gang had become Christians, and for sure not Janine.

"Excuse me, Janine." Not wanting her friend to see her cry, Carly hurried through the long narrow dining room, recalling scenes from high school. There was even one in the bathroom stall. A piece of deeply etched graffiti claiming "Liam Dunn was here" made her retch. She'd gone with Liam briefly during her senior year. Pressing the jiggly handle, she wished she could flush away the image of her old boyfriend, but the water ran as sluggishly as ever. And of course, there was still no soap in the dispenser.

She glanced at her face in the blurry mirror. She'd changed more than Janine. Grays messed up a haircut that was doing nothing for what they used to call her "fairy princess curls," and a slight double chin lowered her once heart-shaped face. Carly used to be the knockout and Janine simply a pushy blonde. And just like the Janine of old, Carly could tell she wanted something. She'd put up with Carly's complaints for almost an hour, and the old gang never gave up a thing for free.

Carly slid back into the booth, straddling a rip in the turquoise vinyl. The speakers on their private little jukebox pumped out James Brown. "Isn't it a little early for 'I Feel Good'?"

"I'm trying to get you in the spirit."

All Carly had wanted from her old friend was someone to talk to, but Janine kept bringing up some big party. Getting together with her hadn't been wise. They no longer had a thing in common. Except maybe for this. "Janine, speaking of spirits—"

"No, no, no. You promised—no preaching. I've already heard all your Jesus talk, and I know where I stand."

"That's not what I mean. What I'm trying to say is, I saw something bizarre out in the river a few weeks ago."

Janine leaned forward. She'd always been into spooky stuff. The two of them had conjured up a real live spirit once, up in the Spinners' attic. They'd asked her Ouija

31

board who Carly would marry, and some weird force guided their hands to the letters *R I C K*. It had scared the pants off them. Janine leaned forward. "Do tell."

"Remember how peaceful it felt sitting out at the end of our dock?"

"Sure, as long as you ignored the old Huntly Plant. But yeah, that spot was magical. What did you see?"

"Someone in a boat."

"So what?"

"So, he showed up out of nowhere, then, poof, he was gone—no man, no boat, not even a ripple."

"Ah-ha! A ghost." She snatched a forkful of Carly's pastry. "No doubt, someone died there. Could be a portal. What did it look like?"

"It happened too fast for me to get a good look, but I'm pretty sure it was a man. The first thing that came to my mind was an angel."

"What made you think that?"

Another record dropped on the turntable. Carly's favorite oldie, "Under the Boardwalk" by the Drifters. Janine hummed along, and for a minute Carly got distracted. "Oh, yeah—I was angry that day. At Rick, the church, even at God."

Janine's ice-cube eyes mocked her like they used to when she failed to act tough. "If you were mad at them, I'm sure they all deserved it." She tapped Carly's elbow. "Since you insist on seeing everything through those dorky religious glasses, how do you know your angel wasn't really a demon?"

Carly shoved away her coffee cup. "I never thought of that."

Janine crooned, "Down by the sea-ee-ee, yeah, on a

blanket with my baby is where I'll be.' Hey, Carly, either way. If it was an angel, maybe he had a message for you. That's what they do, right? Bring messages?"

Carly laughed for the first time all morning. "You still remember your catechism!"

"What if what you saw in the river was your guardian angel warning you that if you don't lighten up soon, you'll need stronger meds? Who knows? Maybe he was the one who sent me to the library the other day."

"I doubt it."

Janine leaned even farther forward and whispered, "What if I told you somebody we used to know really wants to see you again?"

"Who?"

"That, I can't say."

"My family thinks I'm assisting a midwife with a home birth."

"A what? Isn't that against the law? If not, it should be. Oh, Carly, you're still such a nerd."

Carly took a swig of cold coffee. Who in the world would want to see her again?

Janine continued. "Last year, we had a blast. A bunch of girls from our class showed up. We played volleyball down at Beaver Island—very wholesome, all on the up and up, I swear. Had a few drinks—well, maybe more than a few—joked around, reminisced about the old days. Those were some good times, La Nova, you know they were. Remember when we got picked up hitchhiking by those millionaires and they took us to a party at the Knox mansion?"

Carly wiped away a tear. "I thought that would be the last day of my life."

"But you have to admit, we had a blast!"

"They all ended up in the pool, evening gowns, tuxes ... what was that all about, anyway?"

"I have no idea, but you never forgot it."

"No, I never forgot the old days. But a few of them, I wish I could. Anyway, things are different now. We're about to turn forty."

Her old friend jammed the rest of Carly's pastry into her mouth. "Carly, back then we did something I now call 'living.' Sounds to me like all you do these days is exist."

Carly squeezed her eyes shut.

"Listen, La Nova. Correct me if I'm wrong, but didn't you just say that you think you're losing your mind? Maybe going out with us tonight is one way to stay sane."

"Will there be drinking?"

"Well, yeah, but no one's going to put a funnel in your mouth."

"After all these years, I'd feel out of place."

"Stubborn as ever." Janine snapped her fingers. "I have an even better idea. Why didn't I think of this before? Not even a killjoy like you should have a problem hanging out with us at the old Fourth of July parade!"

~

The year Carly and Rick moved to Grand Island, she'd noticed someone following her around town in a bright-blue Buick Skylark. When the same car screeched to a halt in her driveway the next day, it had hit her like a punch in the gut that he'd been the one behind her at the drive-through teller, round the corner when she filled her tank at the Mobile station, and in the parking lot when she stopped for milk and bread at the 7-Eleven. Her cheeks burned.

"Hi, Carly." The driver reached over and opened the passenger door.

When she saw his face, she nearly threw up. Liam Dunn. "Hi. After the parade, I need to come straight home." Janine and a man she recognized but whose name she couldn't recall took up the back seat, so she was forced to sit next to Liam.

Janine piped up. "Come off it, Carly, it's the Fourth of July!"

"Babies don't care what day it is. When they're ready, they want out."

"Whatever, La Nova."

"The name is Green, Jan."

Liam stretched his arms and rested a hand on Carly's shoulder. "No sweat, Carly, I'll get you home on time. Didn't I always?" She cringed at the memory of their very last date. They'd messed up the hull of her father's precious Craftsman cruiser. After that night, the boat was never the same. "Carly La Nova. My, oh my. How long has it been?"

Not long enough. She shrank from his touch.

"I heard you married a preacher."

"He wasn't in the ministry when we got married, but yeah, he's a preacher."

"So, where is he?"

Carly's hands made sweat prints on Liam's leather upholstery. "What difference does it make?"

Liam turned on the radio. "So defensive, Carly." He lit a cigarette, blowing smoke sideways. "Don't know if you heard, but my father died a few months ago." Before she had a chance to respond, he continued, "And I have some questions, you know."

"About what?"

"Like, what happens after we hang it up down here? Heaven and hell, all that stuff."

She'd cursed herself for letting Janine talk her into this stupid parade, but she hadn't held a gun to her head. Janine had been right about her state of mind. Her husband, the church, even her sons—who Rick accused her daily of turning into momma's boys—were driving her nuts. Half of her life was now down the tubes, and she didn't have much to show for it.

Spending a little time on her own wouldn't make the earth crack open and swallow her whole, but with the old gang, you never knew. She'd been intrigued by the idea that someone desperately wanted to see her. What a let-down when she caught on that the person was Liam Dunn.

Too late for regrets. But maybe if his questions were sincere, she could make her mistake count for something. It had been years since she'd given her testimony, let alone led anyone to the Lord. Now, of all people, Liam Dunn wanted to know the future of his immortal soul.

"Do you really want to know what happens after you die, Liam?"

The man in the back seat, whose name she recalled was Travis, issued a warning, "Don't believe a word he says, Carly. If I know Liam ..."

"There's where you're wrong, buddy. You don't know me at all, not anymore. I've changed, haven't I, Jan?"

"Sure. Whatever you say, big guy. Hey, where are we going?"

Instead of heading to the parade, Liam had taken a

meandering route through Falcon Wood Estates, mean-ing Carly would be forced to spend even more time with them. Mick Jagger's complaint "I can't get no satisfac-tion" blasted from all four of Liam's speakers.

When they finally reached the boulevard, there was no place to park, so he drove over a patch of grass alongside Tops Market as if he owned it. *As entitled as ever.* Carly wondered why he bothered locking the doors when all the windows were rolled down. If Liam really had changed, it hadn't been for the smarter.

Janine pointed across the street. "That's the best place to watch. Not too sunny."

"On the shady side, just like you, Janine." Travis grabbed her by the hips.

"Knock it off, we're in public."

"As if that ever bothered you."

Carly pulled up the collar of her blouse as the first band marched passed. It would be just great if someone she knew saw her now.

"Girl, remember the year we twirled for the fife and drum corps?" Janine tapped her foot in time with "Yan-kee Doodle."

"Yes. We were awful!" Carly welcomed this less tar-nished memory. Too bad she and Janine hadn't stuck with flaming batons. It might have kept them out of trouble.

An old Shriner, the tassel on his fez hanging in his eyes, grabbed the arm of a teenage girl standing next to them in the street, pushing her onto a float decked out like a cage. The poor thing looked terrified. *How dare the old bully play a trick like that! Is that supposed to be funny?* Liam sure thought so. He followed the cage for half a block, pretending to be part of the act until he stepped in a pile of manure left by a cowgirl on a feisty palomino. *Now that was funny.*

Carly hadn't been to this parade since she was sixteen and still living with her parents. Like most things since then, the tradition had changed: politicians instead of cowboys, boom boxes instead of bands, and vehicles plastered with advertisements instead of tissue paper flowers. But at least this version might be over faster, she reasoned. She'd wait for the right moment to answer Liam's questions, go home, and drive out to camp. If anyone asked about the twins, she'd be honest—they weren't ready yet.

When the sirens finished blaring and the horns died away, when the kids at the curbs had snatched the last of the candy, the four of them walked back to Liam's car. He waved to stragglers as if he was some local hero while Carly tried steering the conversation back to spiritual things.

"I'm sorry to hear about your father, Liam."

"Yeah, well." He revved the engine and took another slithery route back to the river, this time shooting right past Carly's house. Her heart pounded. Like the girl snatched by the Shriner, she was being kidnapped. Trusting Liam to do what he promised was like chugging cheap wine and believing you could keep it down.

They careened down West River. Carly closed her eyes and tried not to think of the queasiness in her stomach. As if she could read her mind, Janine tapped her shoulder with a bottle of what she called "juice."

"No thanks, Janine."

"Oh, come on. It's good for you! Just a squirt of gin in the mix."

"But I don't drink anymore."

"That's too bad. Remember holding each other's hair back after getting so drunk we had to throw up?"

Her mouth watery, Carly took a deep breath, trying not to gag. Janine had said going out with them would loosen her up, but she couldn't imagine feeling more up-tight than she did now.

Her old friend shook her shoulder. "La Nova, are you OK?"

The answer was no, but the only thing to do was wait until Liam stopped the car, then jump out and walk home with her tail between her legs. "I will be if you'd talk about something else."

"OK. Travis, remember when you dared all the guys to jump off the Grand Island Bridge?"

"That wasn't me."

"Yes, it was. And every one of them did except you."

All their shaggy heads had come bobbing up, except the one poor kid who'd nearly drowned. Janine had con-veniently left that part out. Then Carly asked a question. "What about the time you all tried swimming around the island and not everyone made it back?"

"Thanks for that, Miss Debbie Downer." Liam stepped on the gas, going too fast around the curves. When he slammed on the brakes at the bottom of a hill, Carly guessed his destination—the beach under a huge sys-tem of gnarly roots where they used to hang out and get high. *So this was it all along.* Making her believe he'd spent even one second contemplating spiritual matters had just been a ploy to get her down here, but why her? Why now?

Liam rolled off the road, but before Carly could open

the door, he pressed the automatic locks. "Speaking of memories, Carly, remember the time we took your pop's boat out to Navy Island?"

"Yeah," said Janine. "The story I heard was that you guys were too scared to moor."

"Janny," Liam said, shaking his finger, "don't believe everything you hear."

But Janine was right. Liam had either been too scared or too drunk that day to make it to the last big island before the falls. "If I'd been there," Janine continued, "we'd have nailed it. Unlike some people I know, handling a boat comes natural to me."

Travis choked. "Baby, you have no idea what you're talking about."

"So maybe I'm exaggerating, but how hard can it be? Anyway, I've always wanted to explore that island. It sounds like Middle-earth or something. And Liam promised he'd take us to see the castle." The four of them had grown up hearing the legend of a huge Victorian mansion on the otherwise uninhabited island right before the international boarder.

"Carly, don't believe a word of this. I have it on good authority that the place burned down ages ago. Not a timber left standing. As a matter of fact, I've got a pile of money riding on it," said Travis.

"And before this day is done, every cent of it will be right here." Liam patted his pocket. All we need is a suitable vessel. Carly, I noticed the old *LaLa Nova* still moored at your dock."

At last, they were getting down to what the whole day had been about. Using her father's prized possession that Liam had already damaged once just to settle some bet. "It's still there." No use denying it, she knew. He'd seen it already. "But we've never taken it out. It hasn't been driven in years. I'm sure it won't start up."

"Oh, well. Just a thought."

Carly was amazed that he'd given up so easily until she caught him winking at Travis. The doors clicked open and the four of them jumped out of the car. Travis and Janine headed to a fire pit in which wood had already been stacked, and Liam spread a blanket over some ground that had been cleared. The whole thing had been a setup. She'd been a fool.

Inching toward the road, she prayed they wouldn't try to stop her. Her body trembled. She needed to stay calm. Nothing would happen that God did not allow. She'd been less than steadfast in her faith recently, but at least she could count on that much. Then Liam did something so out of the box she couldn't help but stop to listen.

Pulling out a New Testament, he announced, "It says here, right in Corinthians One, chapter seven and verse fourteen, that 'from now on, those who have wives should live as though they have not.'"

Janine was the first to protest. "Come off it, Liam. When did you ever care what the Bible said?"

Carly got in his face. "Liam, you're taking that verse out of context."

Hopping on a rock, he continued, "No doubt. But what I know for sure is that your husband has been living as though a wife he has not ... got."

"What do you mean?"

"I've seen the good Reverend Green out with a girl, more than once."

Carly collapsed onto the blanket. Travis began

massaging her shoulders. "You know what I think, Carly? Old Liam is making up another of his fractured fairy-tales, like the one about the magic castle. The dude's a natural-born liar."

Liam tossed away the New Testament. "Think what you want, my friend. Just make sure you deliver on your bets. I've seen Carly's husband hanging out with another woman, and they seemed real cozy, too."

Carly covered her ears. "I don't believe you! Rick wouldn't do that to me or our kids." *Although that would explain the missing money and the nights he's gone missing ...*

"I've got an idea," said Janine. "Let Mr. Know-It-All here prove he's not a liar. But to make it happen, Carly, we're going to need that boat."

Allegany State Park

"Keri Ann, I've been looking for you."

"Ricky! It's about time you got here. I'm supposed to be playing tennis with the girls. Where's Nate? He said he'd be right back." She swatted a fly off Benny's neck.

"I'll tell you where he is—across the creek with the Wilson boy! And I'm telling you, whatever is going on there has got to stop."

"Stay on track, Ricky. One son at a time. If you want, I can come up with a babysitting schedule for Benny."

Moving in close to Keri Ann, he ruffled the boy's hair. "No. Taking care of Ben is Carly's job."

"Nate thinks you're glad she's not coming."

"Maybe I am. So many of his problems are her fault." He set Benny on the ground.

"Rick, should I make a babysitting schedule?"

"Oh, yeah. Sure. Benjamin, can you say thank you to Keri Ann for watching you?" No response. He tried again, louder. "Benny, say thank you."

"It's OK, Rick. I know how he feels."

"You do, eh? I wish I did." He rubbed his eyes. "In some ways you're lucky, Keri Ann."

"You think so?"

"No one to worry about except yourself."

"That is not true, Ricky. I worry about you all the time."

He stroked the cheek of his oldest friend in the world, and they kissed. Out of the corner of his eye, Rick noticed movement at the top of the hill. He led Keri Ann further into the forest, following Malcolm's daughters with whom, to their surprise, Benny had begun to play.

Keri Ann took off her sunglasses. "It's great to see the little guy having fun." When Rick failed to reply, she added, "It's an answer to your prayers."

"That's not what I pray for Benjamin. That would be giving in to the idea that there's something wrong with him."

"Maybe not wrong, but definitely different. And it's time you faced it."

"I don't know about any of that. But if the boy has trouble, it's because his mother spoils him rotten."

"Let's sit." She carefully lowered herself onto a huge rock.

"We're far enough away. Tell me what the doctor said."

"I'm in the very early stages."

"Meaning what?"

"I'm OK, for now. If necessary, they can operate. The team sounded very upbeat."

"I should have been there for you." He'd let down his best friend in the world, the woman he'd almost married—and probably should have. "When am I going to learn?"

"Ricky, get a grip. Here come Malcolm's daughters."

Pauline and Grace Worthy hopped from stone to stone, closing in on them. Rick sprang to his feet. "Girls, where's Benny?"

"Out in the woods."

"What?"

"We told him to come back, but he wouldn't listen."

Rick towered over them, shouting, "Why did you let him run off by himself?!" Pauline started to cry. "Keri Ann, take the girls to the lodge."

Word about the pastor's son going missing spread, and soon all the men crawled through the woods, Rick leading the charge. He'd asked Anya Worthy to call Carly, but since no one's cell phone worked up there, she used the landline at the lodge.

There had been no answer. Hours later, she still didn't answer.

Grand Island

Her body on autopilot, Carly found the key for her father's Craftsman outboard motorboat and threw it to Liam.

"Your pops sure took good care of the old girl." Liam swished gas around in the rusty can.

"Yes. He did." Carly recalled the old man's lectures about how wooden boats were special, that the Lord himself had ridden in one, and how taking time to perform regular maintenance on a vessel as fine as the *LaLa Nova* was better than having a mishap out on the river. "Remember that the Niagara is a force of nature. It deserves, you know ..."

Respect? Yeah, sure, Pop. Don't we all.

Her parents had decided not to take the boat with them to Florida—too much work to move and store it. Plus, they thought their youngest and most adventurous daughter might want to take it out sometime. It had been a different story when she was seventeen.

Liam started the motor. "The gauge says half full."

"Then what are we waiting for?" Janine tossed her cigarette smack into Carly's mother's rose bush, which had just begun to revive.

"OK, Travis, now we'll see who's lying." Liam backed out of the boathouse, the *LaLa Nova* bumping and scraping against the walls. "Come on, get in."

Dodging anchored yachts too close for comfort, he pushed his way into the mainstream and then opened the throttle to the max. Janine handed her the flask, and Carly's reflection in the stainless steel looked like a death mask. The boat smacked the waves, *bam, bam, bam.* Spray hit her face, which was already a mess. Right now she couldn't care less.

The afternoon was winding down, but boats positioned to see the fireworks clogged the river. Liam drove like a man dead set on giving each of them a heart attack. Carly sprawled out on the life preservers, which her friends clearly had no intention of wearing. "Fine," she mumbled, "let's all drown."

"Why are you heading west?" Travis yelled into the wind.

"Shorter distance."

"Yeah, but—"

Before he could object, the bow banged against a breaking wave, throwing Travis to his knees. Nauseous, Carly crawled to the boat's edge and hung her head over the side. *This must be how Jonah felt before getting tossed into the brink.*

Liam was still driving like a maniac. They were aiming toward Navy Island, alright, but against a strong current. Once they passed the tip of Grand Island—if they ever did—they'd be in international waters, the river pushing them forward instead of holding them back.

"Look!" Janine had to yell to be heard but kept it bright and sunny. "There's Canada! Maybe the boys will stop at the duty-free so I can buy some more of this." She shook her flask. Carly closed her eyes, pressing her back against the hull.

Liam shouted, "We'll be there in no time!"

True, but at the speed he'd been going, Carly wanted to know where he planned to moor. No such question had occurred to the others, of course, who were getting drunker by the minute. Navy Island loomed ahead, a dense fortress of trees. If Liam was going to take a stab at parking this thing, he'd need to start soon, but instead he tipped his head back to drain the dregs of whatever Janine was passing around.

"Liam, start turning." Travis finally caught on that they were flying by the island.

"Not yet. I know just the spot."

Carly assumed that there had to be somewhere to moor, but a boat this size had no chance of veering over in time. Now that they were racing with the current, the *LaLa Nova* had stopped flopping up and down, but it would take a much stronger engine to push it to shore. Liam tossed out his cigarette and gripped the throttle with both hands.

"Steady it, Liam," ordered Travis, "you're cutting too sharp!"

"I know what I'm doing."

They sped along, but Navy Island's shore never looked more than a few yards closer. It quickly became obvious that Liam had no idea what he was doing. Janine shrieked, "Turn left, you're passing it! You're passing the island!"

In minutes, they'd be caught in the rapids. How many times had the La Novas watched the scene from the movie *Niagara* in which Marilyn Monroe gets hung up yards away from the falls? Carly used to laugh at the official-looking sign visible from the Robert Moses Expressway commanding boaters to "TURN BACK." Now, the sight of it sucked the breath from her lungs.

Liam had lost all control. The *LaLa Nova* hurled past Navy Island and into the rapids—next stop, Niagara Falls.

All of them screamed at the Department of Transportation sign "POINT OF NO RETURN" that stood up amid the rocks. Carly cried, "Oh, Lord, please, PLEASE!"

In an instant, a gray military vessel rushed toward them, the insignia on its sides instantly recognizable: the US Coast Guard.

~

The Park Police escorted Carly safely to her doorstep before eleven that night, but it took another hour for her to gain the presence of mind to check her answering machine. She stood under the shower so long, she lost track of time and stepped out still smelling like seaweed. Wrapping herself in a robe, she went outside. The yachts were long gone, and moonbeams twinkled on languid waves. If the coastguard had not been on alert that afternoon, Carly and the others would have ended up floating face down in the Lewiston Gorge. They'd have gotten top billing on Eyewitness News as the latest holiday fatality.

Janine had called the rescue extremely good luck. But then luck was not what had sent Carly a vision of a man in a boat three weeks ago. Was there a connection? Maybe. But God had certainly seen fit to spare them that day, and Carly owed Him all the thanks in the world.

Somehow, though, the only words she could summon sounded more like complaint. Amateur fireworks across the river popped and sizzled. She tried to concentrate, but her thoughts never got past how the air smelled of sulfur and how they'd messed up her father's boat—again. Why couldn't she pray? She should have been dead, yet there she was, safe, clean, and comfortable.

Through ribbons of cloud, the moon seemed to smirk down at her. For some reason, God had saved her life. If she had died, would anyone have missed her? Her sons would have been devastated, though according to Rick, they'd be better off without her anyway.

When approaching the point of no return that afternoon, desperation to live had surged through Carly like electricity. God had shown up in an amazing show of force. Still, tonight, her thanks to Him sounded hollow.

Liam claimed that he'd seen Rick out with another woman. She'd be lying if she said this was a surprise. Rick thrived on attention, and with his muscular build, square jaw, and hair just as dark and thick as when they'd met, women gave him plenty. Not to mention that his desire for Carly had dried up to the point that most nights, he slept on the couch.

Thick smoke blew in from across the river, chasing her back into the house. Only then did she notice the blinking light.

CHAPTER FOUR

Carly's fingers shook so badly after listening to Anya urge her not to be alarmed that it took her three tries to get the camp's number right. Something bad had happened to one of the boys. What else could it have been?

The phone rang and rang. Finally, a tired voice answered. "It's about time you checked in."

"What's going on, Keri Ann?"

"Calm down, please. Thanks to Ricky, everything's under control."

"Anya said don't be alarmed. Alarmed about what?"

"Benny was lost for a while, but we found him."

"Oh no! Nathan was supposed to watch him."

"Yes. He was. But that's a lot to expect from a seventeen-year-old boy, don't you think?"

Lightheaded, Carly sat on a kitchen chair. "Where was Nate when this happened?"

Keri Ann's sudden laughter turned into a coughing

fit. "You need to speak to Ricky about that."

"Is Benny OK? How long was he gone? Can I talk to Rick?"

"Both of them are sleeping. It's after midnight."

"I can be there in an hour."

"Carly, there's really no need."

"Yes, there is. I need to be with my son."

"But it's late. And we've all had a long day, even you, delivering those twins. Suppose you fall asleep at the wheel and crash your car. Then who'd be there to help Ricky?"

Carly could name a few women who'd step right up.

~

"Who's that?" asked Serena as Carly ran toward her dying campfire. "Oh, it's you. Mrs. Green, you missed all the excitement."

"I got here as soon as I could. But Benny's OK—that's what counts."

Serena waved away the smoke. "You call that OK? The kid was hysterical."

"Keri Ann said he was fine."

Serena offered her a lawn chair, but Carly pushed it away. "OK, Mrs. Green, sit in the dirt if you like. But I'm telling you that your little boy was *not* fine. And what's more, if you trust that Keri Ann character, you're in for a big surprise." Serena looked her up and down, from her cut-off shorts to Rick's cast-off flannel shirt.

"Our secretary wouldn't lie. We've known each other for ages—she and Rick go back as far as grade school. If not for her, we'd be … well, let's just say she's always been there for us, like part of the family."

"Well, you better start taking a closer look at that

part of the family, especially when she's alone with your husband."

Carly's breath caught. "What do you mean?"

"Just that I saw the two of them together in the woods today. It freaked me out so bad that I ran away before they even knew I was there. Everyone's saying he was 'counselling' her—that's what the two little girls called it. But what I saw was not that."

Carly sat on the ground. "Are you saying that my husband was acting inappropriately with Keri Ann McGraw?"

"I know it's hard to believe, but one thing I'm catching on to around here is that there's no accounting for taste."

"You know what I think?" Without waiting for an answer, Carly launched in on her. "I think you're jealous."

"Of who?"

"Of Keri Ann's and my relationship with Rick. Keri Ann for being like a sister to him, and me for being his wife. I trust Keri Ann." The pastor's wife hesitated before adding, "We've meant a lot to each other over the years."

"That's funny. You don't act much like friends. Then again, a lot of people around here don't." Kicking apart the coals of her little fire, Serena shook her head. "I really hoped this church would be different, you know. More caring, like the one I've been reading about in the Book of Acts. Guess I was wrong. Pastor Rick says my expectations are too high, but you'd think that if everyone loved God as much as they say they do ..."

"This has nothing to do with the church."

"If you say so, but to be honest, I followed your husband and that Keri Ann into the woods. I know it sounds bad, but I'd asked Pastor Rick earlier if he could help me with the verse in Acts that said the people sold all they had and shared everything. Anyway, the two of them sat down almost on top of each other and he started crying and kissing and hugging her."

"An unusually long hug?" Carly pointed her finger at Serena.

"Whatever, Mrs. Green. Who knows, I'm new to all this. But I'm telling you, your Benny was one angry little boy when they found him. He kicked and screamed and beat his daddy like a punching bag. If you ask me, he wasn't lost. He was running away."

"That just doesn't sound like Benny."

Serena stood up and stretched. "I don't know, Mrs. Green. Maybe I'm wrong. It's late. Go see your son. And when you kiss him, thank God for how lucky you are that he's not still out there alone in the woods."

"Wait, Serena." Carly choked out something like an apology. "I'm not myself. Please forgive me."

"Hey, it's OK. I heard you stayed home to deliver a set of twins." She pointed to a stream of smoke rising out beyond the camp. "Guess we're not the only ones still up."

"Serena, about those twins ..."

"They're OK, I hope."

"The truth is the twins aren't due until August. It must sound awful, but I used them as an excuse to stay home." She yawned and continued, "I just didn't think I could deal with camp this year."

"I can buy that. I'm not doing so well with it myself. I guess church camp is not all it's cracked up to be. At least not when you're on your own like I am, and it looks like maybe you are, too." Serena held out a hand to help Carly off the ground. "Don't worry about the little white lie. I'll keep your secret."

~

Past the bend in the creek, inside of a circle of pines, Keri Ann McGraw sat across from Nathan Green at their own campfire. As the stars slowly bent toward dawn, she waited for him to decide on his next course of action. They'd been talking for ages, but Keri Ann had not made much progress, even considering their special bond that she made sure he never forgot.

Unfortunately, Nathan was as stubborn as his mother—never willing to compromise. "If you tell your father what you just told me, there is no way he'll understand. I know him."

"But Mom will. I've been *this* close to spilling my guts with her many times." He held his forefinger and thumb one inch apart.

"At this point, what Carly thinks doesn't matter much."

"I hate to hear you talk that way about Mom."

"I'm just stating facts."

Nate jabbed a stick in a tiny cave of embers, some so hot that they squealed. "Sure. Facts. I could use a few of them right now. All I have are feelings. But one thing I can tell you, this is a bad time to dump one more problem on my parents' backs. They've already got enough to deal with—my dad trying to make one church out of two, and Mom walking around so stressed out, she jumps when you touch her. I'm afraid she's going to crack. You know the two of them don't even sleep together anymore."

Keri Ann raised a threadbare eyebrow. That was something she had not known but was happy to hear.

She tossed a log on the fire. For a while, neither one

spoke. A loon uttered its crazy laugh in the distance. She'd watched Nate grow for eighteen years and knew he'd never forget how she'd risked her life for him once. These days Nate came to her more than ever, mostly to complain. According to him, she was the only adult who understood him. No wonder—for years, she'd treated him like the son she never had. Tonight the kid wanted her opinion about all this talk of him being gay. What interested her more than that, though, was how hard he'd bite the hook that she planned to dangle.

"Keri Ann, I almost wish I was. But if I was, telling them would only be stooping to their level."

"How do you know you're not?"

The boy looked shocked. "Good question. I don't think I am, but how can you know for sure? I mean, there are guys who have wives and kids who end up coming out as gay. Were they always that way, or did they change?"

For a while, the two of them stared at the fire. Keri Ann snuck a look at her watch. "It can't hurt for the two of you to go out and experience life on your own. You know, to find some answers. It's what I should have done at your age. If I'd have been willing to drive to Texas with your father when we were eighteen, things would have turned out very differently—for all of us."

"You mean, you think we should run away?"

"Did he ever tell you he begged me to go with him?"

"No. The story I heard was that Dad went with Mom. The car broke down and a guy named Chuck picked them up hitchhiking, shared the gospel with them, got them saved, and the rest is history."

"You sound a little cynical."

"What if I am? You don't know what it's like, having to

measure up to his idea of Christian manhood."

"He wasn't always like that, Nate. In the old days your father was so gentle, a breeze could knock him down."

"What happened?"

No way was she going public with the secrets she and Ricky held in their hearts. Nathan was one person who might understand—someday, but not now. Tonight, her goal was to steer him in a particular direction.

"I don't want to bore you with all that, Nate. Trust me. Things are just different now. Period." She swatted a spark. "I do get that you kids must feel like you missed the glory days."

"Well, yeah. The whole Jesus movement. Guys throwing their drugs down the toilet, burning records, getting healed, traveling to festivals in beat-up vans. Your generation comes off as pioneers. The problem is, you didn't leave us much to explore."

Though she found the idea ridiculous, Keri Ann nodded. She had him just where she wanted. "I get why you feel that way, Nate, but you're wrong."

"As usual." He chewed on a piece of grass. "Dad says I should join the army. Yeah, right—as if that would solve anything. Besides, I just can't see myself all decked out like a soldier." He stood, stretching his arms over his head.

It was now or never. Keri Ann went for broke. "How do you see yourself, Nate?"

"On the stage, or at least behind it. But not much chance for that."

"Yes, there is. Benny got lost today. Maybe now it's your turn."

"You mean run away? That's crazy. I don't have

anywhere to go. I don't know anyone who lives farther away than Buffalo, except my grandparents, and with them I might as well be home."

"How about New York City? It's not too far. The theater capital of the world."

"No way."

"Then somewhere else. There's a lot of unexplored territory out there, Nate."

"But I'll be alone."

"You'll have the Wilson boy, right?" When Nate didn't seem convinced, she added, "And you'll make new friends. Besides, I promise you I'll never be more than a phone call away."

"You sound like a commercial!" He folded his blanket.

"Going to bed?"

"Not yet."

"Well, if I don't see you, good night."

"What? Oh yeah. Good night, Keri Ann, and thanks. For everything."

"Any time, Nate."

Before heading off in the opposite direction of his family's cabin, he kissed Keri Ann on the cheek. His face was wet with tears.

He'd bitten the hook, alright.

That long taxing day had been worth it. She had Rick eating out of the palm of her hand about her cancer—which was only a bit of endometriosis she'd known about for years—she'd made sure he was hopping mad at Carly, and now it looked like Nate would soon be out of the picture.

One less obstacle in her way.

PART TWO

LOW TIDE

CHAPTER FIVE

Twenty years earlier, Louie La Nova rose early to comb the sand on his tiny beach. First, there was the task of removing debris. The river at low tide never failed to drop leftovers from the Fourth of July. He welcomed the seashells and driftwood, but the beer cans, hypodermic needles, and used condoms caused him to worry about his youngest daughter, whom he hadn't seen since she drove off in her new car the night before.

Bottles went in the trash, along with firecrackers washed to shore from his neighbors' docks. Some items were more of a problem, like parts of his own boat. Yesterday he'd found its windshield wrapped around the peers of the state dock two lots upriver. Carly had taken it on a joyride with her knucklehead boyfriend. Louie bent to pick up one of those wire sparklers in case Carly came down later with bare feet.

As he worked, he sang softly so as not to wake his wife, who was asleep with the windows open. She teased

Louie for his singing, although he was the only one in the family who could hold a tune, especially compared to Carly, whose voice was so bad she'd been told to just move her mouth during chorus.

Carly, Carly. His chest hurt when he envisioned his little girl at one of those pot parties the kids had. Maybe he should have waited to give her a car. He'd hoped it would take her mind off boys for a while, especially that Liam. It hadn't occurred to him the little Mustang might make things worse. "Oh Lord," he whispered a line from the mass, "I am not worthy to receive you, but only say the word ..."

He'd been starting prayers all morning for his youngest daughter, but when he tried putting his thoughts into words, they unraveled at the end like a piece of fraying rope. So instead, he whispered bits and pieces of the liturgy, knowing that God would understand. "But only say the word and my soul shall be healed."

His little girl was restless, but wasn't everyone at seventeen? They'd hoped after graduation, she'd stay on with her practical nursing course. At least it was something, better than nothing. The last time he mentioned this, she'd laughed. "Is emptying bedpans what you have in mind for me, Pop? Really?"

Her test scores showed that Carly was every bit as smart as her sisters, but from the start she'd hated school. If anyone compared her to Annette or Amy, both teachers' pets who never missed the honor roll, she'd go out of her way to be different. The math teacher failed her in ninth grade when she announced that what he taught had nothing to do with real life and was just a big waste of her time. It was like that in every subject except for

English, in which she'd always excelled. Stories, she'd said, meant something. What that was, she had a hard time explaining—a problem she must have gotten from him.

Carly's washing out in high school, however, was not his only worry. After her confirmation, she'd hidden in the pew far away from the other kids. He'd yelled at her for ripping up the paper that Father Tom had signed saying she'd received the Holy Spirit and was now officially part of the church.

"But Daddy," she'd said, trying hard not to cry, "it didn't work. The Holy Spirit must have skipped right past me." She wiped her nose on the sleeve of her blouse. "Or maybe the rest of them were faking it, too."

When the rest of the newly confirmed stood for pictures and went off to celebrate with their families, Carly would have none of it. She begged Louie to ask the guests he'd invited to just go home.

Carly had come along so late in their lives that he and his wife no longer worried about money. They'd given their youngest everything a little girl could want, but for Carly, that was never enough. What made one child so different from the rest? Louie shrugged and picked up another beer can. As her father, Louie was the one responsible. Her mother was too sick, too weak to argue. All Louie could say was that he'd done his best. "Lord, I am not worthy to receive you," he whispered, "but only say the word ..."

A car skidded along the gravel in front of the house. His Carly jumped out, wearing a ripped T-shirt and shorts so small they hardly mattered. She ran in the front door. It sounded like she was heading straight for the phone.

Did she know he could hear her? His children accused him of being deaf, but if anything, his ears were as good as they'd been when he first started in business and spent hours cutting deals with vendors, but he let his girls think what they wanted. After all, being considered half deaf came in handy sometimes, and what they didn't know couldn't, well, you know.

Carly was on the phone talking to a friend—about him.

"Trust me, he won't ... why? Because he's old and slow. You have no idea what a drag it is being stuck alone with him. And she's even worse, dragging herself around and coughing all the time. Next thing you know, they'll be asking me to stay home on Sunday nights to watch Lawrence Welk... . No, I am not exaggerating... . And Ricky, please don't forget the cash ... I'm a little short ... we won't get far without it. If I stay in this house, on this island, another day, I'll lose my mind ... what? OK, one more person is cool, but that's all—there's not much of a back seat... . Does she have any money? Good. Every bit helps... . Tonight, then. And listen, if you don't show up, I'm leaving anyway."

After hearing this, Louie lost his balance, almost taking down his wife's rose trellis before collapsing on the chaise lounge.

~

Across the river, in the kitchen of his family's ramshackle house, Ricky Green looked over his shoulder before continuing his conversation with this crazy little rich girl from Grand Island. Her name was Carly La Nova, daughter of Buffalo's pasta king, who was always on TV pitching his noodles. "Eat oodles and oodles!" His mother was pretending to be making coffee, but he could tell she was listening.

He'd met this Carly while hitchhiking. She'd been racing her hot little car almost fifty miles an hour down Abbott Road and had to slam on her brakes to pick him up. Good thing, though, because Ricky and Carly soon found out they had something big in common: they both needed to get as far away from home as possible as soon as possible.

His mother had been the only witness to the way his father had beaten him the other night. Even if she hadn't seen it, the bruises were proof. The poor old girl had cried, her face all red, her mouth saying things like "He was drunk, Ricky" and "He doesn't know what he's doing when he gets like that. Tomorrow he'll come to his senses." *Tell you what, Mom, I've finally come to my senses, and I'm out of here.*

She had been following him around all morning. He'd just finished washing and drying his own laundry for the first time ever. That alone must have made her wonder.

He stretched the cord as far away from her as it would go, but it could never reach far enough, not while he was still in Buffalo. He'd leave for Texas that night with this La Nova girl. She was cute enough, but he already had a girlfriend, one who he'd been trying to convince to come along. The deal with Carly was she had a car, a '67 cherry-red Mustang classic clean under the hood with new tires, new brakes. Something that would get them to Texas—hell, maybe to Mexico. Better than waiting around until he saved enough working at Champion Outlet to get his own wheels.

"Ricky," said his mother, "you're wrecking the phone."

He lowered his voice. "How do you know your old man won't come after us?" Because, she said, her father was too old and slow. If that was all that was wrong with his old man, Ricky wouldn't be in such a hurry to split. If the old bully hadn't threatened to kill him last night, he just might've hung around a little longer, at least until Keri Ann finally decided that enough was enough with her own family.

"I'd take Lawrence Welk any day over getting pulled out of bed in the middle of the night by a drunken SOB who thinks you stole his wallet ... yeah, that's my pop, the fireman... . Hey, what if I bring someone else along? Only one ... . yeah, she's got money. I do too. . . . Of course I'll remember the cash... . My girlfriend's not a sure thing, but I'll be there. You can bet on it... . Alright, then. See you tonight."

He wondered if his mother had noticed the suitcase under his bed. Didn't matter either way—his father was the only one strong enough to stop him. But since she'd been so nosey, he would take it with him to Keri Ann's house and ask her to come along one last time. So far, his girlfriend's solution to the mess they were in at home was to find jobs in town, get married, and move into some dive of an apartment. He'd tried explaining there was no way could he wait that long, that an apartment where his Pop could find them was too close, and as far as marriage went, no one got married at eighteen anymore. After that, she'd started to cry.

She'd been complaining about being late for her period. If his buddies knew this was the only thing keeping him from skipping town, they'd say he'd fallen for the oldest trick in the book: a girl claiming she was pregnant only to get an engagement ring. But he loved Keri Ann and would marry her pregnant or not. Just not then, and just not there.

Keri Ann let him in the side door, whispering for him to hide the suitcase in the coat closet. "Don't slam the door. Daddy's asleep and I want to keep it that way."

Keri Ann's "Daddy" was a class A perv, although his neighbors had different names for fathers who snuck into their kids' beds at night. All their lives she and her brothers had dealt with being woken up at night, though it had always been worst for Keri Ann. Many times, Ricky had fantasied about killing the bastard, though there was a rumor in the neighborhood that he packed a gun. He had even been arrested a few times, but just like Ricky's old man, he always managed to beat the rap. Word was they both had dirt on the Lackawanna cops. This whole town stank to high heaven, in Ricky's opinion, and he couldn't understand why his girlfriend wasn't jumping at the chance to escape.

"Come upstairs, quick."

Keri Ann whisked him into her bedroom and pushed him down onto the bed. "So, you're really going."

"Yeah. It's all set."

She sat up. "Nothing I can do to make you stay?"

"No. Come here." He pulled her down with him.

"So, Ricky, tell me more about little Mustang Sally."

"Why? She's OK. But her car is off the charts." When he kissed her gently on the neck, she turned away.

"Is she pretty?"

"Who cares?"

"That means yes. Ricky, while you were making plans with some little Barbie doll from Grand Island, I found out they need a delivery man down at Sattler's. The pay's good. We can find a nice apartment—not here, down in Hamburg—and if you don't want to get married right away, that's OK. We can wait. All that matters is being together." She flipped him on his back and started rubbing his shoulders.

"Wow. That feels good." He turned his head to the side, drooling a little on the pillows she'd embroidered with pink flowers. "But do you really think they want a girl delivering couches and chairs?"

"No, stupid." She poked him in the ribs. "You're the delivery man. I'll find something else."

"Sounds like you got it all figured out." He rolled around to face her. "How about that other situation?"

She sat up again. "Yes."

"What do you mean, yes?"

"I'm pregnant. The test was positive."

He pounded the bed. "You're sure."

"I'm sure the dot turned pink."

"Can I see it?"

"No ... gross. I threw it out."

"What are you going to do?"

"Don't you mean what are *we* going to do?"

"Babe, I've told you a thousand times, I'm going to Texas. And I want you with me, pregnant or not."

"Right. Cramped up in the back seat of some little princess's car for two thousand miles. No. I need to think about it. Anyway, all this you have in your head about things being better down south is not a real plan. Sattler's is. They're paying a dollar more than minimum."

Ricky pushed her off him. "Keri Ann, I'm not going to work at Sattler's."

"Not forever, just until we can save up enough …"

He sat up. "No way. I'm leaving tonight, with or without you. I know you don't trust me to get something going down there, but I will. And then you'll have to join me, even if it's just to see for yourself that I'm telling the truth."

"What about the baby?"

"Bring it. We'll be like … a family."

"Quiet! What about my father? He'd kill me if he hears we've been talking about running away."

"If the old bastard gives you any trouble, hop on the first bus. Here." He dug a fifty-dollar bill out of his pocket and laid it on the bed. "I want you with me."

Keri Ann watched her best friend in the world barrel down the stairs. Straightening her bedspread, she arranged the pillows exactly how they'd been before he messed them all up. She looked out the window as he marched down the street with that silly-looking suitcase. For once, it seemed Ricky Green had actually made up his mind. But she'd see about that.

The last pregnancy test she'd bought—number three, but who was counting?—was tucked in a drawer under her panties. She took it into the bathroom, opened the box, and for the third time that week completed the tedious procedure. After five annoying minutes, Keri Ann forced herself to accept the fact that once again, the dot had not turned pink. Ten minutes later, still no plus sign; a half an hour, later the line remained flat, blue, and infuriating.

CHAPTER SIX

Unaccustomed to city streets, Carly blew right past the corner she'd agreed to meet this Ricky Green. She drove around the block, slower this time, noting the abandoned buildings and vacant lots. Apparently, the boy lived in the slums. No wonder he wanted to hit the road. She knew very little about Buffalo, let alone Lackawanna, and not much more than the name of this kid she'd given a ride the other day. What mattered was that he was also headed to Texas, had a driver's license, and offered three hundred dollars to pitch in for gas. Bringing him was a risk, but so was a girl on her own trying to make it across the country without getting stolen from, lied to, shot at, or worse. If he didn't show or ended up being a jerk, she'd dump him and drive as far south as possible, then call some people she knew who'd already made it to Houston.

There was the boy now, leaning up against a streetlamp. Rumpled and shaggy, he was the opposite of

Liam with his creased chinos and sculptured hair. *Ugh, Liam.* The main reason she couldn't wait to leave town. As it was, living on an island meant you were closed in, and being closed in with Liam was no longer an option. It was up to her to leave. Liam wasn't going anywhere fast. Why bother when he had such a sweet deal working for his father?

"Hi," she said to the shaggy-haired boy. "You're alone."

"Yeah."

The eye that had been swollen shut the other day looked better. She wanted to mention this but instead asked, "Where's the girlfriend?"

"Look, I said I'd be here, with cash." Ricky pulled a plug of bills from his back pocket. "Is that good enough for you?"

Kind of defensive, but honest. The money's all here— no, wait, he's fifty bucks short. She sighed. It would have to do. He'd barely shut the door when she shoved off in the direction of the skyway.

She made a sharp turn, and the boy held the bucket seat with both hands. "Do you know where you're going?"

"Doesn't it look like it?" She said a silent prayer that the entrance ramp she'd picked was the one heading south. Hard to tell, given the way they all twisted around. Good news—according to the sign, she'd nailed it. As she flew over the city, she noticed the boy looking out at the lake. "So, what about this mystery girl who decided not to come? Did you guys break up or something?"

Instead of answering, he said, "Look at that skyline. Sure is a better last impression than the steel plant."

Interesting way of avoiding the question. And downtown did look beautiful in her rear-view mirror. Maybe he'd just made up this girlfriend, she thought. She really wanted to ask what had happened to his eye, but she doubted he'd tell the truth. People lied all the time, but this boy was especially hard to read. He impressed her as someone like her, a person who'd rather keep their secrets secret. As long as he behaved himself, she'd let him stay.

For eighty miles down to the state line, they talked about Houston, the haven the boomtown kids from Buffalo were flocking to by the hundreds. Carly's friends already down there said she'd get a job in a minute, making good money, too. And she'd need that cash to move on to her real destination: Mexico, Brazil, Australia, Antarctica, or wherever else, as far away from Grand Island as she could get.

As far as she could tell, for Ricky it had been a choice between the Alaskan pipeline and the Texas oil fields, but the ten months of deep freeze in the Arctic Circle helped him make up his mind. He'd had enough of long winters.

By the time they zoomed past Erie, PA, Carly needed to pee. She got back from the rest stop to find Ricky sitting behind the wheel. She threw him the keys and he looked almost happy for the first time, revving the engine with a twinkle in his eyes, which Carly had observed were clear and blue.

"How does a girl one month out of high school end up with a Mustang classic?"

"Luck, I guess."

"No, really."

"Yes, really. I'm lucky. Everybody says so, anyway. My father gave it to me. He gives me whatever I want."

"Just what I thought. You are a little rich girl."

"What you mean by 'rich'?"

"Didn't know there were different kinds."

"Well, yes, there are. Pop has money because he's good at making it and saving it. Plus, he was lucky in his business. Though you'd never know it by looking at him. I'm sure you've heard his commercial."

"Sure. 'La Nova noodles, eat oodles and oodles.' Who could forget it? The daughter of Buffalo's pasta king. See, you are a princess."

"Hardly. But he has made a lot of money. So much, he gives it away like it's nothing. The only cool thing he ever bought for himself was that old boat."

"You have a boat?"

"He did, until I ... I don't want to talk about it. But boats are no big deal. Almost everybody with a house on the river has one. Most of them live in mansions. And guess what? They're no happier than ..." She stopped.

"Finish your thought. No happier than who?"

"Poor people."

"You mean losers from Lackawanna like me."

"I didn't say that. But if that's what you think. Money can't buy, well, you know."

"You're not so good at explaining yourself. You mean that money can't buy you love, like the Beatles song."

"Yeah. I guess so. I'm more like my dad than I like to admit ... Pop never finishes his thoughts. It drives us all crazy."

"You mean that weak old man who forces you to spend Sunday nights watching Lawrence Welk?"

Carly covered her face. Her shoulders shook, but she refused to cry. By now Pop would know she was gone.

Fortunately, the boy changed the subject. "Next stop, Cleveland." He switched on the radio. The only station that came in without static was in the middle of "Under the Boardwalk." He reached for the dial, but Carly caught his hand.

"No, leave it. I like this one." She scrunched down in the seat and closed her eyes.

Ricky started to ask her what was so special about some old song, but she'd checked out. Just as well. They had a long way to go.

Her face reminded him of a Valentine he'd given Keri Ann once—sweet, almost too sweet. No one back home would believe that he was driving a Mustang classic across the country with a little rich girl on her way to the end of the world. He almost didn't believe it himself. After all the talking they'd just done about his job prospects in Texas, he'd never thought to ask her why she'd decided to run away in the first place. Leaving a father who gave her anything she wanted meant she was either stupid or lying.

When the song ended, Carly sat back up and turned off the radio. "If you want to know, the reason I like it so much is that it reminds me of being a kid."

"Yeah, they used to play the Drifters a lot back then."

"Not just that. It's all about summertime and being free. No one bossing you around, nothing to worry about, not a care in the world."

Ricky couldn't remember a time like that in his entire life. His parents had always been at each other's throats. His mother hated his father for refusing to get a real job, instead letting the family suffer while he waited to be called up by the fire department. His father hated his mother because she considered him a good-for-nothing drunk. Ricky sided with her, which was why his old man had beaten him up so badly the other night.

Even now that his father had his dream job, he wasn't happy. He came up with these crazy ideas that Ricky's mother was messing around behind his back and that Ricky and his brothers were stealing from him. When any of his stuff went missing because he lost it when he was drunk, he roughed them up, especially Ricky. One reason he and Keri Ann had become friends was that he never had to explain what it was like living with a psycho. She already knew.

As they exited Interstate 90, Ricky filled in the silence by rambling on about the steel plant closing. "The only chance for a guy like me to make a go of it these days is to leave town." When he tacked on the part about sending for Keri Ann, Carly asked him why he was so sure about her. If she'd been another kind of chick, he'd figure she was coming on to him and just laugh it off. But her cute little face scrunched up so tight, he could tell she was serious.

Funny . . . he'd never been asked what it was about Keri Ann. Her looks were average on a good day, her figure on the skinny side. If he were honest, he'd say it was because she was the only real girlfriend he'd ever had, and that they knew things about each other that no one else would believe. If that wasn't enough, now she was pregnant. Things being as they were in that house, Ricky couldn't even be sure that the baby was his. It was his turn to get all quiet, but he made a stab at an answer. "It's like this—Keri Ann and me, we understand each other."

"That's something, I guess." Carly pressed her knees against the dashboard. "Do you have a favorite oldie, Ricky?"

"Hmmm. Never gave it much thought." Relieved that she'd let him off the hook about Keri Ann, he rubbed his chin. "How about 'Alley Oop'? You know, the one about the caveman?"

"Wow. That *is* old. OK, at the next rest stop I'll call the station and request 'Alley Oop,' for Ricky Green. Is that the one about the Neanderthal who drags his wife around by the hair?"

Ricky nodded. "Maybe that's what I should have done."

"What do you mean?"

"I don't know. My girlfriend—I always let her get her own way. She should be here with me."

"Guess you're not much of a caveman."

Ricky gripped the wheel, zoning in on the road so hard that he felt like part of the car. He zigged and zagged around slow movers, but when it came to the big rigs he stayed in his lane. A caveman, he most definitely was not.

Keri Ann liked to make her own choices. He'd stuck with her when rumors spread about her father being into kids, and when no one in school would sit next to her at lunch. Most of all, he'd been there when her mother died, leaving her in charge of the house. Ricky was the one she held on to when things got crazy. Still, she was her own girl, and she'd never let him tell her what to do.

If she was pregnant, having a baby was even more reason for her to get out of Lackawanna. Who'd want to bring up a kid anywhere near her father, or Ricky's, for that matter? But, as usual, reasoning with Keri Ann had been a waste of time. She had her own ideas—about everything. If she wasn't ready to be a mother, there were things she could do. As he saw it, if she wasn't willing to make this trip, she didn't trust him. Not enough to marry him, anyway.

~

Carly liked that when they passed the first sign for Cincinnati, Ricky said he was going to stop and fill the tank. When she went for her purse, he grabbed her hand. "No. I said I'd pay." His skin sliding against hers sent a tingle up her spine. Liam never thought about things like filling someone else's tank or picking up a check. This boy, who actually worked for his money, had a lot more class.

"You want me to take over?"

"No, I'm good. Catch a nap. I'll get us to Louisville."

Carly leaned her head against the window. When her parents realized that she was really gone, her mother would cry, and her father would lay down some Louie La Nova wisdom like "Maybe it was our Carly's time to fly the ... you know."

She hadn't wanted to hurt them, but it couldn't be helped. At least now they wouldn't have to worry about what to do with her anymore. She wouldn't embarrass them around their friends. Without Carly in the house, they could live like normal old people who played golf and went on vacations to Florida. For a long time, she'd been holding them back.

What Carly was especially looking forward to was never again being compared to her brilliant, successful sisters. No more embarrassing BOCES nursing program for girls whose grades wouldn't get them into regular college. And best of all, no Liam Dunn.

The streetlights on the interstate flicked by at a steady pace. Ricky was an excellent driver. He kept it steady at just a little above the limit. Better than Liam, who believed it was his civic duty to shoot the bird at any type of limit. *Whoever gave Ricky that shiner is probably an idiot.* She hoped Ricky had gotten him back good.

With him at the wheel, Carly let her body completely relax for the first time in days. The words "From the park you hear the happy sounds of the carousel. You can almost taste the hotdogs and French fries they sell ..." flowed out of her mouth. In a dream state, she was floating in a pool of crystal-clear water.

~

Ricky glanced at the girl with her knees propped against the dashboard, humming way off-key, and checked himself. He'd just begun cutting the strings holding him to one crazy chick. This was no time to get tangled up with another—not yet. He planned to keep on his side of the car and make sure she stayed on hers. Her pretty mouth was open, and no longer singing, she'd begun to snore. *She must really be out.*

He shook himself awake. It was all on him now. Keri Ann might not trust him, but this chick did. And he'd keep it that way.

Across the median, a pair of headlights came barreling toward him. He swerved to avoid a crash and ended up sideswiping the guard rail, making a total about-face as the other car corrected itself and sped away. The impact pushed Carly smack onto his lap, who woke up with a scream and beat his chest. "What did you do?"

He couldn't answer that, but if they didn't want to get hit again, he needed to move the Mustang out of the way of oncoming traffic. He turned the key. Nothing. She screamed louder. He tried a second time, but the engine was not responding.

She started calling him every crummy name he'd ever heard and a few he hadn't, and when she stopped to catch her breath he said, "OK, now we're going to have to get out and push." The little rich girl from Grand Island looked at him like he'd told her to drink poison. "I mean it, Carly. I'll steer and push at the same time. You go back there and push."

Carly couldn't believe her ears. This boy from Lackawanna had just crashed her little pony car, and now he wanted her to stand in the middle of the highway and move it? This couldn't be happening. A truck whizzed by, barely slowing down to veer around them.

"What are you waiting for? Get back there and push!" This time she jumped to it. In a minute, the wheels started rolling, and somehow the two of them managed to slide the Mustang over to the guardrail.

"What now?" Carly asked.

"We're going to need a tow truck."

"Can't you fix it?"

He stepped backward to look at the damage. "Even if I could, I'd need tools."

"Where do you think you're going? Don't walk away! You just wrecked my Mustang classic and you're walking away?!" She began to sob. "OK, fix it or don't! Just like the boat. It'll never be the same. You couldn't even get us to Louisville without ruining everything!"

"I'm sorry, but it was either swerve or hit the guy head-on. If we'd done that, at least one of us would be dead right now."

"Dead, huh. Like my car. Look at it."

Ricky had to admit, the paintjob was destroyed, and the front end would need major work—that is, if whatever damage the engine had suffered could be repaired. "It's only a car."

"My car that *you* just crashed. This model is considered an expensive … investment."

He hung his head and kicked one of the tires. "So much for not caring about money."

Wind rustled the dark treetops. Carly shivered. The sky was full of foreign stars, and who knew what was hiding in those woods, or those hills? There was a strangeness to it all, like the strangeness she'd often felt at the end of her dock while imagining sitting on the smokestack of the old Huntly Plant, or like thinking of what lurked below the seaweed in the river's hidden depths. Being out there made her tremble. She held on to the guardrail.

Just as her loser of a traveling companion suggested that they'd need to hitchhike to the next town to get help, a pickup truck pulled to the side of the road. The driver, whose face Carly couldn't make out in the glare of his headlights, said, "Looks like you'ns could do with a tow. Name's Chuck Davis." The faceless man held out his hand. The boy who'd just crashed her car shook it.

"Yes, sir. Rick Green here. Some nut jumped the median and I had to swerve to dodge him."

"Yeah, I saw that fella a while back. Drivin' like a bat outta hell. Looks like you got the worst of it, but he'll be lucky if he makes it wherever he's going in one piece. Let's get this thing hooked up."

While the men attached her car to what she now could see was an honest-to-goodness towing mechanism, all Carly could think about was how much it was going to cost to get it back on the road. What if it took more than she had? Did they throw you in jail if you couldn't pay? Would they make her call her father? The car had insurance, but she doubted it was in her name.

"Carly, let's go." Rick waved her into the cab. With the door open, she could see that this Chuck character had a beard just like Santa Claus. But this old fat man would be expecting payment for his presents.

~

Chuck was usually home in bed with his wife at this hour of the night. He'd been called by a friend to pray for a sick child who, thank God, had recovered quickly under the touch of his big work-worn hands. Farmer hands, Mabel called them, though it had been years since he'd grown actual crops. For a while now, he'd been more involved with planting seeds of faith.

He figured these kids with New York license plates were in trouble in more ways than one. Looked to him like they were running away from home. Judging by his fat lip and shiner, the boy had been in a fight, and the girl was angry enough to spit. At what, Chuck had no idea. But what he did know that these two did not was that taking off to someplace new usually didn't solve the problem. "So, where you two headed?"

"Houston," they said at the same time.

"Sure. Boomtown down there. 'Course, where there's

a boom, there's bound to be a bust." The girl let out her breath in a huff. "Listen, the service station in town don't open till eight. The wife and I can put you up till then if you don't mind sleepin' on a couch."

"No, sir," said the boy. The girl stared out the window, kind of a blank look on her pretty little face. From the looks of it, they didn't like each other too much, which was rare with these kids flying down south or out west, far away as they could get from the place they were raised. He whispered the beginning of a prayer without knowing what for, and then it came to him. "Tell you what, young lady, there is someone I know who thinks you're just great."

"What on earth are you talking about?" She looked straight at him for the first time.

"Just what I said. Someone who knows you better than your folks, your friends, even better than you."

"And who would that be, Santa Claus?"

The boy's face twisted up at the girl's attempt to mock him. Chuck dealt with plenty of mockers down at the mission, and he could tell this little girl from New York was a champ at that sport. The boy, on the other hand, looked like he'd just as soon throw her out of the truck.

"No, although I always had a soft spot for old St. Nick, seein' as he's a dead ringer for me." This made both kids laugh. "The one I'm talking about is Jesus." The cab got so quiet at the mention of the Lord's name that Chuck could hear the tree toads chirping.

"Well, I'm Catholic," she announced.

"That's OK. I'm Baptist, and God don't hold that against me." The boy laughed. "How about you, son? You believe in anything?"

"Myself, I guess."

The young man's sweaty handshake made Chuck doubt this. "Well, if that's true, it's a start. God did create you, and he don't make junk." This got a rise out of the girl.

"How do you know?"

"What do you mean, darlin'?"

"That God doesn't make junk."

Ah. That was why these kids in nice clothes driving a fancy car thought they didn't amount to a hill of beans. "No, kiddo. He knew you when you were swimmin' 'round like a tadpole inside your momma. And not only that—he said you were good. *All* good. Not a drop of bad in the mix."

"I'm sorry, mister, but I don't buy that," said the boy. "Where I come from, nobody's good. In fact, most of us are just plain rotten."

"Well, son, that might be true." Chuck paused as he zipped off the interstate and slid to a stop at the only traffic light in town. "But not a one of you started out that way."

"What difference does it make?" said the girl. "So you're innocent when you're born, and maybe for a few years after that. Then stuff happens—even to my supposedly perfect big sisters, the best at everything they try, voted most likely to succeed. Everyone thinks they're all that, but I've got some really bad dope on both of them."

"You know, that's just the thing." Chuck turned down the road to this house. "Jesus sees right through ... what did you call it? 'Bad dope.' Don't bother him in the least. When he looks at you, he sees the one who God made, the child who runs to him, not a care in the world, because she knows he loves her so much." He heard what sounded like sniffles. *Must have struck a root.* She'd hidden her eyes. When he pulled into his driveway, the house lights went on.

"Carly," whispered Rick from his made-up La-Z-Boy.

"What?" she said from the couch.

"Do you buy any of that Jesus stuff?"

"I don't know." Carly calculated the odds against a tow truck pulling right up behind them at the perfect time. "I've got an idea. Let's test it out. If the car gets fixed and we have enough money left to make it to Texas, then there's something to it."

"Don't you need to say a prayer or something, first?"

"How should I know?"

"Some Catholic. I'll try." He pressed his hands together. "God, if you're really there and what Mr. Davis says is true, make it all work out."

"You left out the 'amen.'"

"Fine. Amen."

CHAPTER SEVEN

After the biggest breakfast either of them had ever eaten, consisting of biscuits and gravy—a combination Carly would have turned up her nose at if she hadn't been so hungry—bacon and eggs, juice, and slices of apple strudel, of which Ricky took seconds, they towed the car to a town that looked so much like *Mayberry RFD*, Carly expected Andy Griffin to pop out and say "Howdy."

The man they did meet was a bone-thin raisin-faced mechanic. Carly explained her problem, but the man stared at her like she was speaking Chinese. Chuck Davis took over. "Everett, this little girl and her friend here ran into some trouble on the interstate last night. Can't get the engine to turn. Wonder if you can look under the hood."

Carly watched the man's lipless mouth form something resembling a smile as he strolled around her little red Mustang. He whistled. "Nineteen sixty-five."

"Sixty-four," corrected Carly. "A classic."

"So she is, so she is. Well, now, young man," he said to Ricky, "if you and Chuck can set her down over there, I'll see what I can do."

The two of them wedged her poor little car into the greasy old garage, letting it plop down like a bag of trash, and then didn't even bother telling Carly where she should go to wait. She ended up on the edge of the only chair in a grimy room with a cash register and a cigarette machine. The only wall décor was a calendar, this one curtesy of Quaker State Oil, featuring a blonde wearing leather boots but not much else straddling a motorcycle. *Hmmm. Would Sherriff Andy approve of that?* She then wondered if Chuck Davis would. *Probably not.*

Against the wall, a sagging bookshelf held pamphlets on local tourist attractions. She pulled a few out. The only one that seemed mildly interesting had a sticker on the back with the name Chuck Davis Ministries. She stuffed it in her purse as the men returned, the crotchety mechanic wiping his hands on a black rag.

"I got her goin', young lady, but if you're plannin' to drive any kind of distance like your friend here says, you'll have to leave her here till I can get parts. And I don't do bodywork. So, unless you're interested in sellin' …"

"No!"

"I told you she'd say that," said Ricky. All three men shared a chuckle at her expense.

Carly tried to control her tone. "So what do we do until then?"

"Carly, Chuck's offered to let us stay with him."

"That's nice of you, Mr. Davis. But I have no clue how

I'm going to pay for all this. We were stretching the budget as it was just to get where we were going."

Mr. Davis held up his hands. "You never know, young lady. Maybe it was meant to be. And as far as the money, when some friends of Jesus needed cash, he told them to open a fish, and what do you think was inside?"

She sucked her teeth. "Ok, I have no clue. What was inside?"

"I know the answer!" said Ricky, raising his hand as if they were in second grade. "It was gold. They found coins in the fish."

Carly scowled at him. "I thought you didn't know squat about this stuff."

"When I was a kid, a lady in our neighborhood had an afterschool club at her house. I brought Keri Ann. I told you about her, Carly."

"Your girlfriend."

"Anyway, it ended up being a Bible club."

"If you're interested," said Mr. Davis, "we have the adult version of that going on over at the city mission tonight."

"I'm in," said Ricky.

Carly's scowl deepened. What was a mission, anyway? Like a church? And why was this old man being so nice to them? Her father had made her promise never to go inside a Protestant church. He said all they cared about was getting converts. But what else was she going to do? Besides, anyone who thought they were going to convert her was in for a big surprise.

Ricky didn't know why, but hanging around Chuck Davis all day, feeding chickens and picking beans, checking his creek and riding around land as well-kept and green as a golf course—a day that should have settled him right down—had made him more anxious than ever. He needed to talk to Keri Ann. In private.

A few times, he almost confessed to Chuck that he'd gotten a girl back home in trouble. He'd been justifying leaving Keri Ann behind by saying if she really loved him, she'd have followed him to Texas. And if wanting to be with him was too much to ask, she should just go and get an abortion. Everyone knew someone who'd done it—it wasn't a huge deal. Although, something told him that Chuck Davis would disagree. So, he kept his mouth shut.

But Chuck, being a great storyteller, talked enough for them both. He told Ricky all about how he'd courted his wife, Mabel, and how after more than thirty years she was still his sweetheart, and that even though their lives hadn't panned out how they expected, they'd learned that God was great at turning tough scrapes into blessings. Ricky didn't buy how a guy with a beautiful house on land that rolled on forever could have ever had a tough scrape. "So, Chuck, what didn't turn out the way you expected?"

The old man's voice came out softer than before. "See, me and the missus always wanted children."

Ricky's breath caught in his throat. If his nerves had been tight before, now they were ready to snap. He'd never heard a story like this before. Most adults he knew wished they'd never had kids; they blamed them for never getting what they really wanted out of life.

Chuck went on about how he and Mabel had taken in foster children for years, adopting one outright, and eventually ending up with more young'uns calling them

Mom and Dad than anyone could hope to and now even younger ones who consider them Grandpa and Grandma. "They're the joy of our old age." The old man told one story after another about the blessings of children while Ricky paced around the barn yard, his hands behind his back.

He really needed to talk to Keri Ann.

~

Inside the house, Carly spent the day learning how to can peas with Mrs. Davis, who asked her over and over to call her Mabel or Mom. She wasn't even pretending to be OK with being held hostage in a steam-filled kitchen in the middle of nowhere waiting for her car to be fixed.

The gang in Houston would be expecting her soon. And there she was, hundreds of miles away, standing at a sink splitting pea pods, tough and stringy little buggers that only held a few tiny green pellets. In her opinion, hardly worth the effort for what you got out of it, although Mrs. Davis found it hilarious, popping almost as many veggies into her mouth as she did into the pot. They were doing something the old woman referred to as "putting them up," a process involving water and jars and billows of steam.

It was so hot in Mabel's kitchen that Carly's vision got blurry. Everywhere she looked, she noticed something that ticked her off: a tiny little black-and-white TV; a bookshelf holding mostly Bibles; a cupboard full of jars; yellow, red, and green food that has apparently already been "put up"; and worst of all, pictures of each of the Davis's kids. Carly counted fifteen different faces. *Mrs. Davis must have started having babies when she was sixteen.* She thought only Catholics had families that big.

In Carly's mother's dining room, there were only three pictures—one of each of the girls in their graduation gowns, which were only drapes that the photographer pinned around your shoulders. The wall hanging that got the most attention in the La Novas' house was the print of Raphael's *Madonna* hanging smack in the middle of the living room, which Carly was always able to see from her bedroom. The beautiful Italian-looking mother of Jesus followed you with her eyes wherever you went, and in one of Carly's worst nightmares the lady's face had turned into a death mask with a smile that seemed to mock her. In the Davises' living room, the only picture not of children was of an old man and woman looking at the ground, praying over a garden they must have just planted.

"So, young lady. Tell me about your family. Do you have brothers and sisters?"

Carly tapped her fingers on the table. For some reason, this was something old women always wanted to know. "Yes."

"How many?"

"Two."

The next thing she'd ask was where Carly fit in.

"Where do you fit in?"

There it was. "Youngest." Now came the hard part. She'd want to know what it was like being the baby in the family, so Carly beat her to the punch. "My oldest sister, Annette, was valedictorian of her class. Now she's a doctor married to another doctor, making tons of money out on Long Island. My parents are very proud of her. The next in line, Amy, always wanted to be a teacher, but not just any teacher—the best one of all time. She just got a job at a big fancy school that only rich families can afford."

"And what about you, Carly?"

"Me? The only thing I'm good at is getting into trouble."

The old woman dabbed sweat off her forehead with a dainty little hanky. "Do you want some lemonade, dear?"

Carly had been making it a point not to take anything more from these people than absolutely necessary, but it was so hot in that kitchen, she expected the rooster-print wallpaper to start sliding off the walls. "Yes. That would be fine."

Mrs. Davis took a cut-glass pitcher out of the fridge and poured two glasses of what Carly would bet money was fresh-squeezed juice. They sat at an old-school red-and-white linoleum table with matching chairs. "Is that why you're running away, child?"

Choking on her first sip, Carly put down the glass with too much force. "What do you mean?"

"Sounds to me like you think you don't belong in your own family."

Discussing her personal problems with strangers, however well-meaning they might be, had never exactly turned Carly on, but the question was hard to resist. "Mrs. Davis, all I ever wanted when I was a kid was to feel like part of my own family. And I did for a little while. But things changed. As far as I can see, you have lots of kids. Do you love every one of them as much as the others? Tell the truth. Are there some who made you proud and others who embarrassed you?"

The old lady didn't answer right away, taking time to carefully open a tin of shortbread cookies and arrange them on a cobalt-blue plate. "Dear, are those the children you mean?" She pointed to the row of photographs.

"Yeah, I guess so."

"Each one of those young'ns was the sun and the moon and the stars to me."

"Was?"

"While we had the good fortune to know them."

Carly didn't know what to say. Had they all died? Every one of them? She'd wanted to keep the conversation as light as possible, but this was weird. "Don't you still know them?"

"Oh, sure. Some come for Christmas. And just like your family, not all of them did as well as the others. Some are better at keeping in touch, but we believe that God handpicked each one to be a part of our family for a season."

This was blowing her mind. "You mean some of your kids only lived with you temporarily?"

"Yes. We were only able to adopt one of them outright, but we loved them all just the same. When I was told that I'd never have children of my own, I cried for weeks. For years I shook my fist at God, accusing him of breaking his promise to give me the desire of my heart. All I ever wanted as a girl your age was to get married and be a mother."

Carly blinked back tears. She guessed she'd had this old girl figured wrong. The kids on the wall belonged to other people who couldn't or wouldn't take care of them.

The old lady was not finished. "I can't tell you why the Lord let me go through those lean years, but there's a song we like down at the mission." Mabel Davis began to sing, "There is a river that flows from deep within, there is a fountain that frees the soul from sin. Come to this water, there is a vast supply. There is a river that never shall run dry."

"I'm sorry you couldn't have kids of your own."

"Did you hear the words of that song, child? I've had more joy in my life than I can hold." Now Mabel had tears in her eyes.

Carly didn't know what to make of it. But if Chuck Davis Ministries was all about old ladies singing and crying, she better get a tight hold on herself before stepping foot into this "meeting" they were being pressured to attend.

~

Her hopes of getting to Houston on schedule shrank as the city of Cincinnati grew on the horizon. Soon, she'd be asked to disobey one of her father's few hard-and-fast rules: never step foot in a non-Catholic church. She'd stopped believing in the God she'd heard about in First Communion class when she was seven years old and the wafer Father Frank put on her tongue made her feel no different at all, zero effect. She'd taken care not to chew it, but rather let it melt slowly in her mouth, just like the nuns had instructed. Still, no change. Soon, she began believing in another kind of god. One who allowed terrible things to go on in the world, like war, hunger, sickness, and hatred, one who didn't care either way what she did or how she felt.

Carly had no idea what to expect at this Protestant meeting. She was beyond worrying about dropping dead like her father used to threaten, but he'd also warned her not to get mixed up with people with different beliefs. "Stick to you your own, you know ..." *Your own what,*

Pop? Race? Religion? Side of the street? Old-school ideas.

Anyway, all this was supposed to be was a meeting. She'd give anything to be on the way to Houston right now instead of downtown Cincinnati, but it was just one night. What could happen in one night? If anyone tried to put something over on her, you better believe she'd set them straight. She took a deep breath and tried to relax in the back seat of the Davis's old Buick but had to keep reminding herself not to clench her teeth.

~

Ricky recognized this Cincinnati skyline from having passed it the night before. It was longer than the one in Buffalo, but just as boxy and bright. He'd driven over this same stretch of Interstate seventy-one minutes before crashing the Mustang. "Chuck, I hate to say it, but I feel like Carly and I have come a long way and now we're going backwards."

The old man stroked his beard. "Well, son, that's true. But think of it this way: maybe you missed something the first time. Come to think of it, I've been travelin' this route all my life, and every now and then something still takes me by surprise. You two, for instance."

"How's that?"

"I never expected to find a pair of young folks from New York broke down right in front of me last night. And if I recall, the car was swung backwards, right to where we're headed. Maybe you went by too fast. Maybe there was something down here you were supposed to take a closer look at."

Ricky glanced at the run-down tenements lining the city's eastern edge, just like they did back home. He'd grown up in the mirror image of all this. And even if what Chuck meant was that God wanted to interrupt their trip just to let them hear the gospel preached, he'd already done that as well. He and Keri Ann had both accepted Jesus at the Bible club when they were eight. But then the lady died. Even with no adult to help them, the two of them remembered to pray occasionally, mostly for Keri Ann's mom to get healed of cancer and Ricky's parents to stop fighting.

Neither of those things had happened. As far as Ricky was concerned, God's record was 0 and 2.

Still, he had a reason to go to this meeting. He needed to make a phone call somewhere no one could hear him, like at a pay phone in the city. What he had to say to Keri Ann couldn't wait. She was bound to do something stupid if he didn't make things right between them soon. Knowing Keri Ann, she very likely already had. He wasn't sure about this whole God business, but he didn't want anything to do with killing a baby. He'd been in a hurry the other day, and Keri Ann could be so pigheaded. Anyway, she'd dropped the news on him like a bomb. What was a guy supposed to do?

Chuck slowed to a ramble as they bounced off the expressway. "How you'ns doin' back there?"

"Just fine, honey," said Mabel. "Enjoyin' the lovely sunset."

Carly couldn't imagine what Mrs. Davis was talking about; all she could see were the roofs of a bunch of ugly old buildings. But then Mabel would call falling in a mud puddle a good thing because mud was so good for the skin. She'd been chatting Carly up about how wonderful this meeting would be. Carly didn't believe her, but she did sense that something interesting was about to happen. As they got out of the car, she caught a bad case of hiccoughs.

She would have liked to talk to Ricky in private before going in, maybe arrange a signal between them so they could sneak outside if things got out of control—all she could think of was a movie she'd seen of a church with people shouting and turning cartwheels in the aisles—but he'd stepped out. Said he'd be back in a minute, that he needed to stretch his legs. *A lot of help he's turning out to be.*

~

The nearest phone booth was less than a block away. "Hey, Chuck, I'll be right back. I've got to make a quick call."

"You sure? We've got a phone in the office."

"Thanks anyway. This is kind of personal," he said, trotting down the street. "I won't be long."

He was surprised when one of Keri Ann's brothers answered. Whichever one it was laughed when the operator told Ricky to insert one dollar and eighty cents. The coins took forever to drop. "Is Keri Ann there?"

"Who's this?"

"Ricky. Get Keri Ann." He could hear arguing in the background and then finally, his girlfriend's voice. "Keri Ann?"

Silence. Then a sharp click.

CHAPTER EIGHT

No posse of crazed Bible-thumpers pulled Carly off into a dark room with a bright light to brainwash her into selling her soul to some cult the minute she walked into Living Water Mission. In fact, the only one who even spoke to her was a man in a wheelchair who just smiled and said, "Hey!"

The windowless place had a scent she recognized, a blend of strong coffee and dusty wood, like the roller rink in Tonawanda where she'd skated as a kid, but that building had been painted a bleak beige. These walls were lined with red and gold tapestry that looked old, very old. Little balconies in the corners sagged down so low, you'd risk your life standing in one. But the thing that held her attention the longest hung in the middle of the farthest wall, over a little stage—a huge cross made from what looked to be scrap metal. No dying Christ hung from it, just an awful lot of rusty old pieces of steel.

Chuck guided her to a table in the back where the

man in a wheelchair sat, straightening stacks of books. "Carly, this is Marcus, the resident assistant here at the mission. He can show you around. Where's Ricky?"

"Out looking for a phone booth."

"Oh yeah. I thought he'd be back by now. This isn't the best place to be roaming around in at night."

"I'll seat the young lady, Chuck," said the man in the wheelchair. "Go get the show on the road."

Carly followed hesitantly as her host rolled down the aisle between a dozen or so rows of folding chairs, most of them empty. She'd been hoping there'd be a crowd so she could blend in and dream about Texas until it was over, but nope. She was out in the open, an easy target.

And this Marcus parked her right up front beside a group of tough-looking women who were not smiling. She clung to her purse. Marcus winked. "Don't worry, miss. My friends here will be on their best behavior to-night, right, ladies?" When the largest of the three stuck her hand in his face he laughed again, but not in mean-ness. "We're watching you all tonight, and so is He," said Marcus, pointing to the huge metal cross.

When he zipped away, abandoning her to these strangers, Carly's heart pounded. Were these women criminals? Ex-cons? Hookers? All three? Maybe. Maybe sitting next to someone whose sweaty skin spilled over their chair onto hers was Carly's punishment for enter-ing this building and disobeying her father. She scanned the growing crowd to look for Ricky.

The woman next to her tapped her on the shoulder. "'Scuse me, miss, do you have a cigarette?"

"No. Afraid not."

"This your first time at Livin' Water, huh."

"How'd you guess?"

"I don't know, the way you starin' up at the walls and all. You know this place used to be a whorehouse?" The other two chuckled.

That explains the red velvet and little rooms off the balcony. Who would have thought? "Can't say that I did."

"Sound like you from up north. What you here for, anyway?"

Her traveling companion finally showed up at the door in the middle of a line of people. Waving in his direction, she said, "I've been taken prisoner."

"Ain't we all," said the one wearing a wig and a rhinestone tiara.

Carly stood up quickly. "Excuse me."

"OK, baby."

The aisles were now so full, Carly had to work her way to where Ricky Green stood chatting away with this Marcus like they were long-lost comrades. She said, "Hey. What took you so long?"

Ricky's face twitched like he'd been caught stealing the collection money. Marcus shook his head, his smile fading. "Miss, I thought I already got you seated."

Carly's mouth hung open. "I didn't know it was, like, permanent."

He pointed to the rapidly filling rows. "Do you notice a pattern?"

She did—boys on the left and girls on the right. "You've lost your place. Now you'll need to stand."

What she really needed to do was get out of there. But up from behind charged Mrs. Mabel Davis. "Sweetie, you're just who I was looking for. Would it be too much to ask to have you pour coffee tonight?"

A table with Styrofoam cups and a big stainless-steel urn was set up near the door. *Perfect.* Carly said yes while planning her escape.

"All you need to remember is one cup per customer, and everyone must be polite."

Carly had rarely been put in charge of anything, and never anything like this. "Sure, but Mrs.—Mabel, I don't know how to make—"

"Don't worry, dear. The coffee's already perking. You'll know it's done when it stops whining like a spoilt child." And she was off again, even happier than she'd been in the hot kitchen putting up peas. Someone started playing piano and the crowd quieted somewhat. Marcus led Ricky off to the boys' section, once again leaving Carly on her own.

From behind the coffee bar, she could see that not everyone in the audience was as rough-looking as the ones she'd already met. A row of girls sitting near the back weren't much older than Carly but looked more like hippies, bandanas holding back long hair, patches on their jeans. *Jesus freaks?* She'd run into a few of those in Buffalo, on the Elmwood Strip. They did their thing outside the college bars like the other religions, TM, Baha'i, and the Moonies. Not much difference between them, as far as she could tell. They all claimed to have the truth, but at least the Moonies handed out flowers.

The old guy up there playing piano introduced a new song, Jimmy Swaggert's "There Is a River." This song was slower, with words that Carly had heard somewhere before. *Ah.* It was the one Mabel sang while they were canning peas. A few in the crowd started up the chorus, "There is a river that flows from deep within ..."

~

Ricky had never heard the song they were singing, something about a river, though the old folks around him all knew it by heart. His favorite number at the Bible club was "Stop! And Let Me Tell You What the Lord Has Done for Me," especially when he was the one picked to hold out the big red stop sign. Sweat dribbled down his face. Why had Keri Ann hung up on him?

She must have gone through with the abortion. He'd been OK with this yesterday. It had been her decision— her body, her choice and all. So why did he feel so lousy about it now? If it meant the two of them were through, that might be a good thing. But if she had been pregnant, it wasn't about just the two of them anymore. Could be that the kid had been his. He had no idea what to do. If someone would only listen to him, *really* listen, maybe he could come up with an answer.

Another row of guys pushed their way down his row, not giving two hoots who they bumped into in the process. Ricky stuck out his arm. "Hey, watch where you're going." The kid who'd pushed him snarled in his face like a cornered dog. Maybe, like he and Carly, this guy had been forced to come. No one to the right or left looked like they'd give him the time of day, let alone advice about his girlfriend.

A minute ago he'd asked that Marcus if he could run something by him, but the dude blew him off. "Maybe later," he'd said. "Too busy right now." All the older people were doing something, checking sound systems, pulling out extra chairs.

When the song was over, Chuck Davis walked onstage

to welcome everyone to the meeting. He said something about switching things around that night so that a few kids who were going to be baptized could give their testimonies. "Linda, you want to come up here and share what the Lord has done for you?"

Ricky leaned forward when a tall girl with very straight hair walked on stage, her tie-dye shirt clashing with the red-and-gold wall behind her. She picked up a guitar and sat on the step so he could no longer see her, but her voice rang out loud and clear even without a mic. The song was hard to understand except for the line "Those who come to me like a little child, I will not turn away."

For some reason, Ricky got a little choked up. He fought back tears, glad when she put the guitar to the side.

"My name is Linda. I'm from Fairfield, and I can tell you life isn't that much better there than it is here. People might have more money, but they've also got a lot of hate and fear. Anyway, I was walking across the Roebling Bridge a few weeks ago, thinking how easy it would be to just jump off and end it all. You know, it was going to come to that soon enough anyway—why not just get it over with? Then I got to thinking how beautiful the scene was, the Kentucky shore, birds in the sky, clouds floating by. It made me remember the time my stepfather took us scuba diving.

"You'd be amazed at all the garbage at the bottom of that beautiful river. I mean, they always say you only see a tiny bit of an ice burg. Same goes for rivers. What's underneath the pretty surface would change your opinion of the Ohio entirely. Anyway, I got to thinking that was just like my life. People only see the outside, my clothes and makeup. But you know, while I stood on that bridge, crying my eyes out, wondering whether or not I should jump, it came to me that there is someone who knows what's down there. The shipwrecks and the lost treasures, the scary creatures, and the ones so beautiful they take your breath away. He knows it all. And suddenly, I didn't feel so alone. Something inside of me said, 'Don't give up. God loves you just the way you are, seaweed, black goo, and all.'"

Just when her story was starting to get interesting, Ricky felt a tap on his shoulder. It was Marcus. "Hey, man, your friend—Carly, is it? Anyway, she just took off. I mean, this isn't a cell block or anything, but I don't think you want her walking around out there all by herself."

"Oh, thanks." Ricky excused himself.

Outside, the streetlights made the sky look even darker. Sure enough, there was Carly La Nova trotting around as if she were back on Grand Island, with not a clue about the stuff that happens in the middle of cities at night. "Hey. Stop!"

She waved her hand. "Go away."

"Where do you think you're going?"

"Why should you care?"

Good question. "If you get mugged, how will I get to Texas?"

"I had to get out of there. That girl, it was like she could read my mind. I swear something fishy is going on."

"What do you mean?" he asked, trying to catch his breath.

"What that girl said about the river. It's exactly what I think about. All the time."

Something the girl with the long hair had said up on that stage had really gotten to Carly. "So, maybe you should go back and tell her. Maybe she can help you."

She looked at him like he had a screw loose but agreed. "OK ... if I can be sure the whole thing isn't some sort of racket. You know, I think she's one of those Jesus freaks."

Before he could answer, a pair of guys jumped out of a car near them, too close for comfort. Ricky grabbed Carly's hand. "Let's get out of here." He didn't look back until they made it safely through the mission doors.

For the miracle of not having to face off with any of the locals, Ricky Green thanked God, something he hadn't done in a long time.

CHAPTER NINE

Meanwhile, on the East Side of Buffalo, Malcolm Xavier Worthy ground out his third cigarette while waiting for the last of his students to finish their test on the history of the Civil Rights Movement. Though the desk that he'd reclaimed from a pile of junk had suffered many a burn, he was careful to use an ash tray. One of his mother's from the Toronto Exhibition, a souvenir he knew she wouldn't miss. Unfortunately, the relic's clean post-modern shape and bright-orange glaze only emphasized the dinginess of the office.

It amazed him that with all the corporate donations the local chapter of PUSH received, they couldn't afford better equipment. The main goal of the Liberation School was to inspire kids, to expand their horizons, to "push" them forward. But even the posters of his parents' heroes staring down at him from the pockmarked walls—Eldridge Cleaver, Jesse Jackson, Malcolm X, and Bobby Seale—were wrinkled and tattered. Brother Calvin, the director who he rarely saw, told Malcolm most of their funding went toward overhead. Malcolm stared at the ceiling where a water stain in the shape of South America had been since they built the Panama Canal.

The Black Power movement had influenced Malcolm greatly as a child. When he was little, he ate a free breakfast every morning gratis the Buffalo chapter of the Black Panthers even though his parents fed him well enough at home. Dr. and Mrs. Worthy wanted their son to witness the strength of the people united firsthand. Things sure had changed. Malcolm couldn't put his finger on it, but ever since corporations got involved, the movement had become more about money and less about people.

In his father's opinion, the powers that shouldn't be were secretly trying to enslave people all over again by making them dependent on government handouts. Malcolm suspected his father had become paranoid because of all he'd been through as a political radical. He insisted that he had been arrested back in '68 because the CIA had infiltrated the Black Panthers. Malcolm supposed he should be glad nothing like that had happened to him, but still he'd heard of so many bad things—hush-up things, like his namesake being shot by men supposedly walking the same path, or clean-cut pop stars like Franky Lyman dying of a heroin overdose.

At least Malcolm, like his grandfather, Reverend Malcom Russell Worthy, was trying to advance the welfare of the people and getting paid at the same time. Not very much, but it was something. At least, he told himself, his job had a degree of meaning.

Promoting social justice, equal rights, and affirmative action to kids from the East Side and making enough money to put gas in his car were all well and good, but he looked wistfully out the window at the hazy summer evening. The sun still shimmered over the rooftops but was sinking fast. On a night like this, a young lady who he knew could still take him or leave him might be leaning toward the latter. If he didn't make it out of there before eight, no way would he and the most beautiful girl he'd ever had the guts to date get to the club before the tickets ran out like they did anytime Sonny Rollins came to town.

In exactly one minute, Malcolm would kick out the two jokers pretending to work but really just wasting his time.

"Mr. Worthy, does this grade count?"

"You know the answer to that, Reginald. What counts?"

"Everything."

"Yes. And you have exactly one minute before I turn out the lights and lock the door."

"If we don't, will you make us stay here all night all by ourselves?"

"If that's what happens, it will have been your choice."

"What if we want to spend the night?"

He hadn't thought of that. Some of his students had little to no home life, and though Malcolm hadn't managed to teach them much about the need for self-determination, they were still waiting for him at the door every day. Could have been for the chips and pop that he bought with his own money, he supposed, but Malcolm hoped it was more about hanging out with an older guy who dressed well, drove a car to work, and addressed them by their proper names. Which was why he'd let them linger over an assignment that the rest of the boys had handed in half an hour ago. "I meant that as a threat, Mr. Sikes."

"What's a threat?" asked Sikes.

"Something you don't want. Now finish up. Your momma's going to be worried."

The young man laughed. "For real, can we go home with you?"

"Not tonight, Reginald. Hand in your work. I'll see you tomorrow."

"Sure thing, boss."

"Stay cool, boss."

Boss, is it? If you judged by how many of his students were grasping the PUSH agenda, Malcolm was no more than a babysitter. But at least he'd been keeping a few hard-luck cases off the streets in his time here.

Malcolm usually graded papers before going home, but that night Anya was waiting for him. The only phone in the room sat on the corner of Brother Calvin's desk, and though the old pickleface protected his side of the room like a junkyard dog, this was an emergency. He took his chances that Supervisor Calvin had not installed a closed-circuit camera and sat down on the man's dangerously wobbly chair.

Dialing the number he'd memorized, he waited for someone to pick up and noticed the disengaged latch of a drawer that was usually carefully locked. He nudged it a little with his knee, suspecting that brother Cal would dust it for fingerprints if he suspected anything.

The only item in the drawer was a ledger, plain and neat. Ever since he'd started working for PUSH, Malcolm had wanted to get a look at this. It might contain the secrets of whatever happened to the checks coming in from

M&T Bank, Peter J. Schmidt, Rich's Products, the Rockefeller Foundation, and other fat cats' charitable trusts. All that his students ever saw of those sizable donations was a sorry excuse for a teacher making less than minimum under the table in a substandard rented space with books and supplies sent to them from the Chicago chapter.

"Hello?" said a lady with a heavy accent.

"This is Malcolm Worthy. May I speak to Anya?"

He heard foreign chatter. Anya's family had recently emigrated from Russia, although you'd never know it by listening to her. While the family sorted things out on the other end of the line, he carefully opened the ledger, expecting to see rows of numbers in black ink.

"Hello, Malcolm. Where are you?"

"Just leaving work. I'm about ready to fly."

"Sure, Superman, get your cape. But I still don't think we're going to make it."

Vowing to put everything back just the way he'd found it, Malcolm flipped the cover of the ledger. He blinked. Not one number in the book—no writing period. Only an unsealed envelope. Malcolm peeked inside: two tickets to Las Vegas, Nevada. Delta Airlines, first class.

Anya Elena Patrovich sat on the stoop in front of their building when her date finally arrived, his shirt damp and his glasses fogged up. Why she was attracted to a character like Malcolm X. Worthy, she couldn't pin down, but it had started last spring in AP history. Malcolm didn't fit in neatly with any one group, and neither did she. Maybe that's why she liked him. After what she'd gone through getting out of the USSR in one piece, it had been tough sympathizing with entitled Americans.

Tonight the boy ran down the sidewalk, out of breath,

with a worried expression on his face. Her mother yelled to her out the window. She was glad Malcolm didn't speak Russian.

"Let's get out of here." He swung her around and down the street.

Anya was wrong about it being too late to get into the concert, although the bouncer at the Tralfamodore gave them a once-over. A very white girl with this very black boy, as if they were freaks who'd escaped from the circus. The bouncer demanded that they show some ID. Anya resisted the urge to give the big bully the finger as Malcolm pulled out his driver's license and she, her fake sheriff's card.

Malcolm paid for the tickets, and she winced just a little. She was the jazz fan. Malcolm's idea of a swell date was going to Ted's Hot Dogs, then walking out to the pier to feed seagulls the last of their soggy rolls. The Tralf itself was about as different from the outer harbor as a place could be. The twists and turns you had to go through to get inside the place reminded her of the tunnels of legend used by the KGB. Narrow and darkly lit, this passage finally opened to a cave-like room with a low stage, filled with little round tables and uncomfortable chairs. Tonight, the room was packed out, and Sonny's hometown fans were anxious. So was Malcolm. He hadn't said a word all the way uptown.

They made their way through the crowd to one of the last remaining tables and once they claimed it, Malcolm looked at Anya over his glasses. "Hey, you want something to drink?"

"No, but you do."

"I'll be right back."

Maybe a rum and Coke would lighten him up. One thing she enjoyed about Malcolm was what he referred to as his "gift of gab." The boy could talk to anyone about anything; he was as open to new people as her family was closed. She assumed it was due to his abnormally clear conscience—he had nothing to hide, no skeletons in the closet, no locked boxes in the basement. So tonight, this silent treatment was bugging her. Could it be something she'd done? Maybe he was mad that it took almost all the money he made in a week to do the kind of things she liked to do in one night.

She scanned the dim room of the Tralf, or the Tralfamodore, named for the imaginary land whipped up by Kurt Vonnegut in the novel *Slaughterhouse-Five*. They must have been the youngest couple in the house. Other than that, Sonny's fans were as different as they could be: black, white, and in-between. Fashion statements galore, from sheik to grunge, Sonny united them all. A middle-aged man in front of them held hands across the table with a girl young enough to be his daughter. The man's profile looked familiar.

Malcolm returned with two glasses, and she pointed to the older man. "Hey, Malcolm, isn't that Brother Calvin?" Her date let the glasses drop, grabbed her hand, and got her out of there so fast, she thought the building was on fire.

~

With so many big, dangerous questions about his boss running through his mind, Malcolm needed to talk. The problem was, except for his grandfather, most people he knew were either running some scam themselves or too cynical to believe justice could ever exist on this earth.

Anya had listened to enough of what some claimed were Malcolm's paranoid delusions: the one about secret government ops being responsible for turning kids all around the country on to drugs, his assessment that most politicians were selected rather than elected, and so on. He didn't think she'd put up with another one, especially not about a guy they both knew. Instead, he apologized profusely before dropping her off at her house.

Taking a chance that his grandfather, Reverend Worthy, had not yet gone to bed, he knocked on his door.

"Grandpa?"

"That you, Malcolm?"

"Yes. May I come in?"

Before he knew it, he was sitting in the kitchen drinking milk, eating homemade snickerdoodles, and spilling his guts to the patriarch of the Buffalo Worthys, Reverend Malcolm Russell Worthy.

When he finished his story, his grandfather took off his glasses and wiped them clean with a napkin. "Son, you've made some heavy allegations against your boss. Do you have proof?"

"The airline tickets."

"Circumstantial. They won't hold up in a court of law." He took of his glasses and rubbed his eyes. "I had a treasurer once who'd taken to dipping his hands in the collection plate."

"What did you do?"

"Well, just like you, I had no hard evidence. So I waited it out, till he made a mistake. Thing was, he was careful to cover his tracks. I figured if I didn't get him, the Lord would."

Malcolm braced himself. Now was the point in the conversation when his grandfather would begin to preach. The old man had a habit of including the larger-than-life personage he called "The Lord" in every important discussion. Malcolm had grown up agnostic; the question of whether there was an actual creator mattered little to him. But some poser taking money from kids so poor, they dreaded going home at night sure did. "So that's your answer, Grandpa? Wait for God to get him?"

Reverend Worthy, a man who had grown up in the Jim Crow South and moved to Buffalo only to find things were not all that different in the segregated North, regarded his grandson. "He will, you know."

"Well, I can't wait that long, Grandpa. How am I going to look those kids in the face tomorrow knowing this PUSH program is all a big joke?"

"Malcolm, you act as if what you've run into tonight is something new. Do you know the reason why your daddy left the church back in the day? Because, just like you, he'd figured a few things out. Big things, like the real reason our country went to war in Vietnam."

"Yes, and the real reason President Kennedy got shot, and his brother Robert, and Dr. King. I've heard it all before, Grandpa, but knowing things and not being able to change them only makes the knowing worse."

"War is tough, son."

"But we're not at war anymore, not the last I looked."

"'For we wrestle not against flesh and blood but against principalities, against powers, against the rulers of the darkness of this world, against spiritual wickedness in high places.' Ephesians 6:12."

"Only words, Grandpa."

"'The words I speak unto you, they are spirit, and they are life.' John 6:63."

"Whatever you say, Grandpa. Thanks anyway. I shouldn't have bothered you so late."

"I know what you think about the scriptures, son. How they're used to keep poor people in their place. How they're racist, sexist, and all that."

"Yes, sir. That's about right."

"You know that treasurer I mentioned earlier? He ended up doing ten years for embezzling money at his next job."

"That's good to know, Grandpa. It's past my bedtime. I'll see you later."

Reverend Worthy locked the door behind his grandson, smiling and thanking God that the wall of deception the boy continually banged his head against was beginning to crumble. In his studied opinion, it was only a matter of time.

~

On the other side of town, Keri Ann McGraw scrubbed the kitchen floor while her younger brothers ran around looking for matches to light their leftover firecrackers. "Get out of here before I call down Daddy!" That sent them packing. She wiped away their crazy footprints, but the smell seeping inn through the window couldn't be dealt with that easily. If there was a hell, it was the West Side of Buffalo the first week in July.

Just looking at it, no one would ever guess how filthy their house was. The stink on the couch, the rugs, even the walls. She used Lysol, but nothing ever got out the deep-down stench. If she really had been pregnant, living here would have been hell on earth.

But no way would she have considered moving out. Not without Ricky, not in this neighborhood of lock-pickers and window-smashers. *Good thing my boyfriend is such a softy.* He'd be calling her again soon, begging to make things right. She'd only been hanging up on him to make him want her more, and she'd bet a hundred bucks it was working. She'd known Ricky Green for so long, she could predict what he'd do next. He'd start feeling guilty about what he thinks is his baby and want to be involved in some way. If he wanted her to get rid of it, she'd refuse. If he wanted to keep it, she'd threaten an abortion to guilt him out even worse.

Anyway, with or without Ricky, her father had put his foot down about her moving out. "No daughter of mine is going to make it easy for the neighborhood hoodlums." Of course, this was a bunch of garbage. Her father couldn't care less about the local hoodlums; he just didn't want to lose his housekeeper.

The phone rang, the sound ripping through the air like a fire alarm. It had to be Ricky. She'd let him wait a while before picking up. Just before the last ring, she answered, "Who is it?"

"Come off it, Keri Ann. Can you talk?"

"I don't know. Depends."

"I haven't got much time. And don't hang up on me again."

"We'll see about that."

"You need to be straight with me."

"Oh, really? Just how straight are you being with me, running away with some girl you don't even know? And with me pregnant with your baby."

"It's not like that, Keri Ann. In fact, I won't be seeing her much. She's staying with another family. The Fellowship keeps the men and women separate."

"What's this about a fellowship?" Sounded like her boyfriend had gotten hooked up with some religious cult. *Something he would do.*

"We broke down in Ohio and met up with a bunch of Jesus freaks."

"Great, Ricky. Just great. And you expect me to trust you not to do something stupid?"

"Yeah, well, they're actually pretty cool. They invited us to stay with them for a while, until we get a better idea of it means to be a disciple of Christ."

"Ricky, don't you remember? We've been through that whole routine. They're all phonies. Get a grip."

"That's what I thought at first—I mean, what I thought they were. But all I can say is these people are different, Keri Ann. Remember Bible Club, back when we were kids?"

"Who could forget that old hag with the green teeth? She still shows up in my dreams—I mean nightmares. 'The B-I-B-L-E, that's the book for me'—what a crock."

"You didn't think so then."

"I believed in fairies and angels back then, too." There was someone singing in the background from wherever he was calling. It was hard to hear. He mumbled something about having to make it quick.

"Keri Ann, I need to ask how you're doing with the— you know …"

"The baby?" He was so easy to read. He'd gotten hooked up with Bible-thumpers and was now going to ask her to keep it. "You want me to give it to you straight, Ricky, so here it is. I've decided to get an abortion."

"Oh, no. I mean, you can't do that! Not without me …"

"Without you is where I am right now. What did you expect me to do? I've already made an appointment. I can't wait much longer. After three months, I'll have to leave town to have it done."

"Please don't. At least wait until I get back."

"You're coming back? I thought you were dead set on Texas."

"Right now I'm not sure about anything. All I know is that killing a baby is not a good idea. Will you wait?"

"I'll think about it."

"Please. Maybe we can come up with a different—" He said as she banged down the receiver. Keri Ann completed his sentence in her head: *We can come up with a different plan. Right, Ricky?* How many were there? The boy was nice to look at, but not much for common sense. He let people take advantage of him. And when he finally caught on, he blew up, as if none of it was his fault. *Blame, blame, blame.* That was Ricky Green.

She could just imagine the leader of whatever new scam this was working his way into Ricky's brain. He'd find out that holding up a bar but making it just a little too high was the best way to keep Ricky Green in the game. It had always worked for her.

CHAPTER TEN

Three months later, inside a tent on Chuck Davis's land, Carly stood next to Rick as the elder of Living Water Fellowship put Rick's hand on top of hers and joined them in holy matrimony. So far she'd hung in there, but when they sat down and listened to the preacher point out that once a man and woman begin an intimate relationship, they become one flesh and are married in the eyes of God, an image of Liam Dunn—the first boy Carly had been intimate with—went wide-screen in her head.

During her time at Living Water, she'd been assured that whatever sins she'd committed before giving her life to Christ had been forgiven. In God's eyes, she had a clean slate. So why was she still so uptight about Liam? She wished the elder had stuck to that. Instead, he was drilling down on the "one man, one woman, one flesh" thing. She looked to her left to see the face of the boy she'd just married was wet with tears. *Maybe Chuck was right about taking such a big step so soon.*

Carly had been taking tiny steps in faith ever since that night at the mission. The girl who'd shared her testimony about the creepy things at the bottom of rivers had really gotten to her. Going into that meeting, she'd told herself nothing anyone could say would change her mind about God. But this stranger's story had been identical to Carly's, down to her wanting to jump off a bridge. Anger she'd felt since forever came pouring out that night at the mission and she'd cried and cried.

A lady from Chuck Davis Ministries had put her arm around her. She told Carly that Jesus loved her and had a wonderful plan for her life. Carly had listened, *really* listened to an adult for the first time in a long time. When the lady prayed for the Holy Spirit to come in and heal her heart, Carly asked to be forgiven for being such an ungrateful little brat to her parents. A warm feeling came over her like a wall inside had broken. Instead of anger, love came flowing in. This, she later realized, was what Jesus freaks meant when they talked about being "born again." The leader of the Living Water fellowship offered her a place in a household of single women for a while until she got her feet on the ground spiritually speaking, and Carly had been genuinely thankful.

Later, at her baptism, the head of her household had a word of knowledge that she would marry Rick Green, the guy she'd shown up with a few weeks ago, who had given his life to God the same night she had. Carly found this odd; after all, the two of them had never even been on a date. But in a way, if it worked out, it would solve a lot of problems. She had no reason to doubt that these people had her best interest at heart. No way would her father approve of her marrying someone who didn't even have a job, let alone a non-Catholic, but God would have to sort out the details.

So, Carly's final step toward giving the Lord complete control of her life had been agreeing to marry her former traveling companion, who was good-looking enough, nice in his own way, and apparently now believed the same way she did. Yet here she was on her wedding day, afraid she'd wandered too far into the unknown to ever find her way back. It was cool in the big tent, yet her sweaty hands were wilting her bouquet.

Carly could see that Ricky was not the only one whose face looked all wrong. In the front row, her father, who'd driven with her mother all the way to Ohio to see their youngest daughter tie the knot, looked like he wanted to take a swipe at the elder. Her mother was hiding her face behind a handkerchief.

Then there was Chuck Davis, who had objected to how fast she and Rick had gotten engaged. He believed the Lord was working in the Living Water community, but the whole shepherding thing they'd been doing with the young people was too pushy for his taste. New believers, in his opinion, could hear from God just fine on their own without a third party always filling in the blanks.

Her new husband, on the other hand, could never get enough blanks filled in by the leadership. According to him, in eighteen years no one had ever bothered giving him a single word of advice, and these guys had been willing to spend hours listening to his problems, praying for him, and coming up with answers.

Carly liked the man Rick was becoming. He was more confident, deliberate. That is, up until the minute they met each other at the altar. Instead of looking at her, he'd turned his head to stare at some girl in the front row. At any wedding she'd ever been to, it was the bride's parents that got emotional, not the groom. The person Rick was looking at was wearing a dress showing too much skin and glaring at him with X-ray eyes. *That must be his old girlfriend, Keri Ann what's-her-name—the one who didn't want to drive to Texas.* Carly's knees weakened, and her own stiff smile turned upside down. Rick's hands shook as he slid the ring up Carly's slippery finger.

Louie La Nova's eyes were too bleary to zoom in on his daughter's face, but he thought it odd that the young man hadn't kissed her when they were pronounced man and wife. This whole production was strange to him, especially the sermon. Louie almost got up and walked out when the preacher went on and on about the woman, Eve, being the one who sinned. If he remembered the story correctly, the man was just as guilty in the Garden of Eden, if not more so. And what was all that about women keeping quiet in church? If that sad sack of a groom tried to keep his Carly quiet, he was in for a big surprise.

Louie had put off sending back the little card in the wedding invitation hoping that his own bride of thirty-seven years would decide not to travel halfway across the country for this non-Catholic wedding, but she wouldn't hear otherwise. They both wanted the best for their little girl. And she had promised them that the ceremony would be in a tent, not inside a Protestant church.

This certainly didn't look like any religious service they'd ever seen. But at least the people were all talking about Jesus. The La Novas agreed this was a good sign. Still, Louie's blood pressure had been rising by the minute while the preacher drove home his opinion that a woman must be quiet because she was the one who had listened to the devil. Louie wanted a good look at that Bible.

The whole thing was so confusing—no priest, no communion, no organ music, just some hippies playing guitar. When the service finally ended, his daughter and this Richard Green walked down the aisle to a song sung by a young man whose hair was so long, Louie would have had to turn him away for a job in his noodle factory. As she passed him, his daughter looked like she had as a little girl, petrified of a storm coming in off the lake.

Carly's sister Amy, who'd just flown in from New York, hadn't had a chance to eat or change her clothes, which were at least business casual, a step up from the floppy, flowy garb her sister's new friends were wearing. Amy had spent more time looking at her watch than at the preacher who'd just finished delivering the most sexist rant she'd ever heard. At least plates of food were being laid on long tables in an adjoining tent, but what Amy really could have used was a drink.

She followed her parents as they got in line to congratulate the new couple and at the same time looked around for a glass of something stronger than coffee. The only option was punch, but to her dismay, the kid ladling it out informed her it was mostly ginger ale. She grabbed a cup anyway, plus one for her mother who, she feared, might never recover from this experience. But her father looked to be in an intense conversation with a guy next to him in line, one of the hippies her little sister had gotten mixed up with. Poor Carly never could catch a break.

The conversation was getting heated. Amy hadn't

heard her father raise his voice in public like he had just then since ... well, ever.

"How can you say that?" Her father stuck out his arms.

"It says right here, 'For the woman was deceived—'"

"Let me see that book."

The man who'd introduced himself to them as Carly's "shepherd" handed her father the Bible. "But they aren't the only ones who sinned. And one more thing—my daughter is no sheep!"

Then, to Amy's amazement, her father stepped out of line, sat down, and ripped open the card he'd intended to give to Carly. He wrote a quick note, stuck it back in the envelope, and returned to the reception line. When the three of them reached her sister, he hugged and kissed her and then slipped the envelope into her hand. At his insistence and Amy's dismay, he hustled her and her mother back to the car before dinner was served.

Hemmed in by her Christian friends, Carly couldn't stop her father in time. When she did escape those gathering around her to give words of encouragement, her parents' car had already disappeared. She opened her father's card. On the left side he'd scribbled, "Sweetheart, we love you. You are always welcome back home, with or without that sad sack of a young man."

Carly returned to the tent to find her new husband crying on the shoulder of that girl in the plunging neckline wearing way too much makeup.

CHAPTER ELEVEN

Keri Ann shook her head. It was just like Ricky to run away from home and hook up with a bunch of religious loonies, but to *marry* one? That took the cake. Riding a grimy Greyhound bus all the way down here, sitting next to people whose smelly bodies touched hers, and then having to waste money on a cab had all been a royal pain, but getting herself to Ricky's wedding had taught her something very important.

According to Ricky's new spiritual leader, he hadn't really married this stranger after all. He was already married—to Keri Ann. He'd read it straight from the Bible for all of them to hear. Once two people made love, in God's eyes, boom—they were married. *So there. Forget this whole wedding thing.* She and Ricky had been made one in God's eyes years ago, the day they buried her mother. Keri Ann had been his real wife all along. This mousy little prep was an imposter. The realization calmed her nerves.

She weaseled her way to the front of the reception line and when she made it to Ricky, his phony wife took off. *Right on schedule.* She had him all to herself.

"Keri Ann, I didn't expect you to be here." He took out a handkerchief and wiped his nose.

"I didn't either. The last time we talked, I thought I'd made myself clear."

"Yeah. You said you were having an abortion."

"Not a done deal. Still haven't made up my mind. I only said that to get you to come home. What I didn't say was how much I've missed you." She clung to his neck, bringing his head down low enough to whisper in his ear. "You know, Ricky, it's like the priest said."

He pried her fingers off his neck. "What do you mean?"

"About the first person you have sex with."

"You need to calm down, Keri Ann. It may not look like it, but this is a church. *My* church."

People behind her in line began to whisper. The priest— minister—whoever snuck up from behind and guided her away. "Hello, young lady. Please come with me."

Did she have a choice? He led Keri Ann by the elbow to a table covered with little pamphlets. "I take it you're an old friend of Rick's."

"More than a friend. He and I have a child together." *Wow, that really snapped him to attention.*

"Rick never mentioned a child."

She patted her stomach. "Well, it hasn't been born yet. He ran off with a stranger, so I guess I have no choice but to, you know, get rid of it."

His eyes popped out of his head. "You do know what God says about that."

Some lady waved for the guy to follow her. "Not really

sure, mister," said Keri Ann, "but I got the gist of what you said about marriage."

A lady ran to the table, her face all red. "Pastor, we need you up at the head table."

He put his hand on Keri Ann's shoulder. "Excuse me, dear. What is your name?"

"Keri Ann."

"Keri Ann, please read this. It explains in detail what God thinks of what you're planning to do."

He tried to give her a booklet, but she jammed her hands into her jacket pockets. In a hurry, he propped it up on the table she could see it.

Everyone was sitting down to eat, but she'd rather starve than swallow anything these hippies were serving. *Probably moldy.* She did, however, pick up the booklet the pushy priest had tried to give her. The full-color pictures got her attention.

~

A man in Rick's accountability group had given him the keys to a cabin on the Kentucky side of the river for a brief honeymoon. Carly's car now ran great thanks to Chuck Davis, but Rick still couldn't get comfortable in the driver's seat. Something was up. His new bride hadn't said a word since they'd started out, and he wondered which one of them would pop first.

She did.

"Why were you staring at that girl all through the ceremony?"

"That girl is carrying my baby."

"From what you've said about her, it might not be yours."

Rick smacked the steering wheel. "It makes no difference. She's had it rough."

"Haven't we all?" said Carly, her voice a sigh. "But as far as I'm concerned, she ruined the whole day. No one expects a scene like that at their wedding. Rick, she was acting crazy. Maybe she needs counseling or medication."

"Could be."

Come to think of it, Keri Ann had not looked pregnant, but he'd heard girls didn't show much with their first. One thing was for sure: Since he'd left Buffalo, his old girlfriend had been coming unglued. She'd refuse to talk when he called, but then called him and hung up. He figured she was playing cat and mouse and that this pregnancy thing was all in her head. That had been his conclusion back in July when he decided, with encouragement from a few of the brothers, to stay in Cincinnati. The guys he'd moved in with agreed it was better for him to push on with his new life. He'd done all he could to help Keri Ann. What was left except to pray?

"You know what I think?" said Rick.

"What?" She leaned against him.

"I think we should forget about her and concentrate on enjoying the night."

"OK, Rick. I'll try. Hey, check out the river."

"Just like back home."

"Moonbeams are my favorite."

"Who knows—I might have been watching the moon the same time you were, only from the other side of the river."

~

The cottage Rick's friend had lent them was just as cozy as Rick said it would be, and their first night together turned out better than Carly had expected. Her new husband was patient and gentle, and more than exceeded what she'd hoped for in a lover. In the morning they prayed together, remembering to include poor Keri Ann. Maybe getting married had been the right thing to do. At least she wouldn't have to go home to her parents, admit defeat, and take her place once again as their only failure.

Over coffee and pastries they found in a basket tied with a blue ribbon, Rick talked about returning to Buffalo someday and opening an evangelical coffee house. "Some of the brothers are into the idea. They might even drive up there and help me out."

"You think they would really do that?" Carly dipped a bowtie into her coffee. "So you aren't kidding about going back home."

"Well, yeah, not right away or anything. I've still got a lot to learn, especially if I want to get into the ministry myself someday. I mean, you never know."

One thing Carly did know is that she'd come to appreciate the five hundred miles between her and Grand Island, New York. But that was selfish. God might want her to suck it up and go help the people back home to come to the Lord. A sobering thought, but quite possible.

She whispered in his ear, "Chuck says you have a heart for the lost."

"Really? He never mentioned that to me. And he was so quiet at the wedding. I thought he might stand up during the reception. You know, make a toast or something."

Carly sipped her coffee. "With what, ginger ale?" This

made her new husband smile—perhaps a good time to bring up her own ideas about the future. "Mabel took me aside and said she's praying that I'll think seriously about finishing my nursing program and maybe go on to get a degree. She said it might come in handy someday. Not sure what that was all about."

"Could be she's right. Men who run street ministries don't make much money. For a while, maybe you could work, at least until we have kids."

Carly had nothing to say to that. Her attempts to picture going back home as a married woman kept coming up blank. Rick took her hand and led her to the sofa. She laid her head on his chest. They looked out the sliding glass doors as clouds gathered and broke, rain falling softly on fields of Kentucky grass.

"Isn't it supposed to be blue?"

"Looks green to me."

Later that afternoon, they began opening cards people at the wedding had stuffed into a big white box. There were so many beautiful thoughts and blessings. Rick especially liked the checks. Then Carly pulled out something oddly different—a tract. From an organization called the Right to Life Coalition. On the front was a grisly picture of a fetus destroyed by a late-term abortion. Shocked, she tossed it away.

Rick picked it up and read the handwritten note on the back, "Carly, you are responsible for this. Enjoy your honeymoon! Keri Ann."

CHAPTER TWELVE

Four Years Later

Malcolm had mourned the loss of his grandfather, but while the family patriarch was still alert, he'd made Malcolm promise that he would find a place to grow in his newfound faith. Unfortunately, everywhere Malcolm took his new bride, the folks in the pews looked at them cross-eyed. The Bible taught Christians to welcome outsiders, but he and Anya had been all over Buffalo—East Side, West Side, and all around the town—and had yet to find one place where a biracial couple could let down their guard a little. His grandfather had warned him that marrying a white girl wouldn't be easy.

Too bad the old man was no longer around, but at least he'd lived long enough to know that his prayers for Malcolm had been answered. After his eyes began opening to the corruption in the Black Power movement, they opened to a lot of other truths as well, including the ones about Jesus Christ, the son of God.

Though old Reverend Worthy had been right about so much, he'd had no idea how hard it would be for someone like Malcolm, with more than the average amount of insight into systemic corruption, to find a group of like-minded Christians. The process had grown wearisome to him, and when his lovely wife insisted that they find a church before Christmas, if for no other reason than to properly celebrate the holiday, he tried distracting her with an offer of dinner and a movie.

"Sounds fantastic, Malcolm, but first let's check out this House of Light."

"That coffeehouse on the strip? I got that it's Christian—who could miss the cross. But what makes you think it'll be any better? Might even be worse. It looks kind of like that Baha'i temple over on Bidwell."

"They have a lunchtime Bible study, open to the public. I stopped in once."

"You didn't tell me that."

"You're my husband, not my handler."

What he loved most about Anya, her hardheadedness, was also sometimes the thing he loved least. "Did they pressure you into compliance?"

She laughed. "No. A lady named Betty sang a song, then a guy named Rick read a few Bible verses. They wrapped it up by praying for everyone who came. Short and sweet."

"Describe their clientele."

"A real mix. A few college kids, a guy in a suit, a girl who looked a bit dazed and confused, and me."

"And they prayed for each other?"

"Yes, I already said that. And there was a poster on the wall that you'd approve of: 'QUESTION EVERYTHING.'"

"Hmmm. Interesting."

"I knew you'd think so."

~

Keri Ann watched snow piled up outside the store-front coffeehouse run by Ricky Green, the love of her life. As a new team member, it was her responsibility to keep the front step clear. Neatness came naturally to Keri Ann, but not when the one telling her what needed to be done was Ricky's phony wife. She stuck the shovel back in the coat rack. Instead of the task Carly had given her, Keri Ann began snatching up trash the college kids had left on the sidewalk last night. Inside the storefront, baby Nathan cried. Keri Ann was quite sure she could do a much better job caring for Ricky's baby, which, by rights, should have been hers anyway.

She scooped up a soggy North Buffalo Rocket wedged under the stoop. Keri Ann wouldn't have even known that Ricky had returned to Buffalo if she hadn't read about his coffeehouse. The article had included a picture of her handsome boyfriend holding baby Nate. Carly, standing alongside them, ruined the picture, but Keri Ann simply cut her out of it before sticking it on her fridge

If it hadn't been for Carly, things would have been great right now. She and Ricky would have started up where they left off four years ago. When Ricky was in Ohio, she'd burned every letter and card he'd sent that included anything about Carly La Nova. The only good fortune Keri Ann had run into in the meantime was her father dying and leaving her his car and the house. If her brothers ever complained they'd gotten cheated, let them. They'd all taken off and left her to deal with the old bum by herself. Now, she was alone and glad of it. In her perfect world, only two people existed anyway: her and Ricky.

Keri Ann had been the first to arrive at the House of Light on their opening night and, before leaving, had even said a prayer with one of the scraggly-looking hippies who helped Ricky run the place. She wasn't sure why, but her just repeating the words the kid told her to say had made him so happy that he gathered the rest of Ricky's new friends around her as if she were queen for the day. She guessed that this was all it took to join their group, but their sweaty bodies closing in on her all at once had almost made her change her mind. That is, until Ricky stepped in to hug her so tight that she thought she might burst. He said she'd never regret giving her life to Christ.

That was what Ricky called it—giving her life to Christ, just like they had done at Bible Club when they were kids. Had he forgotten? But this time, it had drawn Ricky to her like a magnet, almost as close as they used to be. She was trying hard not to screw things up. Working at the coffeehouse was no picnic, though. Just like with her other jobs, no one filled her in on all the rules or, even better, left her alone long enough to make up new ones. Too bad, because that was one thing at which she excelled.

From the start, she'd walked a very thin line as a member of the House of Light. Trying to fit in with these Jesus freaks had made her so nervous that she'd landed back in the Community Mental Health Center for a while. The good news was they'd let her put Ricky down as her next of kin. Since he was that kind of guy, when her doctor recommended some volunteer work to keep her busy, he'd agreed to let her serve coffee at night and clean the place up during the day.

Her job with the ministry would always be touch and go, however, since Ricky's phony wife did not approve. The reason she gave was that Keri Ann should be spending her time recuperating from what she referred to as her "nervous breakdown." What Miss Carly Preppy Pants didn't know was that these days, Keri Ann had all the time in the world. *Too* much time. All she did was think. And some of the things she came up with weren't all that great.

The terms of her discharge from the hospital included showing progress on her behavioral goals. This week, she was working on resisting the urge to buy every baby toy in every shop on the strip for Ricky's son. This was especially hard since it was so close to Christmas. On Monday, she fell into temptation and bought him zip-up pajamas with little reindeer antlers. This sent Carly into a hissy fit—surprise, surprise. Ricky said it had been very thoughtful, but that Nathan had more than enough clothes and that she should save her money. *For what? Going out? Fancy vacations?* Without Ricky, those things meant nothing.

Today was Tuesday, and she'd managed to walk by Claytons Toys twice without going inside. *Not that anybody could care less.* But if she ever tried anything like accidentally starting a fire in the kitchen while Carly was back there baking, they'd notice.

Funny how these nasty ideas came when she was trying her hardest to please.

Before Keri Ann had stepped out, Miss Preppy Pants had been in the kitchen with Ricky's little boy strapped to her back. Keri Ann had watched her rival light the stove, an old gas monstrosity that could easily blow the place sky-high if given a chance. Keri Ann had been working hard to push away bad thoughts like these. Since Ricky had been in and out, she needed to be on her best behavior.

Scanning the scene through the front window, she opened the door. The way everyone threw big pillows here and there around the stage drove Keri Ann nuts, but Rick was sitting on one talking to some guy holding a guitar. She'd need to wait to fix them. The smell of burnt sugar in the air told her that Carly had ruined the cookies—again.

You'd think a trained nurse could follow a simple recipe. Keri Ann's doctor had assured her that her resentment toward Ricky's wife would lessen over time, but she'd been hanging around this group for months, and her fantasies had gone from slapping her rival in the face to watching her die a slow and painful death. Thank God—or whoever was in charge—that Ricky couldn't read her mind, otherwise he'd have no choice but to ban her permanently.

Even so, his love for her hadn't changed. He was as gentle and quick to come to her defense as ever. Sometimes she caught him looking at her, his eyes sad, as if to say he was sorry that things had ended up the way they had. Keri Ann understood—what could the poor guy do? His phony wife had him trapped. It was up to Keri Ann to convince him that he'd made a mistake. That in God's eyes, she was his real wife and Carly was, well, a mistake. There she was now, Keri Ann noticed with a scowl, looking frumpy as ever wearing an apron covered with dough.

"I burnt the cookies. Keri Ann, can you run out and buy some?"

If Ricky had not been right there watching, she would've make up an excuse to say no. "Sure. How many?"

"Five—no, six dozen. Last night we ran out. Here's some cash."

"No. I've got it." She glanced up to make sure Ricky was listening.

Out on the Elmwood Strip, big wet flakes covered everything. It wasn't even seven o'clock and the Buff State students were already in front of Mr. Goodbar, stinking up the air with their joints. Each time the bar door opened, loud music blasted her eardrums, but the idiot playing "God Rest Ye Merry Gentlemen" on the tuba across the street was even more annoying. Her sneakers were doing a lousy job keeping out the slush, so her feet would be frozen by the time she got back. She should have told Carly to go to hell.

Radio Shack's windows were fogged up, but kids crowded around them anyway. Keri Ann stopped to see what all the fuss was about. The TVs were all turned on to the news. One of the boys shook his head. "Can you believe it? Why him, of all people?" She caught on that a gunman whose identity had not been released shot and killed a rock star.

"Why would anyone do that?" the kids asked. Never having been a fan, Keri Ann had no clue.

A man in a suit shook his head. "Someone up the food chain must have put a number on him and found a stooge to do the deed." The group looked at him like he was nuts. But Keri Ann pressed in, hoping to hear more.

~

Malcolm and Anya had to wait in line in front of the House of Light that evening, but when they made it inside, he went for the table closest to the door. Anya teased him about preparing for a quick exit. "Just looking out for you, babe," he said while looking around. *Batik curtains and Oriental rugs.* Cool enough, but he could live without the cheap tinsel garlands wrapped around the doorframes in honor of a holiday he objected to on historical as well as Biblical grounds. At least there was no vestige of Santa Claus on site. Anya pointed out the poster she'd mentioned, a man with glasses as thick as his watching TV with a thought bubble over his head which said "QUESTION EVERYTHING."

An anxious-looking person introducing herself as Keri Ann approached asking them if they'd like coffee. "No," said Malcolm, "maybe just some conversation."

"You'll get plenty of that here." Her smile was just a shade off from a grimace.

Anya pointed to the far wall. "My husband likes that poster."

The woman looked over her shoulder. "You do? Why?"

Malcolm sat up straight. "In my opinion—Keri Ann, is it? We're all being lied to constantly, by the TV, the newspapers, even the movies." Malcolm paused to check his wife's reaction. "And most people are content to believe everything they hear."

A guy about Malcolm's age joined them. He introduced himself as Rick Green. "Keri Ann, did you offer our guests coffee?"

"She did," said Malcolm, "and we declined. Malcolm

Worthy here, and this is my wife, Anya." The men shook hands.

"Nice to meet you, Malcolm and Anya. Glad you could make it tonight. The music will be starting soon."

When the girl with nervous eyes stalked off, Anya mentioned that she was the one she'd seen at the Bible study. "Does she or does she not look a little bit off?"

"Maybe. But maybe she's just down on her luck and this Rick Green has given her a job. You can't knock that, Anya. So far, I'm liking the vibe here."

"No ducking out?"

"Not yet."

Another group tramped inside, brushing snow off their army jackets and clearing mist from their steel-rimmed glasses. They mixed in with a few preppy types in button-downs and chinos and a few more grungy types in T-shirts and jeans. So far, no one much older than him and Anya. There was even a man wearing a dashiki who nodded at Malcolm.

The music their host had referred to turned out to be a stream of consciousness thing sung by a long-haired dude with a bit of a lisp. One thing Malcolm missed about the East Side churches he'd gone to with his grandfather was the music. Some of those choirs could blow off the roof. But after a while, Rick took the mic. He preached about the problem with religion, including Christianity, and that what Jesus talked about was not religion, but relationship. Now Malcolm was all ears.

"In the beginning was the Word, and the Word was with God, and the Word was God. Doesn't sound like some religion to me. It's what life is all about."

A guest who must have been drinking something

stronger than coffee stood up. "Dude, you are so wrong!" Then very slowly, as not to slur his words, he put out a challenge. "What about war? Any God who loves us so much and is so mighty and powerful would not allow such ... waste."

The preacher, this Rick Green, mumbled something about sin entering the world but the heckler, who was apparently drunk, shouted him down. "Sin? Buddy, what you call sin is ... what I say life is all about." The audience burst out laughing, and to Malcolm's disappointment, the interruption marked the end of the sermon. The room buzzed, some siding with the preacher, others with the heckler. In the middle of the hubbub, Malcolm caught sight of the girl with crazy eyes heading straight to their table.

She dove into the empty third chair without asking. "Do you think somebody actually paid to have that rock star killed?"

Malcolm hesitated. He'd heard about the shooting and had no doubt that celebrities who threatened the global power structure were assassinated all the time, e.g., Marilyn Monroe, the Kennedy brothers, his namesake Malcolm X, Dr. King—all political hit jobs. The account of the crime in the Buffalo News said a young man with mental problems shot the musician. Anytime a mental patient was involved, Malcolm immediately expected some type of mind control at play. Plenty of psychiatrists would agree to groom an unstable person on mood-altering medication to perform some dastardly deed. "Could very well be, Keri Ann. Anya, are you ready, babe?"

Once again, Keri Ann looked over her shoulder. "Please don't go. That woman over there, the one with a baby on her back, will say I scared you away."

"Not at all. It's just that we have reservations—for dinner."

~

Carly rose early the next morning. Rick wanted the leadership to meet at the coffee house for an emergency meeting, and she was part of the team. When she'd asked why the big hurry, he said they couldn't afford another catastrophe like the one they'd had last night. The next meeting was supposed to be about how to deal with Keri Ann. Carly had made her opinion clear—even after months of counselling and medication, her husband's old friend was still not right in the head and shouldn't have been serving coffee to their guests. If there had been any doubt left in Carly's mind, it was cleared up last night when she'd single-handedly chased away a beautiful young couple who seemed interested in more than the free food.

Bitter wind off Lake Erie blew in the last of the team. "Welcome." Rick closed his eyes and nodded. "I know some of you need to get to work, so we'll keep this short. Last night was a bust. We all know it. I'd like your ideas on how we can move forward in the future." A round of amens rose from the brothers. Rick opened his Bible. "The writer of Hebrews states in chapter five, verse two that those in charge should deal gently with those that are ignorant and going astray. On that note, I'd like my wife to open the meeting with prayer."

He'd put her on the spot in front of everyone. Plus, she was mad at him, so nothing she said was going to sound right.

When they'd gotten home the night before, Carly had asked Rick to do one little favor for her—to string lights on the Christmas tree her father had brought them, a beautiful Douglas fir—and since it was their first Christmas with baby Nate, she'd hoped to decorate it together as a family, maybe take a few pictures. Instead, they'd wasted time arguing about Keri Ann. He'd gone to bed in a huff, and she'd stayed up doing a lousy job on the lights, half of them not even working.

But in her experience, refusing to lead a group in prayer when asked only made things worse. "Dear Lord, we come before you this morning with humble hearts, wanting to do what is best for your kingdom. Please show us how to do just that, and if there is anything we can change for the better, please make it known." Another round of amens. Baby Nate, who'd been asleep in the kitchen, began to fuss. She got up to check him and could tell he wanted to nurse.

When she returned, the group was agreeing on a procedure to handle hecklers in the future. A few of the brothers had already put on their coats.

Carly sat next to Sister Betty. "What did I miss?"

"The men are going to take turns being bouncers. And then he said something about a visit from the Health Department."

"Did he even mention Keri Ann?"

"Nope."

The baby, whose back Carly had been patting, let out a loud burp and the older woman laughed. Rick looked at Betty for the first time. "Everything OK over there?'

"Sure, Pastor," she said, but Carly could see her face turning red. Rick loved to call out the women.

"Glad to hear it. I'm almost done. One more thing about our visit from the health inspector. My guess is he's going to tell me we need a license if we want to continue serving food." Everyone grumbled. "To be honest, I have no idea what this means, so I'm going to need one of you to do a little digging." He glanced at his notes. "Yikes! The guy's coming on Thursday. We'll have to make this quick. Any volunteers?"

Those left in the room got so quiet, Carly could hear wind rattling the windowpanes. "How about you, Carly?"

She stared at a stain on the carpet. Rick knew Thursday was her one day off, and her only chance to spend unhurried time with the baby. Looking around the room, it was obvious that, having recently graduated from nursing school, she was the only one who'd be conducting legitimate research.

"Honey, you're good at stuff like this."

"Who'll watch the baby?"

"I can." Betty pats her knee. "But I'll need a ride to your house in the morning."

Rick's face beamed. The only two women in the room had just agreed to take care of an important task that he'd left hanging until the very last minute. "Thanks, ladies. So, how are we going to work this?" He rubbed the slight bristle on his perfectly square jaw. "Carly, what if we pick up Betty at seven, I drop you off, then take Betty and the baby to our house? I should get back here by eight, and you can call me as soon as you get the scoop."

"Why can't I do it later in the day?"

"I have no idea when they'll show up." He looked back at his notes and then at Carly.

Nothing like flying from the seat of your pants. "Why

don't you tell them we need more time?"

As if Carly didn't know the real reason for all this last-minute finagling. He needed it to sound urgent so she and Betty would think they had no choice, as if the ministry would go down the tubes if the two of them didn't come to the rescue. Leaning on women was easy for Rick. Easier than dealing man-to-man with some bigshot from the Health Department.

Ignoring her question, he thanked everyone for coming as the last few brothers headed out.

"Wait. What about Keri Ann?"

"What about her?"

"We were going to talk about what she pulled last night with those new people."

"Oh, yeah. I forgot."

He forgot. That young couple would have stayed longer if she hadn't run up to them, her eyes like a starving raccoon. And something else—she'd love to bring up how often Keri Ann had been parking her car near their house on Bird Avenue and just sitting there. What was that all about? Asking her was pointless. She denied doing anything wrong and loved to tell Carly that she was imagining things.

"Fair enough, Carly. I'll call her."

"And say what?"

"That she's off the schedule until she checks herself in at the CMHC. It did her good last time."

What would do Keri Ann even better, in Carly's opinion, was to leave Buffalo altogether and make a whole new start with no one around to remind her of her lousy childhood.

With the hand not holding her baby, she pulled over

her Bible that was still open to the book of Hebrews. The passage Rick had kicked off the meeting with was underlined, and she noticed he hadn't read the whole verse. The last line shed light on what the chapter was all about: "He is able to deal gently with those who are ignorant and are going astray, since he himself is subject to weakness." That "he himself" perfectly described her husband.

CHAPTER THIRTEEN

Before Keri Ann knew Carly La Nova even existed, she'd had her life all mapped out: She and Ricky would marry and move away from their families. They'd work until they could afford to buy a little place in a very neat and organized suburb like Tonawanda and have two children, a boy and a girl. Carly La Nova had sure made a mess of that. And now, just when things had gotten back on track between her and Ricky, Carly was messing them up again.

She'd just hung up the phone after talking to Ricky. Miss Preppy Pants had told him that she'd chased people away last night. Thanks to Carly, Ricky had given her an ultimatum—check herself in at the CMHC or forget about working at the House of Light.

There was no time to waste. She had a plan and the sooner she got it over with, the better. There was an out-patient at the day program who'd been on her mind, a wiry old geezer they called the Don. She raced downtown, passing a few her fellow outpatients waiting for the bus, but parking on High Street turned out to be even worse than usual. By the time she charged through the waiting room, the group session was about to start, and the security guard wouldn't let you into the clinic if you were over five minutes late.

She sailed passed reception just as the guard let the patients in the hallway into the day room. "Hey, wait!"

"Let me see your pass."

Just like high school. She flashed her doctor's referral and slipped in as he locked the door behind them. One thing she could say about the CMHC is they ran a tight ship. And at least the stuff they said here didn't make her want to pull out her hair like some of Ricky's sermons. All her boyfriend cared about anymore was God.

Most of her fellow outpatients were OK, too, as far as nutjobs went. The Don, a convicted pyromaniac, was the reason Keri Ann hadn't turned around and gone home when there'd been no place to park. She'd spotted his rusted-out van with the faded logo "D and D Painting and Siding" over on Ellicott Street.

She forced herself to take the chair next to him. If the grimy old coot had taken one bath this month, she'd have been shocked. Leaning as far away from him as possible, she reminded herself that even though he didn't look like much, this little fellow had started some amazing fires. The only reason he was living under supervision in a local group home and not doing life in prison was that nobody had ever died due to his crimes; he claimed to be very precise. Keri Ann hoped the stories about him were true. It was hard to tell with this crew.

Their counsellors never worried much about lies. The

opposite of Ricky, who was always harping on them. What Keri Ann couldn't get over was how the love of her life had swallowed the biggest lie of all—that in the eyes of God, he was married to Carly La Nova.

"Happy Wednesday!" The counselor looked around the circle. "I see an old friend this morning. We haven't seen you for a while, Keri Ann. Is there any particular reason you've returned?"

Keri Ann stared at her fingernails. She picked at a cuticle. "I guess I missed you guys."

"Wrong!" said the Don, swaying back and forth. "The real reason is that you got fired from another job. And they made you come back. That's why, Miss McGraw. You got fired. You can't fool the Don."

"Donald, why don't you let Keri Ann explain?"

"Actually, he's right. But not fired, exactly. Just put on leave because of a certain person who I hate so much, I could ..."

"Finish your thought, Keri Ann," said the counselor.

"So much, I could spit."

"Ha!" Donald laughed loud enough for anyone outside the glass walls to hear. "You mean you hate so much, you could kill."

"One more outburst like that and you will be excused for the day, Donald. Keri Ann, is there anything else you'd like to share?"

"Yeah." She looked around the circle, examining each face. "Does anyone here think the guys who shoot celebrities are the victims of mind control?" Every one of them—the anorexic girl, the five-hundred-pound boy, and the other five loonies—all started talking at once. It took the counselor a minute to calm them down, and

Keri Ann used the time to arrange a private meeting between her and the Don.

There was no way Keri Ann could pretend she was not accompanying the grubby little man as they walked into the Deco Diner. Big deal. What was more important to her was that there were no cop cars parked in front of the place. The Don headed right to a booth and although Keri Ann would have preferred a seat at the counter, due to the nature of her business, she decided to follow him, first checking under the table. The waitress came by with menus.

"Order anything you want, Donald. My treat."

"My, my. This must be a very important job."

"Keep your voice down."

"Anything you say, Princess, but you can't blame me for being excited. It's been so long." He pressed his fingertips together as if in prayer.

No doubt this guy was off his rocker. To think what her life had come to, sitting across a table from an ex-con, all because of Carly La Nova . . .

"Maybe we should talk outside. We could take a walk in the park."

"No! It's too cold. I'll keep it down. I promise."

"Let's get to it, then. I need some advice."

"On how to start a fire?" His eyes gleamed.

"Yes. But I'm in a hurry."

"That, my dear, is a problem. Time is of utmost importance if you want to do it right. You must make sure there is absolutely nobody in or near the building, not even a dog or cat. And that takes planning."

"Tone it down!" she hissed as the waitress came back with a pad and pen. Donald ordered almost everything on the menu. "Don't they feed you at the group home?" His grin flattened. "Sorry, Donald. Get whatever you want." The waitress moved on and Keri Ann whispered, "All I need is a little technical assistance. Can you help me?"

"Of course, Princess. But if what you have in mind is a hit job, you're on your own."

Was that really what she had in mind? One thing she was sure of was the daily routine of the Green family. Sunday through Wednesday, Rick drove Carly to an afternoon shift at Buffalo General, then Rick worked in his office at the coffeehouse while a lady named Betty watched baby Nathan. Thursday was Carly's day off from work, and she always spent it at home with little Nate. But Ricky had mentioned that this Thursday Carly had something important to do, so the baby would be with the sitter. Meaning Miss Preppy Pants would be home alone for a change.

"Explain to me, Donald, how you manage to know for certain who all is inside a particular house?"

"Simple, Princess. You watch. People come and go. In and out, in and out. You wait, and wait, until no one else comes out. This can take days, sometimes weeks. And you must be vigilant. Stepping away for even a few minutes can ruin everything. But it's worth it in the end." His smile, brownish and missing two teeth, made her lose her appetite.

Her first sip of tea burned going down. What had been just a daydream was starting to sound real. The main thing was making sure Ricky's baby stayed safe. She hid her hands, which had begun to shake. She told herself that as insane as the little man looked, he had managed to keep out of prison after clearing the city of a few major eyesores. He knew what he was talking about. She was suddenly out of breath.

"Relax, my dear. You mentioned a house. Considering the time of year ..." He paused to stroke his stringy goatee. "I might be able to do the job myself. That is, if you can personally guarantee no one will be on the premises, not even doggies or kitties." He put his finger over his lips as the waitress laid down two plates.

"What do you mean, the time of year?"

"Christmas, of course. If the address in question is an actual residence, does it feature a lit-up evergreen tree?"

"You mean a Christmas tree?" Keri Ann laughed. "Yes. I drove by last night and they were putting one up. It's real, too. I watched Old Man La Nova hauling it in."

"Do you know how many house fires start every year because of those lovely trees?"

Keri Ann used a napkin to blot sweat off her forehead.

~

At 3:15 a.m. Thursday morning, Donald sat in his van waiting for the man the Princess had assured him would be leaving the house carrying a baby somewhere around seven. She promised that when the man with the baby pulled his Country Squire out of the driveway, the place would be void of all life-forms except perhaps a spider or two. Did he trust her? Of course not. She was as crazy as he was, maybe more. But zero occupancy would be easy enough to verify before he created the spark that would ignite the tree. First, the stage had to be set.

He almost backed out when fresh snow fell. Now, walking around would leave tracks. But those colored lights, which someone had left on all night just for him, were a true delight. He whispered a chorus of "O Tannenbaum" while jimmying open the basement window. Old style, it easily moved. So far, two signs that this job was his own personal Christmas present.

Upstairs, he found another wonderful surprise: one whole string of bulbs was out. A job straight from heaven. He removed a little rag from his pocket, doused it with his secret sauce, unscrewed one of the blown bulbs, and jammed in the cloth. The last and most challenging task was slipping the cord out the window so as not to be detected. From the inside the tree was so big, one would have to strain their eyes to notice the cord. Even better, the outside of the house was surrounded by shrubs. Ideal. After that, he moved fast. If Baby woke up Daddy, he'd need to abort the mission, and all would be lost.

At 6:47, the Christmas tree lights went off and Donald, hunkered down in his van across the street, watched the man carrying the baby exit through the side door. But what was this? A lady, locking the door behind them. The first glitch—the Princess had never mentioned a lady. To make sure there were no more surprises, he'd check inside one more time.

As soon as the station wagon was out of sight, Donald slipped back to the house. No one around, no one awake, and the neighboring dogs had yet to catch his scent, so he made quick work of breaking in. Unless they were hiding in a closet or drawer, there was definitely no one home. But before causing the wires to spark, he'd drive down to WE NEVER CLOSE and call the Princess. He was supposed to wait for her to give the final go-ahead anyway. He tossed his shoes out the window, pulled his featherweight body up and out of the basement, and removed all signs of his presence, except, of course, the fuel-soaked rag.

She picked up on the first ring. "Donald?"

"Good morning, Princess."

"How did it go?"

"Like a charm."

"Did the man leave?"

"Yes, he did. With a baby ..."

"Perfect."

"And a lady."

"A lady! No. No. No. Something's wrong. She's supposed to be ... where are you now?"

"Looking out the window at WE NEVER CLOSE."

"Don't do anything until I get there."

"You're the boss, Princess. But I checked. There is no one inside! All we need is one tiny spark. Sounds almost biblical, doesn't it?"

"No, Donald! No spark ... not yet. Wait until I get there." Keri Ann's heart was pounding. She wasted time pacing her house. *Carly should still be there.* She'd have to make a new plan. But Donald had spent all night on this one. Over the phone, he'd sounded anxious. *After all the work he's done, he might just go through with it anyway.* Even worse, a pathetically honest psycho like him would be only too happy to tell the police who'd come up with the idea.

~

From a stool at the front of the store, Donald had been watching the sky grow lighter and lighter. Fireworks were no good in the morning. Plus, he'd been tired after losing a whole night's sleep. He would be in big trouble when the staff discovered he left the group home without permission. And all of this for no good purpose.

The Princess was going to poop out on him. He could tell by the panic in her voice. She'd wanted to burn someone after all, the lady who'd driven away with the man in the Country Squire. She'd lied to him, and now she wanted to cheat him out of his Christmas present—a blaze that would provide such a glorious memory. He checked his watch. 8:12, nearly daylight. He hopped off the stool.

~

Due to rush-hour traffic, it took Keri Ann twenty minutes to reach the corner of Bird and Elmwood, and to her horror Donald was no longer sitting in the window of the WE NEVER CLOSE.

An explosion rocked the ground as Keri Ann turned her car right onto Bird Ave. In front of Ricky's house, the Greens' babysitter ran out the side door screaming for help. "The baby, little Nathan, is upstairs! Somebody, help!"

Before she could wonder what Betty and the baby were doing in a supposedly empty house, Keri Ann jumped out of her car, ran to the backyard, and kicked open the door. Flames cut off the front of the house from the stairway, and more flames licked at the banister. Smoke filled the air, but she climbed three steps at a time, grabbed baby Nate, and made it outside just as fire engines, their sirens whining, barreled down the street.

Both she and Nate were coughing and black with soot, but according to the EMT, neither had sustained serious harm. Nona Barbie from Eyewitness News stood in front of the charred remains of 592 Bird Avenue, a microphone in her hand. "An overheated Christmas tree is the suspected cause of the blaze that destroyed a West Side home this morning. Mr. Green left their six-month-old son in the care of his babysitter at approximately seven thirty. The fire spread so fast, by the time the sitter saw it, she was unable to reach the boy and ran outside to call for help. A family friend who happened to be passing by ran into the house to save little Nathan before the fire department was even on the scene."

A fireman took the mic. "That's right, Nona. Normally, we would not condone a civilian running into a burning building, but it would have taken time for us to get there, maybe too long to save the child."

Then Carly grabbed the mic, interjecting between tears and laughter, "Our Nathan has been taken to Children's Hospital for observation, but the doctors say he's fine due to the bravery of a long-time family friend named Keri Ann McGraw!" She threw her arms around Keri Ann, who shrank from her touch.

Finally, the reporter handed Keri Ann the mic. "Miss McGraw, what gave you the courage to run in a burning house?"

"Love." Keri Ann's teary eyes were fixed on Ricky.

"Wow. That says it all, doesn't it? Nona Barbie reporting live from the West Side. Back to you, Irv."

CHAPTER FOURTEEN

Present Day/Allegany State Park

Carly crept inside Cabin #3, the one normally set aside for the pastor's family, praying that Keri Ann hadn't switched the assignments to make them somehow more efficient. Moonlight guided her to Benny's cot. Her little boy trembled in his sleep, his chocolate-covered mouth set in a scowl. Serena's words came back to her. "Mrs. Green, just be thankful the poor kid isn't still wandering around in the woods."

Man-sized snores rumbled from the corner. *Rick.* Carly sat down, trying to keep the mattress from screeching.

But Rick woke up and growled, "Benjamin getting lost was your fault."

"How do you know that?"

"You should have been here. Taking care of him is your job, not Nate's or Keri Ann's."

"It's late, Rick."

"Yes, it is. Very late. Maybe too late."

Whatever that meant. Right now, Carly didn't care. An empty cot on the other side of the room indicated her older son was staying overnight with one of his friends, probably David Wilson. Nothing to worry about. She bunched her jacket under her head and fell unconscious.

When she woke, the sun poured in through streaky windows. Rick was already gone. She shook the wrinkles out of her clothes and walked a groggy Benny over to the lodge for breakfast. The minute they appeared, everyone stopped talking. Carly's gang had played a joke like this back in high school, everyone shutting up when a new person walked in. But this wasn't high school.

Benny clung to Carly's leg like a boy drowning, and it was all she could do to shuffle over to the nearest bench. Carly felt Anya Worthy slip her arm around her. "Good morning. Did you get any sleep?"

"A little. But Nate wasn't in the cabin. I'm assuming he stayed overnight with another family."

"I'm afraid not."

"What do you mean?"

"He left camp."

"Did he say where he was going?"

"No one's heard a thing. It must have happened early this morning. They're gone, and so is Mrs. Wilson's car."

"They?"

"He and David."

"They've always been close. I'm sure they'll be back. Why is everyone acting so weird?"

Rick stormed out of the kitchen, his face heart-attack purple. Carly had never seen her husband so angry. Keri Ann stood in the background. Whatever was going on here, she'd bet anything Keri Ann had something to do with it. Carly followed Rick outside, but he let the screen door slam in her face.

The people sitting at the tables returned to their pancakes and private conversations as Carly returned, slumping onto the bench and swaying slightly. Her family was falling apart before her eyes, and the only one who cared was Anya Worthy. Carly's voice broke. "What's gotten into my husband?"

Anya handed her a paper napkin.

"Thanks." Carly dabbed her eyes and blew her nose. "Here he comes again." As abruptly as he'd left, Rick marched back into the lodge.

Anya held Carly's hand as Rick stood before them in his preacher pose, deliberately refusing to look in his wife's direction. The room fell silent for the second time. "Keri Ann will be taking the children to the playground." The secretary Anya had never trusted corralled the boys and girls, including her two daughters. "What I have to say is not for them to hear. The rest of you, stay put. If anyone didn't make it to breakfast, go get them. The entire congregation is responsible for what I'm about to say."

Anya scowled at her husband, who was apparently letting their girls go with this woman who hadn't changed much from the off-balance character they'd met at the House of Light years ago.

Before leaving the building, Keri Ann, who was the only one in the room smiling, grabbed little Benny. The boy kicked and pushed. But since Carly was distracted, Keri Ann got her way. Anya dropped Carly's hand as the children disappeared and balled her own hands into fists.

The pastor closed his eyes, which Anya prayed meant that he'd calmed down a bit, but his voice was still jangling her nerves. "Two situations have recently been brought to my attention." She could feel Carly shaking.

Rick took a deep breath and continued, "My son, Nathan, as you all know by now, has left the camp. Not a serious matter, as he is nearly eighteen. But what we're dealing with here is the reason he left. He told my secretary, Keri Ann, that he wants to find a place where he and his 'friend' will be accepted for who they are, which is a serious matter. Apparently, Nate and one of the Wilson boys have been engaging in an—"

Before the pastor could finish his rant, the other boy's father stood up.

"That's it, Rick. I've heard enough. Where do you get off accusing my son of a darn thing? I've known you for a long time, buddy. Since the beginning. We've given you the benefit of the doubt more than once—me and my family have a lot invested in this church. But you just stepped over the line. Doesn't the scripture say to deal with personal matters in private, brother to brother?" Murmurs broke out all over the room. "Let's go, honey. We're done here." Anya's muscles tensed as Mr. and Mrs. Wilson passed by.

"Fine. Anyone else who wants out, be my guest. I'm tired of pretending what we do here has anything to do with true discipleship, anyway." A few more couples made their way to the door, the men red-faced, their wives' faces drained of color.

Anya heard Carly sobbing quietly.

"Now. Let's get down to it. I'm disappointed in my son, but I can't say what he's done comes as a complete surprise." Anya noticed the bench had stopped shaking. Carly was no longer crying, but rather leaning forward, her face fierce. The pastor continued. "The way some of you mothers, my own wife in particular, have raised your sons, it's a wonder they all aren't running off with each other."

More murmuring between husbands and wives. A few more of them aimed for the door. Anya thanked God that none of her and Malcolm's congregation had been subjected to this carnage.

Finally, Anya's own husband stood up. "Pastor Rick, may I say something?"

"It's all yours, Malcolm. That's all I've got."

Now Anya was the one trembling. How in God's name would Malcolm tame a firestorm like this?

"I can imagine how some of you are feeling right now, but I encourage you not to do or say anything rash." Rumbling spread through the fifty or so people remaining. "If you need to ask questions, please make an appointment with Pastor Rick."

Someone shouted out, "Can we talk to you instead?"

Malcolm turned to Rick, but he had already left the building. "Yes, of course. I'm available as well."

CHAPTER FIFTEEN

N ate corrected his friend, David Wilson, who was in the middle of a list of second thoughts about striking out on their own. "New York is way better than Chicago. For one thing, it's bigger."

"That's the problem."

"So, it's big. I don't like changing things up this late in the game."

"But we'll stick out so bad in Manhattan, the muggers won't be able to resist. Plus, what will we do when our money runs out?"

"Get jobs, of course."

"Where will we live?"

"The Y. Listen, Keri Ann told me if we get in trouble to just give her a call. She'll even wire money. It's all going to be OK. Are you with me?" Nate looked at his friend as they approached the thruway.

"No."

"What do you mean? Last night you were all in."

"I know. I'm sorry, Nate, but now I'm thinking we should have given it a little more time. Let's go back. Last night I was angry, you know—about what people are saying about us and all—but like I said, maybe we need a better plan."

"What about everything we talked about? Finding ourselves and blazing our own trails?"

"We can still do it. How about next year when we've saved up a pile of money?"

"This isn't about money, Dave. It's about right and wrong."

"I know. Still, I don't think I'm ready. Besides, we basically stole my mother's car. How is she supposed to get around now? You know, to go to the store and all?" David Wilson pulled to the side of the road. "We need to go back."

Nate grabbed his knapsack and jumped out of his friend's mother's car. "Nope. Not 'we,' just you, Dave. So, I guess this is it. See you around, buddy. On second thought, I doubt it."

~

After her husband had finished trashing her in public, Carly sat watching the lodge empty out. Even Anya Worthy couldn't leave fast enough. "I'm so sorry," she said, "but I need to find my daughters."

"Of course you do, Anya. It's OK. I'll be alright." Carly sat staring at the floor. As the remaining members of her husband's congregation filed past her, the only one who stopped to offer a kind word was Nate's old babysitter, Sister Betty.

"He was rough on you just now, young lady. How are you holdin' up?"

"Not well, Betty."

"One thing I got to say." She lowered her voice. "Pastor got it all wrong about your boy Nathan."

"What do you mean?"

She pointed out the window toward the playground. "I've known him all his life, along with most of those kids. And one thing's for sure: all you moms have done a fine job raising your babies, just maybe a little too fine. The way I see it is, Nate never got a chance to test out his wings. If you ask me, all that most of them need is a little more time in the deep end of the pool."

Carly hugged her old friend, but when she opened her mouth, all that came out was a sigh. Betty filled in the gap. "Remember how the two of us learned the truth about life? It wasn't in Sunday school, now was it?"

"No. You're right. Nate's not a fool. He'll be OK." Carly nodded. Then again, Sister Betty had never had any children of her own. "Thanks, Betty. For everything."

~

The man in the toll booth commanded Nate to stand so far out of the way of traffic that he wondered if he'd ever get a ride. But just as the pavement got hot enough to burn toast, a car stopped. "How far are you going, young man?"

"All the way."

"You're in luck. Hop in."

Nathan had never hitchhiked in his life. He was so amazed that a car stopped that he never thought to look in the back seat.

"What's your name, son?"

The frigid darkness of the Lincoln Continental was

a stark contrast to the hot brightness of the road. "Nathan." No need for a stranger to know his last name.

"Frank here." The driver stuck out his hand, which Nate shook. His skin was flabby, clammy, and cold.

"So, Nathan, you're traveling rather light for such a long trip."

"It was a last-minute decision."

"Oh, really? I cover this route a bit, you know." He cleared his throat. "For business and whatnot."

"What is your business, Mr... . ?"

"Jakes. Frank Jakes." He flipped on the radio to about the worst kind of music Nate could imagine. All syrupy and sweet, like what they played in elevators. "My business?" He chuckled. "I've got my hand in a lot of things. Just ask my wife. Speaking of the ladies, do you have a girlfriend, Nathan?"

What kind of question is that? "No, not at the moment."

"Good for you. Girls are so ... what's the word I'm looking for? Clingy. Don't you find that to be true, Nathan? Especially to a kid as handsome as you."

"I don't know, Mr. Jakes. I guess I haven't had that much experience." For whatever reason, this got the old guy so excited that instead of sixty-five, they were now going over eighty.

"Care for a smoke?"

"Don't smoke."

"I don't mean cigarettes, my boy. There's a few refers rolled up in the glove box. Help yourself."

Reefers? This guy was too much. "No thanks." Nate tried to open a window but when he pushed the button, nothing happened.

"What's the problem, Nathan? Too hot, too cold?"

"No, I just need some air."

"I understand, but it's brutally hot out there. Hey, if you're not in a hurry, you're welcome to stop for a swim in my pool. My place is less than ten minutes away."

Offering him drugs and now inviting him to a private pool party? Nate clenched his teeth. "Thanks anyway, but I am in a hurry. In fact, I'd like to get off at the next exit, if you don't mind."

The man took off his sunglasses. His face was pale and even flabbier than his hands. "Nathan, you don't impress me as a stupid person. I told you I'd take you all the way to the Big Apple. How will getting off at the next exit get you there any faster?"

"Look, mister, maybe I am stupid. But if you don't let me out of this car, you'll be committing a crime."

"Wait just one minute, young man. There is no law in the books against picking up a hitchhiker."

"There is for kidnapping. If you don't let me out, you are officially abducting a minor. I'm only seventeen."

The man laughed so hard that tears rolled down his cheeks. Nathan continued, louder this time. "And another thing, Mr. Jakes. Luring kids in with drugs and bribes is some heavy sin. Someday you'll have to answer for it."

No longer laughing, the fat man slowed down to fifty. Someone behind them hit the horn. "Answer to whom, pray tell?"

"God, sir. We all will."

"Will we, now?" Frank Jakes's voice turned as cold as his LTC. "So, young man, what do you plan to say when it's your turn?"

Nate hesitated.

"You haven't got a clue, do you, kid? Running away to

the big city, and you haven't got a clue which end is up. You'll be lucky to get as far as Rochester before you run home to Mommy."

"How do you know?"

"Because you're a loser. I knew it the minute you opened your mouth. You say you want to go to New York, but you have no idea what you want. Too bad. I know people—lots of them. I could have helped you." He swerved into a rest stop. "Get out of my car. You're wasting my time."

Nate jumped out and slammed the door. The sudden heat gobsmacked him, and he leaned against a signpost. Maybe he was a loser who didn't know which end was up. But the old man was wrong about one thing—he knew what he wanted. He'd had enough of that look of disappointment in his father's eyes.

Group Camp Twelve

"Mrs. Green, I'm so sorry ... I mean, Pastor Rick going off on you like that in front of everyone ... was just wrong."

"Thank you, Serena." She sped up but was unable to shake Ms. Petrick.

"The good news is, Benny's right there beside you, safe and sound. Is there anything I can do to help? Maybe just talk. I know I do a lot of that, but I'm also a pretty good listener."

"Seriously?"

"Of course. And pray. I mean, all this stuff is new to me, but you can't go wrong by listening and praying."

"No. You certainly can't. Thank you, Serena." She pressed on toward her car.

"So where are you going?"

Good question. "Home for now, I guess, at least to gather a few of my things." Staying in the same house as Rick was no longer an option. "I don't really know, Serena. Normally, I guess I'd go to my parents' house or to one of my sisters', but they all live so far away."

"I have an idea. Come and stay with me." Her smile revealed two even rows of bleached-white teeth.

"Thanks for the offer, but I couldn't. It's too much to ask."

"I don't mean, like, forever or anything, but at least until you've had a chance to sort things out."

When Carly opened the car door, the smell of the river wafted out. "Serena, believe me, the offer means a lot right now." Benny climbed into his car seat. She fastened the belt so tight that he gasped. "But I don't want to drag you in to this mess. There's more to it than you know."

"Does it have to do with Keri Ann McGraw?"

"That's what I need to find out."

"I've got a spare room—with double beds. A little 'you time' will really help. Trust me. I've been there."

"It's tempting. Serena. You need to realize that Rick is not the only one who's made mistakes. I've not always been the best—"

Serena put her finger over her lips. "Shush, now. You're talking to a divorced woman. If anyone knows about a breakup taking two, it's me." She rummaged around in her purse, pulled out a card, and handed it to Carly. "Call me."

On the way home, Benny picked a cassette tape and threw it into the front seat. A well-worn recording of Kid's Praise. "You want to hear this one, Benny?" Silence.

"I guess that's a yes."

She stuck in the tape and the song the children were singing was "Standing," his favorite. "Standing on the promises of Christ my king, through eternal ages let his praises ring, glory in the highest I will shout and sing, standing on the promises of God."

Carly pulled off the road. Leaning her forehead on the steering wheel, she prayed, "Oh, Lord, please ... please!" She'd uttered this same simple prayer only yesterday, right before the coast guard had pulled them out of the rapids, and last month before seeing the figure in the boat rocking in the waves passed the end of her dock. God must have been hearing her, seeing her.

At home, she dialed the number on the card that read: "Serena Petrick, Beauty and Fitness Consultant – 'Cuz as Dolly Parton says, 'Honey, there ain't no such thing as natural beauty.'"

~

At the thruway rest stop, Nathan searched his pockets for a quarter. Keri Ann had urged him to call anytime, day or night, but even she would laugh at him for needing help so soon. He'd only been gone half a day.

The visitor center was packed with families waiting for fast food and restrooms. Grease heated the air that had felt cool when he'd first walked in. He took wide strides from the Roy Rogers on one end of the building to the Friendly's on the other and back again twice, trying to drum up some plan of action, but he was having trouble focusing.

The same question plagued him as when his music teacher back in second grade had touched him the wrong way and his Boy Scout leader had done more than that: Why him?

Some of his friends in drama club were gay. To them, it wasn't a thing. In fact, none of the kids he knew cared much either way. David Wilson had messed around a little with guys. Did that make him gay? And if it did, was that a sin?

People at New Wine Fellowship thought so. That's why he and David had decided to run away in the first place. Neither of them had dated girls in high school. Their female classmates expected them to act all romantic, large, and in charge, traits neither he nor David could claim. And girls from church were more like sisters. How do you explain this to your parents who told you to go out and have fun, just not too much—because that could be dangerous?

He had feelings for girls, strong ones. But how was he supposed to know they weren't, as Dad had put it, sick and twisted? Hanging out with guys was less complicated but, come to find out, even that wasn't safe. *Maybe monks were the only ones who got it right.*

He sat on a stool in front of McDonald's, trying to reel in thoughts skittering around like minnows. A man walked in front of him. He was wearing a badge and looked like some sort of cop. "Hello, son. May I sit down?"

"Excuse me, officer, did I do something wrong?"

"We got a call about a runaway about ten minutes ago. You fit the description."

"Not sure what you mean, sir. I'm on my way downstate, but I'm no runaway. People from home know about it. I can call them if you'd like. Is my sitting here a problem?"

"My report says a boy going by the name of Nathan propositioned a man for sex in return for money. That is a problem."

Holy cow. That jerk called the cops. Talk about sick and twisted. Keri Ann would tell him to blow old Frank out of the water by reporting what really happened. But what if this cop asked for proof? When Nate opened his mouth again, what came out sounded lame. "You've got the wrong person, sir."

A guy in a UB T-shirt stepped in between them. "That's right, officer. You've got the wrong man. This kid is with us, and we're about to bounce in a minute. Football practice. Is there anything else we can do for you?"

"Is that true, Nathan?"

The UB student handed Nate a bag of Burger King. "Yes, sir."

"Well, then." Unconvinced, the cop looked at his watch and waved them on.

"Probably late for his donut break." The guy who'd rescued Nate led his friends outside, where the three of them plus Nate jammed inside a little Datsun hatchback.

The driver zipped onto the eastbound lane as Nate found his voice. "Thanks for that."

"Hey, that's what friends are for."

"Wait—do I know you?"

"Not yet." The way the rest of them laughed at this made Nate's stomach heave. "So, are you the dude he's looking for?" The driver lit a cigarette. Between the smoke and the speed of the car, Nate worried he might hurl.

"Yes. And no."

Another round of their sick laughter. "An anomaly! Yes is no, right is wrong, black is white. Sure. I get it, kid. Still, some questions do require more than one-word answers."

"OK, I did get picked up by an old man, but he's the one who came on to me, not the other way around."

"A fat dude in an LTC?"

"Yeah."

The guy he was squished up against in the back seat grabbed a fistful of fries and howled like a hyena. "Old Frank, still at it. What a clown."

"You know him?"

"Sure. All the boys know old Frank. Even the Thruway Authority, although they won't admit it. So, Anomaly, is your name Nate? True or false?"

"True. Absolutely."

"Absolutely true. Hear that, boys? Except absolute truth is something I myself absolutely reject. Hey, that puts me in the mood for some Talking Heads. What do you say?"

"Stop making sense, stop making sense!" shouted the one with a laugh like a hyena. Music began blaring from a speaker five inches from Nate's ear.

"So, Nate, you may have been better off going swimming with Frank. He is loaded, you know. That is, if you're short on cash, and who isn't? Kit's been in his pool, haven't you, Kit?"

The kid with his elbow in Nate's ribs lit up a joint. "Oh yeah. He pays up."

Nate put his head between his knees.

In between bites of a Whopper, Kit called attention to Nate. "Looks like somebody's getting ready to toss his cookies."

"Oh, hell. Leave it to me to take pity on a little runaway.

Hate to do this to you, kid, but I just had new car scent blown in—costs extra, you know. Can you hold it for a few minutes?"

"I don't think so."

"How about I let you off in Pembroke? Plenty of room out there. You can puke your guts out in a cow pasture. But watch out for those farm boys, Anomaly. Some of them make Old Frank look like a saint."

~

At Group Camp Twelve, Keri Ann folded her laundry in the mesh bag she packed every year just for this purpose. She'd let Rick know she'd be leaving early to take care of a few errands, including a stop at the bank. So many of the brethren had gone home anyway, the place felt like a ghost town.

She'd caused a ruckus by telling Rick an embellished version of what Nate had told her the night before, including why he'd run away with David Wilson. Just as she'd expected, he'd taken the news very badly, blaming Carly for his son's fall from grace. Keri Ann's faith in people getting what they deserved soared. *Too bad the entire congregation had to be in on it, but that's Ricky for you.*

Wilson was right. Situations like Nathan's should be handled in private, but that took patience, something the love of her life had never learned—which was exactly why he needed her. She was great at waiting, and planning, and waiting some more—for years, if necessary, while Ricky's fuse burned for a few seconds—then boom! He blew, leaving an ugly mess.

Keri Ann recalled adding even a little more weight to

tip the scales in her favor, a certain anniversary she'd reminded him about that really lit his fuse. The day she'd found out about their own child, the one that was never to be. Of course, he'd never tell a soul about that.

While crossing the Grand Island Bridge, she debated whether to stop at Ricky's before going to the bank, to gather his mail and whatnot. Of course, she'd run the risk of bumping into Carly, but as their secretary, she had the right and responsibility to retrieve the church mail. After all, buildings had mortgages which would—eventually—need to be paid.

She cruised down East River Road. Seeing that the driveway was empty, she parked near the mailbox and pulled out a week's worth of envelopes. One made her drop all the rest. An official-looking document from the Grand Island Town Court addressed to Carly Green looked a lot like a summons. Had Rick's phony wife gotten herself into trouble? Keri Ann would waste no time finding out.

~

Rick and Malcolm were the last to leave on Saturday. Malcolm insisted on helping his co-pastor scrape the huge kitchen grill, a task Rick said he performed every year with another brother, but only Malcolm had stuck around. He'd been waiting to bring up the one-on-one meetings he'd been having with church members. It was hard for Malcom to believe, but after four days, Rick still refused to face the aftermath of his rant.

Clearing the spatula of grit, he said, "Rick, your people are questioning your lack of tact, and some think you're completely out of your mind."

"They're overreacting. As the pastor, I have every right to call out sin in the flock. Anyway, I was only referring to certain people."

"I believe you, but the way most of them heard it, you were accusing them all of being bad parents. And what you said about Carly, well, that sure didn't help."

"Don't go there, buddy. That's between me and my wife."

"Exactly."

"I could have handled that better. It was just the shock of Nathan running away and proving that he really is ..." Rick lowered his head, unable to finish.

"Tell me, Rick. How do you know what he is? Has he told you? Did he leave a note or something?"

"Nate spilled his guts to Keri Ann. She's the only one he talks to anymore."

"I see." Malcolm attacked a pan with steel wool. "He tells your secretary what he's about to do and why, then she reports back you."

"The two of them have always had a special thing going. You know, since she pulled him out of that fire."

Malcolm stopped scrubbing. What he was about to say might very well cost him his job. But as the week had droned on, his sense that there was a rather odd dynamic between the pastor and his secretary had become more than speculation.

"OK, Rick. Nate and Keri Ann have a special relationship. How about you and Keri Ann?"

"Which is it, buddy? First you think I'm fooling around with Serena Petrick, and now it's Keri Ann. I'll level with you—hundreds of nights I've laid in bed and questioned God about how I ended up with Carly. What if I made a big mistake twenty years ago? We were young, and the leaders were too. The only way I can square the thing is that I missed God's will for my life. Instead of manning up, I left Keri Ann alone to clean up a mess that I caused, then went skipping off with some little dish who I hardly knew and still don't, not really. What does a guy do with a burden like that? Tell me, brother."

Pausing a second, he thought of what his grandfather would have said. "When you marry a woman, she becomes God's will for your life."

Rick jammed the blade he was holding into the wooden counter. "You haven't heard a word I said."

"I heard you just fine, Rick. And I'm telling you, you're heading for a train wreck, and some of your people are bound to become casualties."

"So, Pastor Worthy, maybe it's time you stepped off the train."

Pembroke, New York

Nate surveyed the empty road with fields on each side spreading out for miles. He'd never considered that a walk in the country might be dangerous until the creep driving the Datsun had put it in his head. So far, he hadn't worked up the nerve to stick out his thumb.

Truck stop signs towered far in the distance. The thought of food made him sick. He did, however, really need something to drink. His mouth was dry, and his skin had burnt. Behind him the sound of an engine got louder. *A car.* He considered hiding in one of those corn fields, but whoever it was had seen him already. They slowed down, then backed up in a sloppy zigzag. *Bad sign.* Whoever they were, he'd ignore them.

"Hey there, want a ride?"

Girls. Thank God. Still, he took a good look inside the car before answering. "Um, yeah, thanks."

"Too hot to walk. Where you headed?"

"I had it in mind to get to New York City."

The girls looked at each other and giggled. "You're a little off your route."

"I've had a few setbacks."

They waited for an explanation, but how could a guy go about spilling what he'd just been through to girls— nice-looking ones, at that? The driver spoke up. "Hey, are you OK? You look awful."

"I've felt better."

"Well, you're in luck. We happen to have the best-equipped first aid kit you'll ever find down there under the seat. Aspirin, Tylenol, Sudafed, Imodium ..."

"How about Alka-Seltzer? Got any of that?"

"I think so. If not, there's Pepto and milk of mag."

"What, are you a nurse or something?"

"Actually, yes. We both are. On our way to work."

The one in the passenger seat pulled out a box of first aid supplies. "Two individually wrapped tabs of 'plop plop, fizz fizz, oh, what a relief it is.'"

The driver giggled. "But we'll need some water to dissolve it. I'll grab a bottle for our patient at the 7-Eleven."

"Thanks, that would be great." Nate hopped into the back seat.

They explained that they worked the second shift at Strong Memorial in Rochester and shared an apartment in town, but they were in a bit of a hurry since they'd spent the day at Darien Lake and needed to stop home to shower and change.

When they got to the store, the driver ran out. "Waters for everyone. Looks like they're on sale."

Her friend remained in the car. "I was just saying that there's a bus to New York out of Rochester every day, but I'm not sure when it leaves. You're welcome to hang out with us until then."

His first real break. "That would be fantastic. To tell the truth, getting to New York isn't a huge deal right now. It's not like I'm on a schedule or anything."

"You do have a job, though, right?"

"Not exactly, but I'm looking for one."

"Does it matter where?"

"Nope."

"Fantastic!"

The driver returned and crumbled two tablets into a water bottle. "Here you go."

Her friend said, "Guess what? Our patient is looking for a job."

"You are? What a coincidence. The Strong's been hiring like mad this week."

Nathan glanced up from his drink. "That's incredible. I haven't got much experience. Do you think I have a chance?"

"Never know until you try. Since this young man, whose name is ..."

"Nathan, Nathan Green."

"Nathan Nathan Green"—they both giggled—"is not on a tight schedule, so he should head straight down to the personnel department."

"Great idea. But Nathan," the driver said, peeling out of the parking lot, "Rochester's not even a speck on a seed of the Big Apple."

He burped, making the girls giggle even harder. "The truth is, right now I've got nothing to lose but this sick stomach."

Raintree Apartments, Tonawanda, NY

Serena saturated Carly's hair with natural light golden-brown dye, then covered it with a plastic bag. Benny sat on a kitchen chair halfway interested in what was going on. At least he hadn't left the room, although Carly could tell he was tired of being there and wanted to go home.

Serena asked if he was hungry. He'd eaten nothing except the hard candy in the bowl on Serena's coffee table. Carly guessed it was because he didn't like cheese sandwiches and white milk and was waiting for the frozen waffles and chocolate milk Carly gave him every morning. She'd have gone grocery shopping herself, but she'd been to the ATM and, funny thing, her card no longer worked.

The doorbell rang. "Hang on, Carly. I'll get it."

Carly knew it had to be Rick when the noise jangled her nerves three more times, no break in between. The blood drained from her face. It had taken him a few days, but Rick had managed to find her. She and Serena had discussed what she should and should not say when this moment came. They agreed she should stick to the truth, but keep it simple. If he lost his temper, which he was bound to do after seeing the mangled boat, she'd remain calm and offer to pay to get it repaired. Serena warned her against taking too much blame.

Her husband walked heavily into the kitchen, his face blank, his voice calm. Too calm. "Hello, Carly. I brought these." He slid two documents across the table.

Touching the bag covering her dye-slicked hair, Carly cursed silently. Could he possibly have come at a worse time? "Can you at least say hello to your son?"

Rick reached for him, but Benny shrank from his touch. "Well, there it is. Our son, hanging out with the girls."

"Benny's confused, Rick. He has no idea what's going on. Why don't you sit down? I'll make you some coffee." She gestured for Serena to take Benny into the other room.

"No. I'm not staying. All I need from you is a signature."

"For what?" The first envelope was a summons for Carly to appear in court. The *LaLa Nova* had ventured into a restricted area, a violation of state law. The police had told her to expect one, though they said not to worry; the case against her was mostly a formality since she had not been the one driving the boat. She hadn't gotten to the second envelope yet.

"Divorce papers."

Of course. Serena had warned her this was coming. Carly knew the only Biblical grounds for divorce was adultery, but Serena argued that mental abuse also made a strong case. The question was who had suffered the worst abuse. Carly looked her husband straight in the eye. "You've jumped to this awfully fast, don't you think?"

"Hardly. I'm about twenty years late." He pointed to the bottom line. "Sign here."

"I will not sign there, or anywhere." Carly wiped dye off her cheek. "Not unless one of us has committed adultery."

His voice was so steady, it shocked her. "Of course. And you know the answer to that."

"No. Tell me. And while you're at it, explain why you made such a fool out of yourself at camp."

He dropped his head. "I don't deny that I could have been more discreet that morning."

"You'd just been talking to Keri Ann. Why is she in the shadows every time something awful happens to our family?"

He burst out laughing as if the joke was on her. "She's the one I should have married. I guess that makes you and me both adulterers."

Carly gasped.

"So technically what we're talking about is an annulment, but that takes too long. I've wasted enough time. I need to get my life on track, to make up to Keri Ann what I've stolen—what I've kept from her all these years."

A loud noise from the other room interrupted him. Serena stomped into the kitchen. "Of all the malarky I've ever heard a man spew. To think I looked up to you as the ideal husband! You're nothing but a poser! What a dope I was to listen to a thing you ever said. Get out of my house, right now! And don't ever come here again. You are not welcome!"

Carly was grateful for her friend's support, but when Rick strutted out of the room as if it was his decision, she decided she had not finished talking. She followed him to the door. "Wait, I want to know. Why is Keri Ann always around when something terrible happens to our family? You owe me an explanation!"

"I don't owe you a thing."

CHAPTER SIXTEEN

The first time Ricky Green made love to Keri Ann McGraw was the afternoon of her mother's funeral. As the undertaker at Our Lady of Perpetual Help lowered poor Mrs. McGraw into the ground, a few neighbors and her five children stood near the hole, crying their eyes out. The only one not crying was Old Man McGraw. What her friends knew but were too polite to say was what had caused poor Mrs. McGraw to die so young. Why her kids had never spoken up, Ricky figured, was the same reason why he'd never called the cops himself. Shame, embarrassment, feeling that somehow, some way, it was all their fault.

Rain poured as Father Mack said a few words over the dead lady's coffin, but when a bolt of lightning arced not far from the cemetery, everyone except him, Keri Ann, and the priest hurried off to find shelter.

His girlfriend was still looking for answers. "Why did God let her die, Father Mack?"

"Everyone dies, sweetheart."

"But not this young. I needed her—God should know that! Now I've got no one to ..." She buried her face in Ricky's handkerchief. Father Mack, who Rick considered more with-it than the average priest, handed her his umbrella. What she wanted to say but couldn't was that now there was no one to come between her and the old pervert when he barged into her room in the middle of the night.

"You'll always have someone."

"You mean God. But he let me down, Father. Can't you see that? We prayed, a lot. Ricky and me." She squeezed his arm. "We really believed."

Distracted by the lightning, Father Mack patted her shoulder. "Now what you need to do is believe in your-selves. You look like intelligent young people." Keri Ann shrugged, displacing his hand. The priest tried again. "Jesus never said life would be easy."

He was dodging her question, but the two of them were used to being blown off by their elders. His last words were "Remember, you're stronger together" before running back to his car, leaving them his umbrella but not much else. He hated to think that this guy was just another player, like the cops and the judges and the school principals—big shots who drank together, stuck together, and covered for each other when necessary. But in this town, the odds were for it. Another big phony, just like his own old man.

No one was home at Ricky's house, so they went up to his bedroom. He'd taken her there before, but that day was different. He noticed her looking around at his stack of records, the unfinished model Corvette on the desk.

All stuff she'd seen before, but it was like she was seeing it, seeing him, for the first time.

"Ricky, what was it the old hag at Bible Club used to say?"

"You mean that God works all things for our good?"

"Something like that."

"Do you buy it anymore?"

"Do you?"

"No."

They took off their wet clothes and didn't stop there. When he held her close, it was as if they'd melted into each other. Soon they were on the bed kissing and hugging, and for the first time, instead of pushing him away, Keri Ann wanted more, wanted everything.

Afterwards, she said, "I suppose that's what Father Mack meant."

"What do you mean?" Ricky was breathing hard, still surprised at what they'd just done.

"You know, that whole 'stronger together' bit."

"Do you think we are?"

Her eyes fixing on him for all she was worth, she nodded. "Absolutely."

Ricky held her face in his hands. "Then let's make a pact—the two of us against the world."

"The two of us," she said, kissing his forehead.

Noise from downstairs made them both jump up. Ricky pulled on his pants. "Listen, Keri Ann, if I'd known we were going to … I'd have come prepared. What if you get … you know?"

"Don't worry, Ricky. It'll be fine. If I do get pregnant, at least we'll know who the daddy is."

CHAPTER SEVENTEEN

N athan ran past the visitor's desk at Strong Memorial Hospital. If they were hiring, one of the jobs better have his name on it. As the son of a nurse, he knew more about hospitals than most seventeen-year-olds. His mother always said he'd make a dynamite healthcare professional. Right now, he'd settle for a job as an orderly.

The nurses who had given him a ride agreed to let him put them down as references, though they warned him not to make them look stupid. In other words, he better not mess up. As far as he could see, his only challenge would be convincing whoever did the hiring that he was old enough. He wouldn't be eighteen for another month. He could write in another date, but they'd probably want to see his license. He prayed that they'd be reasonable. After all, how much difference would a few weeks make?

When he got his first paycheck, he'd buy something

nice for the girls who'd let him wash up in their bathroom, given him one of their boyfriend's clean shirts, and dropped him off at the department of personnel with time to spare.

He sat in a room full of other applicants, all of them filling out forms, and watched as the others scratched out a lot more mistakes than he had. If Keri Ann had taught him one thing, it was to be neat. He was confident in his prospects, but when the rest of them were called in for their interviews ahead of him even though he'd been the first to sign in, he got restless.

He told himself that they were saving the best for last. But as the hour hand of the clock edged toward five, he worried that he may have just been forgotten. The walls of the room were covered with facts he could now recite from memory: the five steps in resuscitating a choking victim, the dates of the UAW meetings for 1998–99, and the federal minimum wage scale. But when his name was finally called, he'd been nodding off, a bead of drool on his chin. What did they expect from a guy who hadn't slept the night before?

"Nathan Green?"

"Yes, ma'am."

"This way, please."

The room was pink, an odd choice for the bruiser of a man sitting behind the desk. When he stood, he towered over Nate. He'd heard somewhere that the walls of penitentiaries were painted this color to make the prisoners easier to control. But this was the department of personnel!

"Hello, Nathan. I'm Mr. Hathaway, the one in charge of staffing here at the Strong." He held out his hand, which looked more like the claw of a bear. "Please have a seat."

"Thank you."

"After reviewing your application, I regret to inform you that in order to be considered for full-time employment, you must be at least eighteen."

Nate's shoulders slumped. If they'd known that all along, why had they made him wait so long? He had wasted the whole day. But as he darted up, the huge man motioned for him to sit. "Wait a minute, Mr. Green. How badly do you need a job?"

"The best word for my situation at present is 'desperate.'"

"We thought that might be the case."

Nate turned sideways in the chair, ready to bounce. The word "desperate" might not have been the best choice.

"I've described you to one of my associates, and he thinks he might have something which will suit you even better. Off the books for now, but if you work out, a position with his company is a once-in-a-lifetime opportunity."

Nate tensed up. In what alternate universe did a seventeen-year-old with no experience get a once-in-a-lifetime opportunity? He imagined his grandfather telling him, "Nate, if something sounds too good to be true, it probably, well, you know ..." He would listen to this man's pitch, but if sounded like BS, he'd heard enough of that for one day.

"Nathan, does what I've described so far interest you at all? Would you like to hear more?"

"Um ... OK."

"We at the Strong work with a company that produces simulations of disasters, natural and ... otherwise."

"Like fire drills?"

"We call our simulations live-action role-play, although the purpose is much the same as a drill—to make sure our staff is ready for any type of medical emergencies that may arise. You're familiar with the strategy?"

"Sort of. My mother is a nurse."

"Splendid. Then you know these productions aim to create a sense of immediacy and reality."

"I know they use fake blood. Gobs of it."

"Why, yes. That's true. But our little drills represent only a small portion of the services Global Connections provides."

"Global Connections?"

"Yes. We're talking about a corporation with international scope. The pay is significantly more than you'd make in an entry-level position at the hospital, and traveling expenses are included. Honestly, given your present situation, I don't see how you can lose."

"What exactly would I be doing?"

"Acting, my boy."

Was he dreaming? The director of personnel let his words sink in before continuing. "I notice you've had experience working on theatrical sets."

"Stage crew, yes. But I've always been in the background, never in front of an audience."

"Minor point. My associate and I agree that you're the first candidate passing through here in some time who perfectly fits the profile." Once again, the man paused.

A job as an actor? His father would kill him. He'd blown a gasket when Nate joined the stage crew. Why a son of his wanted to hang out with a bunch of art wimps had been beyond him. Football, swimming, even, but stage crew? It was just one more brick in the wall.

"But I don't know how to, you know … I've never actually performed in front of people." In drama club, he'd learned about lighting and props and how to get on and off stage fast, but not much about pretending to be someone else. Keri Ann had encouraged him to audition for bit parts, but knowing how his father would react, he'd kept his distance. "What kind of acting are we talking—like onstage?"

"No, young man. In front of a camera. Reenactments and such, as I've already explained."

"Oh. So no live audience."

"Not that I'm aware of. Before you decide, I should tell you that their next production is scheduled to start on Monday, so we'll need a commitment today. That doesn't give you much time, but I'd encourage you at least to try it on for size. At this point, there's no binding contract. Although I hear tell …"

"Hear tell what?"

"That if it's job security you're looking for, Global Connections is a very good fit. And if it doesn't work out, for either you or them, your birthday is in October, correct? You'll be eligible to return and interview again for an entry-level position here, although by then what we do at the Strong will strike you as, well, rather mundane in comparison."

"Are you saying that someone you know really thinks I can be an honest-to-goodness actor?"

"Yes, Nathan. What do you think? Shall I call the project manager and say it's a go?"

"On the condition that I can back out any time, I say yes."

"Good decision, Nathan." He picked up his phone. "As far as backing out at any time, that's an issue you'll need to take up with Mr. Yellen." He dialed a number. "Hello, Oscar? Hathaway here. I've got a recruit. Yes ... sure ... of course. Yes, he'll be there ... I don't doubt that for one minute, Oscar." He turned to the wall and whispered, "I scratch your back, you scratch mine"—a message Nate doubted he was supposed to hear. But it probably had nothing to do with him. In any case, Nate was desperate. If he ended up hating the job, it was a free country. He'd just tell them thanks, but no thanks.

He still had a million things to ask about this opportunity of a lifetime, but thinking of Mr. Hathaway scratching some other guy's back was making him fidgety. *No matter.* Striking out on his own and nearly broke, his options were limited. He wasn't even sure he had a place to sleep that night. So, he pared his questions down to one: "When do I start?"

~

Keri Ann sat on Dr. Bernstein's examining table, her backside sticking to the tissue paper. These gowns were disgusting, though for the most part she felt comfortable at Roswell Park Institute. The staff were clean and thorough. Her lab results had indicated something more than abnormalities in her uterine wall. She'd been shocked to hear a diagnosis of uterine cancer but calmed down when told that, in their opinion, her chances were good if they could remove it entirely. The treatment was going to be intense, and it was bound to gain her tons of sympathy from Ricky.

Ricky had asked her to marry him the day she brought home the wig—after the divorce was final, of course. Never mind that it had taken twenty years. The point was, she'd officially won him back.

She'd also managed to convince him not to panic about Nathan's disappearance. The kid had been keeping in touch with her, and she chose certain details from their conversations to pass on to Ricky. Nate had found a job and was doing great on his own but was still not interested in speaking to anyone but her. All true, except for that last part.

Each time they talked, Nate begged her to help him get through to his parents. Of course, she didn't tell the boy that she'd had the Greens' landline turned off. Why pay the bill when Carly had moved out of the house and Ricky was staying with her? She'd also blocked Nathan's number on Ricky's phone and, as the one paying the bills, successfully cut off Carly's phone as well as other accounts. There was no way the kid could get through to them, nor they to him.

Last time he'd called, Nate said he was heading to Wyoming to act in what he referred to as "live-action role-play," whatever that meant. If he hadn't always been so sincere, she wouldn't believe it. But it sounded a lot like acting, and though he'd always wanted to, Nate had never had the nerve to step out from behind the curtains. Could be he was finally learning to reach out and grab what he wanted. If so, it was only because of her.

Keri Ann was pleased at how easily the boy had accepted her story that his parents were the ones who'd had their numbers changed. Of course, he'd asked why.

She said she didn't know for sure but that they were upset with how he'd embarrassed them at camp, basically proving to all of their friends that all of their gossip was true. Anyway, if it wasn't for this stupid hospital gown, Keri Ann would be in a very good mood. Across the examining room, her fiancé chatted with Dr. Bernstein.

Ricky told the doc, who Keri Ann had assured him was the best at doing what it was she needed done, that he was who she'd picked to make any important decisions while she was in recovery.

Bernstein swiveled around in the chair. "Is this true, Keri Ann?"

"Yes. As my fiancé, Ricky has power of attorney. Any questions, ask him."

"In that case, Mr. Green, is it?"

"Yes, sir."

"I'm happy to say that Keri Ann has a very good chance of coming out of this surgery cancer-free."

"That's fantastic."

"Of course, there are no guarantees. Mr. Green, why the sad face?"

"Do I look sad? The truth is, I couldn't be happier. My only regret is that taking out her womb pretty much shuts down our chances of her getting pregnant again."

The doctor raised his eyebrows. "Again?"

Keri Ann's heart skipped a beat. The doctor was closing in on something she'd kept from Ricky since they were in their teens. The fact that she'd never been pregnant—not with his baby nor anyone else's.

She whimpered as if in pain, hoping to create a distraction, but then, pointing to her X-rays, the doctor really sealed the deal. "Due to the endometriosis, see all those shadows? Keri Ann is nulligravida. I assumed that this was something you'd have known."

"Of course, doctor. We have no secrets." Rick quickly nodded his head, and Keri Ann could breathe again. The love of her life had no idea what Dr. Bernstein was talking about but was too embarrassed to ask.

She'd known about her endometriosis for ages and along the way picked up that "nulligravida" meant a grown woman who'd never been pregnant. *Thank God that one went over Ricky's head.* She rustled around on the table. Ricky rocked back and forth on his heels, trying to look in-the-know, which he most definitely was not.

"So, doc, is there anything we can do to get her ready for the big day?"

The surgeon smiled at Keri Ann. "You're lucky to have such an attentive partner. Some women go through this all on their own. It breaks my heart." He turned back to Ricky. "Nothing special. Just be sure she follows the pre-op protocol, stays hydrated, and gets plenty of sleep. Call the office immediately if she has bleeding or an increase in pain."

"Will do, doc. And thanks."

"You're quite welcome. I'll see you next week."

Relieved that her deepest secret was safe, Keri Ann hopped off the table, but Ricky's forehead had broken out in sweat. "One thing I should have asked him—what the heck is endometrionics?"

Keri Ann beamed. "You mean endometriosis? Just a little nervous condition I've had since forever, I guess."

"What does that have to do with your cancer?"

"Nothing, Ricky. Nothing at all."

CHAPTER EIGHTEEN

Anya Worthy surveyed the sprawling living room of their old North Buffalo bungalow. With no idea of how many former members of the New Wine Fellowship would show, she set up a few folding chairs, stiff old things she and Malcolm had rescued from their former church before the building was sold. Some of the brethren might have trouble with such hard seats, but there wasn't much she could do about that now. Malcolm had sprung this meeting on her at the last minute. Hating to see members of Rick's congregation wandering around like sheep without a shepherd, her husband had offered their home as a place to gather.

Malcolm and Rick had mutually agreed to end their partnership, but even if they hadn't, Rick had been kicked out of his building. Something to do with the mortgage being in arrears. That didn't come as a surprise. Keri Ann took care of the bills, and she was currently in the hospital recovering from surgery. Anya would have expected that a grown man whose secretary was indisposed would have the sense to pay the note, but according to Malcolm, the ministry was broke. Rick's "congregation" was down to a few hangers-on, and where or when they got together anymore was anyone's guess.

As a pastor's daughter, Anya was holding a "wait and see" attitude toward Rick Green. Pressure on ministers was just as intense here as it had been in Russia. So were peoples' expectations, and not everyone heeded the biblical admonition to guard their tongues. Her father had been forced to flee his country due to the careless talk of folk who claimed to love Jesus.

Rick had left her husband in the lurch financially by letting him go, but still she couldn't help feeling sorry for him. Problems in churches were rarely one person's fault. David Wilson had eventually confessed what had and had not gone on between him and Rick's older son and that the last he'd heard, Nathan was headed to New York City. Carly was so worried about Nate, she'd taken a leave of absence from work. Praying for the boy was one reason for tonight's meeting.

The other reason was more complicated. Those who'd left New Wine after the disaster at family camp wanted to know how things had gotten so bad so fast. But, in her husband's opinion, these people had been far from one big happy family for a long time.

According to the people Malcolm had counselled, the faithful at New Wine Fellowship had gotten stuck in a rut. Most stuck closely to their own groups, based on family ties. They used to mix things up more, but years passed and conflicts arose. Often, instead of facing them, they brushed them off and retreated to the safety of family.

Malcolm planned to get them back on track. He sounded confident that sitting in the same room, side by side, they'd feel free to open up. Anya wasn't so sure.

All she could do was make them as comfortable as possible. Her husband had only one worry: that Rick might hear about the meeting and consider it an attempt at "sheep stealing." If he did, the poor man was even farther from reality that they thought.

The doorbell rang, and Anya ran to greet their first guests. "Welcome, Carly, Serena! New hair color, Carly? I love it! And who do we have here? Benny! Our girls are looking forward to seeing you again, young man!"

Carly hugged Anya. "Thanks for letting me bring him." She choked up. "Can you believe I've never needed a babysitter before? Keri Ann had always been there."

"No problem at all. Grace and Pauline have big plans for him. Not sure what—all I know is that paint and cardboard boxes are involved." Carly released her hand abruptly. "What's the matter? Have I said something wrong?"

"No, it's silly, really."

"Tell me."

"It's just that Benny refuses to have anything to do with paint. I've never even gotten him to color with crayons."

"That's OK, don't worry. I'm sure the girls will come up with something. They have enough toys up there." She hollered up the stairs, "Grace, Pauline, Benny's here!"

From his study off the living room, Malcolm listened to his wife greet Carly and Serena. He'd planned to start by asking some questions of a practical nature, like whether those who had left New Wine wanted to keep meeting and whether they were still interested in joining Malcolm's congregation, wanted to go someplace else, or had given up on church altogether. But the sadness in Carly's voice prompted him in another direction. As the brethren arrived and were encouraged by his wife to make themselves at home, he scribbled down a few notes.

Only about a dozen people showed up. Malcolm noticed that all of them had figured out which chair was his. He said, "Good. Now I can see all your faces. No one can hide," prompting a round of nervous laughter.

Laughter ceased as Pastor Malcolm began to pray: "Oh, Lord, we thank you from the bottom of our hearts for the love you've shown this body of believers throughout the years. You know how trying the past two months have been. We ask your mercy this evening on our humble efforts to set things right, to rip out any weeds that strangle the good fruit you want in our lives. Please help us to restore unity of spirit and bonds of love. Amen."

Assuming that what people did at a prayer meeting was pray, Serena Petrick launched out after Pastor Malcolm's "Amen" with some intercession of her own. "Oh, Lord, I pray that my friend Carly here will have the courage to open up about a couple of things tonight, enough to lighten her load a little, anyway."

When the room got so quiet that Serena heard cars passing on the street, she stopped. She must have broken some rule or done something they didn't approve of. These people were so uptight. If any of them had a beef to settle, it was Carly. The women had been sidelining her for years, and when she'd finally had little Benny, they acted like the boy was some sort of freak.

194

Serena had helped Carly plan what she should say tonight, although on the way over, her friend hadn't sounded very confident. Serna reminded her she had nothing to lose. The tension between her and these people couldn't get much worse.

Talk about tension—now, Serena was ready to pop.

To end the awkward silence, Pastor Malcolm scanned the room, his eyes settling on the only soul making eye contact. "Sister Betty, can you lead us in a song?"

Betty smiled. "Of course." She closed her eyes and sang their old favorite softly but on key, "There is a river that flows from deep within, there is a fountain that frees the soul from sin. Come to this water, there is a vast supply, there is a river that never shall run dry." Slowly, the rest of them joined her in another round of the old standby.

After the third repetition, Malcolm called the meeting to order. He noticed that singing had made the sadness on their faces fade some, perhaps a sign the Holy Spirit was on the move. If not, there was a chance he might be guiding them all over a cliff.

"Thanks. That was great. To make sure we're all on the same page, I want to assure you that those who have met with me personally are the ones who requested this meeting. In other words, tonight is for you. It's your meeting, not mine." He paused to let this sink in, and it seemed to. So far, so good.

"From what I gather, most of you are still in the dark about Pastor Rick's meltdown last summer. You want to know how your church fell apart with no warning." Another pause. With each of them now on the edge of their seats, it was time to rip off the lid. "But I think the problems that surfaced at camp actually started long ago and involve more than your issues with Pastor Rick. In my opinion, members of your congregation need some serious reconciliation."

A wife crossed her arms. A husband stuck out his chin. Malcolm told himself that most of these folks wanted to do the right thing. They loved the Lord and missed the fellowship of the saints—otherwise, they wouldn't have come. They'd just grown so used to following that they'd forgotten how to lead. So, he soldiered on. "Does anyone here feel a tugging in their spirit, a desire to be forgiven or perhaps a need to forgive? To heal properly, wounds need exposure to the light." Eyes that were fixed upon him a minute ago dropped to the floor as if his wife's Oriental rug held all the answers.

Finally, someone took him up on his offer, though it was not the someone he'd hoped. "I sure do," said Serena Petrick.

"What's on your mind, Serena?"

"I know I haven't spent enough time with you all to, how should I put it, have earned the right to speak, but since nobody else is going to, I'll point out the elephant in the room."

Malcolm wasn't sure which elephant she referred to, as in his estimation, there was a small herd. An immediate negative reaction followed her statement. More crossed legs and arms, a dozen frozen expressions.

Carly interrupted. "Thank you, Serena. I can't tell you how grateful I am for your generosity over the past few weeks, giving me and Benny a place to stay. I don't know what I would have done without it. Not just sharing your home with us, but listening to me pour out my heart about the breakup of my marriage. Then Nathan running away and ... everything.

"I'm angry, alright, at all of you. That's right, folks. You, as my brothers and sisters in the Lord, have let me down, everyone except for Serena, and I appreciate her calling it out. But I really should take it from here. The only problem is, where do I start?"

Malcolm said, "Perhaps at the beginning."

Carly glanced at the pastor. "Do we have that much time?"

Shocking everyone, a woman sitting next to Anya cut Carly off. "I'm not sure if this is what you're mad about, Carly, but I know one thing. When so many of us moved out of the city, you felt left behind. Right?"

"Well, yes ..."

"That's too bad, because it had nothing to do with you. It was about our kids. We wanted better schools. I'd have thought you would have realized that."

Another woman chimed in, "Everything we did was for our kids' sake, Carly. We always wondered why you waited so long to have another one. But since you were the pastor's wife, we assumed you knew what you were doing."

"If this meeting is going to be about confession, I have something," said a man who Carly had known since they all came up from Cincinnati. "I used to think the reason you and Rick never had more kids was because you were under judgment."

"That sounds awful!" interjected someone else. "How do you know it just wasn't something God allowed because, well ... for a reason only he understands?"

The woman on the couch spoke over everyone. "How

could any of us know anything about Carly when she stopped sharing with us years ago? You have to admit, Carly, you weren't much of a friend, either."

This time, it was Malcolm's own wife who spoke up. "So, let me get this straight. Some of you have avoided Carly because you thought she was under divine judgment, but then put the responsibility on her to give you all the full report?"

Malcolm watched Carly shrink like a pricked balloon. And the women were not finished.

Mrs. Wilson, the mother of the boy Nathan supposedly ran off with, was quick to reply. "It's more complicated than that, Mrs. Worthy. Since we're going for full disclosure, I admit that I was jealous of Carly years ago, you know, for being married to Rick and all." She took a shaky breath and continued. "If she had any questions or problems, she had the pastor right by her side to help. What else could a woman want? And I happen to know I wasn't the only one who felt that way."

Mr. Wilson, who had yet to say a word, suddenly erupted. "This is the first I've heard of anyone being jealous of Sister Carly!" He glared at his wife. "If you ladies weren't so focused on yourselves, you many have noticed that all around us, people are having real problems like keeping our jobs, paying our bills, and trying to keep track of our kids."

To prevent what was becoming a landslide of negativity, Malcolm brought the focus back to Carly. "Carly, a while back you had something to say."

But it was too late. Her hands covering her face, Carly backed out of the room and ran upstairs. Silence fell over the group, which Serena was quick to fill. "You know, I thought Carly was exaggerating when she talked about how she feels cut off from everyone. I really did. I mean, how could Christian people be so inconsiderate? But if anything, she was letting you guys off easy. You should be ashamed." Serena left the circle and followed her friend.

~

Upstairs, Carly was greeted by the laughter of children, including that of her own son. She entered the girls' bedroom, wiping tears on her sleeve. "What do we have here?" The floor was covered with snips of construction paper, but the girls had been careful to keep the jars of paint confined to an easel in the corner. They were in the process of dressing up like robots, walking and talking in stiff one-word-at-a-time robot language.

Carly regarded Ben, who she'd never seen this happy. "Look, Serena, he's got paint on his hands!"

"Sorry, Mrs. Green," said Pauline. "We'll make sure he washes them before you take him home."

"No, no, girls, it's great. I love that he's messy—mess him up even more! Don't stop on my account." Little Ben got into his box costume and walked across the room, arms held out straight.

Serena was also amazed. Benny hadn't broken out in a real smile since she'd met him. All he ever wanted to do was watch TV. She made a note to ask Anya if the girls could come to her apartment and play with him sometime, as they were the first ones to coax him out of his shell.

~

Downstairs, Malcolm made another attempt to re-route the group discussion. "I know she was upset, but is it possible that what Serena just said has some truth in it?"

"Not quite following you, Pastor Malcolm," said Mr. Wilson.

"What I just heard from your discussion sounded to me like the result of years of miscommunication."

The oldest participant, another who'd followed Rick and Carly from Ohio to Buffalo, spoke up. "The way I see it, Reverend Worthy, we all get used to things the way they are, and if that means sticking to one side of the church and not worrying about the other, well, so be it. God never said everyone was cut out to be your friend. Hasn't bothered me much, being that I'm used to keeping my own counsel, but I've been close to the Greens since back in Cincinnati, and one thing's for certain. Carly never got used to ... how can I put it? Being on the outside looking in. Yep. That's it. You all pretty much closed her out. I agree she's not the easiest lady to get to know, but some of us could have tried a little harder."

After a long silence, another brother picked up the thread. "I don't know about the rest of you, but I came here hoping to revive some spark of life in what we used to call New Wine Fellowship. I remember when people flocked to us because they sensed so much love. Those were the best years of my life. You could walk up to any one of us and share deep, deep stuff. Trust. Trust is what we had, and generosity. Anyone would give you the shirt off their back."

"He's right. Pastor Malcolm, we were really something back then. No complaining or gossip—no little cliques, and everyone was rooting for you. You'd stand up with a testimony and people would cry—with joy."

"It's been ages since I've heard a good testimony. What happened to us?"

Amazed at their sudden candidness, Malcolm let the men unload.

"We can't blame it all on Pastor Rick."

"Maybe not," said Mr. Wilson, "but from what we've just hashed out, it may be too late."

~

As they put the last of the folding chairs back in the basement, Anya asked Malcolm how he thought the meeting had gone. So far, he hadn't offered a single comment. Instead of answering, he slouched in his chair, pretending to watch the ten o'clock news. She knew better than to push.

If anyone had asked her, she'd say that things couldn't have gone worse. Not only did their guests fail to agree about getting together again on the way out, but they didn't even sound much like friends. And they never even got around to praying for Nathan.

It was unlike Malcolm to watch TV at all. He was usually listening to conspiracy theories on the radio at this time of night, but there he was, vegging out in front of some stupid show.

"Hey, babe, talk to me. What's going on?" She rubbed his shoulders.

"Not a heck of a lot."

"Things could have gone better tonight."

"I really blew it, didn't I?"

As her husband's voice broke ever so slightly, Anya

recalled the moment in her childhood when she knew her father was in trouble. His anti-Communist sermons had earned him the reputation of an agitator. Their family needed to leave the country immediately or her father would be arrested, given a rigged trial, and sent to prison. Her mother had jammed clothes into a trunk, and then they all spent countless days on trains and ships.

Malcolm's problems were minor in comparison, but if she'd learned one thing as the daughter of a pastor, it was that men of faith were not immune to bouts of depression. Anya had seen firsthand how prolonged discouragement could be more dangerous than its cause. "No, Malcolm, you didn't blow it. They did. A long time ago. Don't beat yourself up."

"You're right. This is stupid." He turned off the TV, retreated into his office, and gently shut the door. She resisted the urge to follow.

Reaching for his Bible, Malcolm's eyes landed on an envelope propped up on the desk—a reminder that their own mortgage payment was past due. He'd been confident when they'd signed for the loan that the house was affordable considering his two streams of income. And even after the first church split, his salary agreement with Rick had been more than enough to make up for the loss. But getting fired had been unexpected.

Last spring, he'd projected a big enough income to allow him to quit his day job at Barnes & Noble. But the Worthys were going to be OK; they'd just need to tighten their belts a little. Last time he checked, he still had a management position and a ministry, though the latter was small and shrinking further by the minute.

The bill leaned against a photo of the elders of his

original church, under whose hands he knelt to receive prayer during his ordination. It shamed him to think he'd been so caught up with Rick's group that he'd neglected his own loyal crew. They were waiting to hear their pastor's plan of action. Never mind that he didn't have one.

Anya knocked at the door. "Babe, you OK?"

"Just peachy."

"Honest?"

"Come on in."

Now in her nightgown, Anya let him pull her into his lap. "The kids made a royal mess upstairs."

"Last I heard, that's what kids do."

"Not all of them. Carly said she's never known little Benny to get paint on his hands."

"The girls cleaned him up, I hope."

"That's not the point ..."

"Hey, you guys," their older daughter, Grace, called to them from the living room. "Come here, quick!"

Mr. and Mrs. Worthy jumped up.

"Look, it's Nathan! You know, the boy from camp who ran away. He's on TV!"

CHAPTER NINETEEN

Carly felt more at ease with Serena Petrick than she had with anyone in ages. After straightening things out with her bank account, she began pitching in toward food and other household expenses. Carly had even begun feeling at home in Serena's tiny apartment. Though they had little in common, she shared one thing with Serena: honesty, a trait Jesus referred to as a lack of guile. A good quality in long run, but Carly knew it could also hurt.

On their way home from the meeting at the Worthys', she held her peace. She'd been humiliated—again—and Serena was furious. It didn't help when her friend hit the brakes at each traffic light as if they'd been turning red just to tick her off. She attempted to lighten the mood. "Well, at least Benny enjoyed himself."

"Yes."

On their way to the meeting, Serena had sung along with the Christian music on WDCX. She'd sounded filled with hope that once the brothers and sisters had a chance to hear each other out, they'd all kiss and make up and begin acting like true followers of Jesus. Now, Carly sensed that it was all Serena could do not to cuss.

"I'm sorry you had to hear us at our worst, Serena. Believe me, we weren't always like this." Carly glanced at her new friend, whose mouth was set in a straight line. Once home and certain her little boy was down for the count, she'd put the kettle on. They'd drink tea. Hopefully, by then, Serena would be ready to talk.

~

Tired out from playing, Benny fell right asleep. Carly sat across from Serena at the kitchen table and waited.

"So, Carly ..."

"So what?"

"I've about had it with church."

"Are you joking?"

"This is not something I'd joke about."

"You mean you're turning your back on the Lord because of what happened tonight?"

"Not the Lord, just the church. You people—and I don't mean you personally, but your born-again crowd—are worse than the gang I used to hang out with at bars. What ever happened to Jesus? Isn't it all supposed to be about Him?"

The kettle's whistle sounded like a dying bird. Serena was right. Carly reached for their mugs. "I'm talking about people with genuine faith." Carly's eyes teared up. She cried so much these days, she no longer bothered with mascara. Thoughts of her father, a man full of real faith, often filled her to bursting. He'd been calling her from Florida almost every day to see how things were going and to say he was praying for her and her family. Even for Rick, who, in his opinion, needed it the most. "What'll it be tonight, Serena, lemon or cinnamon?"

"How about Constant Comment in honor of me at the meeting tonight? I couldn't keep my mouth shut."

"But you told the truth, Serena. If the fellowship had more people like you, we might still be a ... fellowship." Carly emptied the kettle into Serena's favorite pot, the red, white, and black one. Bold, just like her. "You know, Serena, I used to speak up a lot more."

"Why did you stop?"

"People tune you out when you talk too much."

"But you were ready to talk tonight."

"Malcolm said he wanted to see where the people were at, and thanks to you, he did. My feelings got hurt, but what else is new? What I'm trying to say is, you shouldn't trash the assembling of the saints in general because of one group." She poured the tea. "Although I have to be honest, last summer I came close."

"When you went out with your old friends."

"Liam said he'd seen Rick out with another woman." Carly paused, remembering that she'd suspected Serena of being that woman. "I was done, not just with church, but with faith and God Himself."

"What changed?"

Carly remembered her vision of a man in a boat, then almost dying before being saved by another man in a boat. "We forget how close God is, you know. Day after day, going to work, coming home, we forget. Then you almost die, and there He is, closer than the air you breathe."

206

Serena stirred her tea. "OK, I get that. But how about before, when God made you wait all those years for a second baby?"

"Who knows? I may never understand what that was all about. Even so, I ended up with two boys. Two times the heartache. Don't get me wrong, I've never regretted having my sons. I'm just saying that looking back on it all, I've finally gotten it though my head that having babies is not what life is all about."

Serena shook her head. "Let me get this straight— you're saying God let you hang out to dry for thirteen years just to teach you something?"

"Sounds like the old 'If God is so loving, why does he allow suffering?' argument."

"Well, yeah, come to think of it, that's something else I haven't nailed down."

"Don't look at me, Serena. I'm no theologian. That was Rick's job. All I can say is, I've been around long enough to know that receiving what God has for you is not always easy, and sometimes it means your prayers aren't answered just the way you want."

"I can buy that, Carly. I didn't want my husband to leave me, and I don't talk about it much. I never told you this, but I hoped to have a few kids, too. To be honest, that's how God got my attention in the first place. I was a wreck after the divorce, didn't have a clue what to do. So one day I'm driving home from work, fiddling around with the stereo, and must have left the dial on Family Radio or WDCX. Anyway, some guy is yelling at the top of his lungs, and this verse pops out at me—you know the one. 'For God so loved the world that he gave his only begotten son, that whoever believes in him should not perish, but have everlasting life.'

"I'd heard those words before, but that night they really got to me. I don't know how it happened, but it felt like God flew into the car and put his arms around me. I had never felt so loved." She wrapped both hands around her mug. "And I still do. So it's not God I have a problem with."

"That's right. You said it was the church."

"Exactly. Is there a way to be a follower of Jesus and not part of the church?"

"Depends on what you mean by 'church.'"

"I know it's more than New Wine Fellowship. I remember Rick preaching on the body of Christ, that the real church isn't stuck in categories like Protestant or Catholic. That made sense to me. In fact, all his sermons did. Even the one about Moses needing his two friends to hold up his arms so they could win a battle. But after how that big bully treated you, I wouldn't trust him to water my house plants."

"I get that, too, but don't focus on Rick. What counts is that you gave your life to Christ and the Holy Spirit came into you. If not, you wouldn't be able to understand the Bible like you do. It's a gift, you know."

"Why can't it just be me and Jesus? Forget church, fellowship, the whole religion thing. After tonight, I'd just as soon never step foot in a church again."

Carly put her hand on her friend's arm. "You're tired. Now's not a good time to make such a big decision. Wait a while. Things always look better in the ... you know."

"Right. The sky is always darkest just before the, well, you know." Serena smiled. "OK, roomie. But I'm too wound up to sleep. Let's see if we can catch *America's*

Got Talent. At least that show's good for a laugh."

Too late for the talent show, Serena flipped to the news. The story of a student about the same age as Nathan grabbed her attention. They had been tortured and left for dead, and the campus was gathering for a candlelight vigil in their classmate's honor. A reporter from the show handed the mic to one of them. Carly spit out a mouthful of tea. "That's my son! That's Nathan!"

Denver, Colorado

After signing on with Global Connections, Nate flew out west for an audition that involved walking into a fake convenience store and threatening the fake cashier with a fake gun. Though the producer called him a natural, he'd had trouble getting into character since his partner, a lady named Jean, couldn't stop laughing. The cameraman was the kind of guy who'd say white was black if it earned him points with the boss, a lot like the wannabes from drama club. It had been hard to tell where exactly he fit in with this "opportunity of a lifetime."

He ended up bombing the robbery scene by flubbing his lines, all of two simple sentences: "See the gun? Now put the cash in the bag!" If this wasn't bad enough, he couldn't resist the urge to throw in some nervous laughter and a Humphrey Bogart accent, which wasn't in the script.

At the end of the shoot, he waited for the industry's biggest insult: "We'll be in touch." What he got instead was a check for five hundred dollars—more money than he'd ever seen at one place and one time, and for less than an hour's work! At first, he assumed somebody had put the period after the wrong zero. And if it hadn't been so much money that he very much needed, he'd have mentioned the error. But like his grandfather used to say, "Never look a gift horse in the, well, you know."

That night when the rest of the crew went out for drinks, he said he couldn't join them because he had another date, which of course was a lie. He knew no one in Denver and didn't have enough cash in his wallet to buy a beer, let alone a round—something he'd always wanted to do. They told him not to be a stranger as he walked out onto a weird-looking street looking for somewhere to cash his check.

Standing in line at a Food King, he saw a familiar face. "Hi, Nate."

"Hi, Jean." His partner, the lady he was supposed to be robbing, walked up behind him. "You didn't go out with the crew."

"Not tonight, kid."

He noticed Dr. Pepper and frozen pizza in her shopping cart. "So, Jean, what do you think of me so far?"

"What do you mean?"

"My performance. Do I have a chance at keeping this gig?"

"No comment."

"Next," said the lady behind the counter. "What can I do for you?"

"I'd like to cash a check." He handed her the envelope, trying to keep it out of Jean's line of sight.

"Do you have an account here?"

"I'm afraid not, but I do have ID."

"Honey, I can't cash a personal check unless you have an account."

Jean pushed past Nate. "Excuse me, ma'am, I have

one. Cash the kid's check. Look, mine is just the same."

The lady stared at Jean, stamping Nate's check without looking down, then shelling out five bills. "Next."

"Thanks, Jean. What a coincidence you were right behind me."

She laughed at him, but not the same way she had during the shoot. "Yeah, sure, kid. So, what are you going to do with all that loot?"

"Buy some decent clothes, and maybe a new phone. I've been having trouble with this one and I want to call my mother, you know, to let her know I'm OK."

"Good idea. When you get that phone, make sure to give me the number. That is, if you decide to stick with this job."

"Why wouldn't I? Hey, do you know something I don't know?"

"No doubt, but one thing's for sure. Nobody on the payroll knows everything. And something else—not everyone is cut out for crisis acting."

Nate wasn't sure what she meant by nobody knowing everything, but if he could expect this much money on a regular basis, he'd do whatever it took to stick around.

The division of Global Connections he'd hooked up with was called Simularity, and everyone he'd met so far, except for Jean, was ready to do or say anything that might help them get ahead in their careers. What these careers would amount to, though, remained unclear.

The next day Nate would stand in as a victim of a generic bomb blast, footage that could be used in a pinch for a number of scenarios. He offered his face to a make-up artist, all set to plaster it with a reasonable amount of blood and dirt. He asked the girl her name.

"Let's see … how about Sally."

"Sounds good. Got a question for you, Sally. When you get paid, who signs the check?" Her hand slipped while etching a cut on his forehead. "Hey, watch it! No one said anything about me losing an eye."

"Sorry. The same guy who signs everyone's. Mr. Yellen."

"Oh yeah, that's right. The CEO. But isn't it strange that it's just a plain old bank check? No logo or mention of the company?"

"Listen, Nate, is it? The best advice I got when I started here is don't ask too many questions. Do your job and shut up. Now tilt your head."

His next simulation, the first that would be nationally televised, was more challenging. In this University of Wyoming shoot, he'd play a clean-cut freshman who was frustrated by the way law enforcement was treating the recent attack on a student. Although he was not supposed to have known Michelle personally, he needed to convince reporters that his fellow student wouldn't be fighting for their life right now if they hadn't been genderfluid.

Jean, who'd been assigned as his mentor, coached him to come right to the point of crying but to hold back the tears. When she signaled that it was showtime, he could hardly breathe. He tried speaking, and nothing came out but a squeak. In a minute, some journalist would stick a mic in his face and he'd need to do his thing. This was the first role he'd play that a lot of people would see, maybe even his family.

He'd hesitated on the part. Old doubts about his own identity had been popping up and he really needed

212

someone to talk to, someone like Keri Ann. But she hadn't even been acknowledging his texts, let alone returning his calls.

At the designated spot, where the angry student body could be seen in the background, Nate saw the heavily made-up lady and a cameraman who was heading his way. God, he couldn't wait until this was over.

Suddenly, the tears were real. This time, he was in way over his head. The words gushing out made no sense, and he prayed that no one he knew would be watching.

The next day, the interview a blur in his mind, he prepared himself for getting the boot. But once again the producer said he did great, though he still hadn't laid eyes on this mysterious Mr. Yellen. Some members of the crew didn't believe the man existed. Nate noticed that people who'd been doing this for a while didn't believe much of anything, and with the way they moved around from place to place, neither did they get a chance to make friends.

Nate was advised this was only for their protection. He wasn't sure why staying anonymous was such a big deal, but along with this bit of information, he'd been given the great news that he was on the short list to fly to Europe for few jobs. In his wildest dreams, he'd never imagined traveling the world as an actor. Yet there he was, just a few months out of high school and in a position to get an all-expenses-paid working European vacation.

On his eighteenth birthday he celebrated by calling Keri Ann, who actually picked up for the first time in weeks. She promised to tell his family that he'd found a well-paid position but that it involved a lot of traveling, and not to worry; he was doing OK, great even. He asked her why the heck everyone back home was so mad at him for leaving. He really needed to talk to them, especially his mom. As usual, Keri Ann said she had no idea why they'd cut him off and figured it had something to do with things being a mess at home. If that wasn't enough, the entire church had split apart. But she promised to get the message to his parents somehow.

Keri Ann told him he'd really hit the jackpot by getting hired at Global Connections. She was jealous, as she'd always wanted to go to Europe. Nate explained that it wasn't for sure yet; Jean had warned him that jobs overseas weren't for lightweights. But he'd also heard that leaving stateside might be his chance to get ahead in the organization, kind of like initiation into a gang. Keri Ann sounded surprised at this, but he assured her that the staff he'd met so far were OK sorts of people. He also reminded her that there was more than one kind of gang in this world, and a better word for it might be "brotherhood."

Keri Ann said whatever else he would get out of it, the experience was sure to toughen him up, kind of like being in the service. "And remember to send me a postcard." Then she said he should stay overseas for as long as possible, since the company was footing the bill.

"Won't you miss me?"

"Sure. Everyone misses you."

"Not Mom and Dad. Otherwise they'd want to talk."

"Oh, I think deep down they do. You're their son, aren't you? They're just going through a tough time."

That didn't sound very reassuring. Then she said the reason she hadn't returned his calls was because she'd been sick, but not to worry, everything was going to be fine. When he came home as a rich globe-trotter with millions of stories to tell, he shouldn't be surprised if a lot of things at home had changed. He'd asked for more details, and she told him for the second time not to worry and that it was all for the good.

Instead of calming him, this conversation only made him more nervous. They'd been doing a shoot downtown, and he told Jean he was heading back to the hotel. "Nate, you know we're not supposed to wander around in public so soon after a simulation."

Jean said she'd been with the company long enough to know what happened when you talked too much, or when your face became too familiar. She'd signed some contract, what they called a nondisclosure agreement, a gag-order type thing.

When he complained about it sounding like a cult, she laughed. "You're not far off. If anything, it's one big dysfunctional family. But like I've been telling you, Nate, not everyone is cut out for this sort of thing."

"So Jean, do you think I have what it takes?"

"Don't know. But you better remember about nondisclosure: the company can sue the pants off you, or worse, if you reveal their secrets."

"I've heard that anyone who's anyone signs them these days. Couldn't be *that* serious."

"You can't say I didn't warn you."

CHAPTER TWENTY

Carly knew right away that the young man on the news was Nate, but she had no idea why was he pretending to be a student at the University of Wyoming. He'd never been that far from home in his life! And everything he was saying—it was all made-up nonsense! She was immensely grateful to see his face again, but what was he doing on TV?

She called her house on the odd chance Rick was there, but when only static came through the landline, she remembered that it had been disconnected. Someone, no doubt Keri Ann, had changed both her and Rick's numbers, but Carly still had Keri Ann's. Rick was probably with her anyway.

When her rival actually answered, she put the phone on speaker and motioned for Serena to listen. "Keri Ann? It's Carly."

"Have you signed those papers yet?" Her rival's voice sounded tired.

"Forget the papers. Put Rick on the phone. Please. It's important."

Dead space. She'd hung up. But not more than ten seconds later, Carly's phone rang.

This time it was Rick. "Carly, what's going on?"

"Nathan was on TV tonight."

"OK, well, that makes sense. Keri Ann says he got a job making public service announcements. He still doesn't trust me enough to talk, but maybe being out on his own will make a man of him."

"He was on Special Edition tonight."

"Well, how do you like that?"

"Not much, Rick. He was being interviewed about a student who was beaten up for being genderfluid, whatever that means."

"What?"

"Our son Nate ... was on TV ... pretending to be someone else, and it was scary. Really scary."

"You sure it was him?"

"Yeah, no doubt. Listen, Keri Ann needs to come clean with everything he's told her. This is no joke, Rick. He sounded out of his mind."

"That's a problem, see. Keri Ann just got out of the hospital. I'm helping her out in what's looking like a tough recovery."

"Wow. I had no idea. Is she going to be OK?"

"It was a hyster—they had to take out her womb."

"Hysterectomy. I'm sorry to hear that."

Rick's voice softened. He said something like "I'll be right back" to Keri Ann and then returned to his conversation with Carly, his voice low. "Listen, Carly, this might sound stupid, but what is nulligravida?"

"Nulligravida. Where did that come from? That's an easy one, a woman who's never been pregnant." Seconds passed. "Rick, are you still there?"

"Are you sure?"

"Come on. I'm an obstetrical nurse."

"I can't believe this ... she lied to me. She's been lying all along."

~

Nathan didn't miss old Jean until they sent her away. She'd taken him out to breakfast to tell him that someone from corporate had decided it was time for him to start getting serious about his career. "It's like this, kid—they want you to poop or get off the pot."

Nate asked her if he were her son, would she have wanted him to stay with it?

"Since I never had children, I can't really say."

"Jean, you know what I mean."

"I guess it depends on what you want out of life."

Nate hadn't thought that far ahead. All he knew was that it took money to live, and so far, he'd been getting piles of it on a regular basis. So far, his only regret had been playing that kid in Wyoming. The project manager reassured him that half the people in broadcasting were reading made-up scripts. After that, he started paying attention and realized that the scripts were often identical.

"What did you think, kid? The reporters still go out and dig up their own leads?"

Actually, yeah. He'd never thought much about it. Another fun fact his manager had popped off was that all the networks use the same sources. That was the way things were done these days; it was simpler and cheaper.

Plus, media moguls didn't like surprises. They preferred to be in control of what the people were told.

"That's why we have jobs, kid," said his manager, punching him in the arm. "Get used to it."

Nate would have felt better if his parents had been around to hear the guy say that. He doubted they'd be overjoyed to know their son was getting paid to present prewritten reality. Hopefully, the writers had the good of society in mind.

Of course they did. Why wouldn't they? Nate figured it was a case of the ends justifying the, well, you know ... and so far, no harm had been done that he knew of anyway. If that changed, he'd heard there were other jobs at Simularity that didn't require being thrown in front of the camera.

He'd also gotten the idea that they liked using teens. "Like you, Nate," said the manager, "not bad-looking but not particularly memorable." A backhanded compliment. He'd have acted a little more grateful if they'd let him hang out with old Jean a little longer. But that morning, after paying for his pancakes and sausage, she was off to another assignment, like a little gray-haired secret agent.

Maybe he'd get a new partner, someone more his age, a girl who was not bad-looking and not particularly memorable, like him. Or maybe not. One thing he'd learned about Global Connections, they kept you guessing. But two could play that game. He'd hang around for this orientation thing and then, if he changed his mind, he'd collect his last paycheck and hop on the next plane, train, or bus back to Buffalo.

~

The guy who met him downtown in front of a building that hadn't had a paying tenant in fifty years was carrying a ring of keys that clinked together as they walked up the dusty stairway. Nate was breathing hard by the time they stopped before door #332. "I'm going to be straight with you, Nathan Green. If you're not one hundred percent sure you want to go through with this, walk away. Now."

Walk away where? How? He didn't even know where he was—someone he'd never met had picked him up at the hotel that morning and dropped him off in front of this building without saying much of anything, not even when or if he'd get a ride back. The job had taken a creepy turn since he no longer had Jean to talk to. It was too late to walk out now, but with Denver being a major city, there had to be a bus station nearby. He might be able to scrape up enough cash to get home if it came to that.

Why was this guy making it sound so scary? What was the big deal? Nate wished the dude would stop fussing with his keys and just open the stupid door.

Last night he'd called Keri Ann again, and she'd finally come out with the reason why his parents were in no mood to talk to him. They'd decided to get a divorce.

The way things had been going at home, this hadn't come as a complete surprise, but he'd assumed they'd just separate for a while, get some counseling, and work things out. They were both so into the Bible, the only way they'd go all the way and split for good was if one of them had committed adultery, and if that was the case, it would be a shock. He'd always figured his parents were too old to go off the deep end like that.

He missed them a lot. But if they'd gone so far as to

have the house phone turned off and change their numbers, they must really losing their minds.

Keri Ann warned him not to let his parents' troubles interfere with his job. "Go ahead and sign anything the company asks you to sign if it guarantees your job security."

"But Keri Ann, money isn't everything."

"Maybe not, kid. But when's the next time you're going to get an all-expenses-paid trip to Europe?"

She'd had a point, but he wished he could at clear it with his parents first. He asked her one more time if there was a way to set up a time to call either one of them at her house or the church, or even a pay phone.

She said she'd try, but that he shouldn't get his hopes up. "When I was in the hospital recovering, neither of them even bothered to visit. After all the help I've given your family over the years. That should tell you something, Nate."

Yeah, that they were too wrapped up in their own problems to have time for him.

She also said his dad thought Nate being out on his own would make a man out of him, and as far as his mom, Keri Ann put it this way: "Carly has always been too far up in her own little head to care about anyone but herself."

His mother and Keri Ann had never been what you'd call "friends," but the next thing Keri Ann said blew him away. "Nate, if you knew what I knew about your mother, what she was doing last summer while the rest of us were at camp, you would have a whole different opinion of her." He remembered his mom telling him that she had to stay home to deliver a set of twins—not much of a crime. Would she have told him a bold-faced lie?

Man, what was up with his family? They were coming unglued—fast! What could his mother possibly have done? And what about his little brother? How was he handling this divorce thing? If he'd only managed to save a little money rather than spend so much on clothes and the phone and other junk, he'd forget this orientation thing and go home right away, but just living had taken more than he'd anticipated. It had been a few weeks since he'd been handed a check.

The man who'd just managed to freak him out even more than he'd been already finally got the door open. He flicked on an overhead light and they stepped into a small room with a chair, a desk, and a computer. He motioned for Nate to sit. So this was it, the grand initiation—just a stupid computer program. The man with the keys looked him straight in the eye. "No going back from here, Nathan."

There he went again with the scary stuff.

"Take your time. Answer the prompts honestly. Don't try to fool the program—trust me, you can't. And one more thing. Before you begin, I'll need to take the phone."

"Why?"

"Don't worry, you'll get it back."

"Like collateral or something?"

"You might say that."

He handed it over and chuckled a little when it took the old geezer a while to find the power button on the dated computer tower. "It's right there, sir."

"Thanks." When the screen jumped to life, Nate felt more in the zone than he had in weeks. He leaned back in the chair as the program kicked off. A handsome man with a voice deeper than Morgan Freeman but smoother than Peter Jennings commanded his attention.

"Welcome. Whatever brought you to this place at this time in your life, the fact that you are here is no coincidence. There are no coincidences. As of now, the level of wealth and success you achieve in the future depends on whether you absorb this and the rest of the truths that will now be laid before you."

This middle-aged Hollywood-style speaker was in great shape, sporting an expensive suit and moving with the confidence of an A-list actor. In seconds, Nate got so swept up he didn't notice the man who'd brought him there had left, locking the door behind him. Soon he got so sucked in that he forgot where he was, and why.

The narrator turned, facing another camera. "Why do so many people fail to achieve their material, professional, and personal goals in life, ending up disappointed and even bitter at the end, while others—the minority, to be sure—move up the ladder of success with relative ease? The answer is simple. When informed that they have been deceived into accepting a false impression of how the world operates, those who are on the winning track accept the correction. They, like you, are willing to adjust their preconceptions and align themselves with the reality that there is one power on earth that controls everything and everyone."

Nate's heart raced. The man was making sense, but something about his message felt off. "Right now," the presenter continued as he turned, facing the camera at a new angle, "you are wondering if what I've said conflicts with the Bible or other religious texts you've been taught to believe, but I assure you, it does not. In fact, religious leaders throughout the ages and to this very day have been in perfect alignment with the information you are about to receive."

Who was this person, and how was he able to read Nathan's mind?

He pressed pause. *This sounds a lot like a pitch for selling your soul to the devil.* The warning he'd received before entering this room came back to him: "If you're not one hundred percent sure you want to go through with this, walk away now." He broke out in a cold sweat.

Whatever was going on, Nate got the idea it was not the kind of thing a guy walking the straight and narrow path was likely to run into, but he reminded himself it was just a video. Anyway, he'd felt this way before while watching a scary movie or a sexy one—he knew he'd regret it afterwards because once bad stuff got into his head, he could never get it out. Still, he couldn't resist hearing a little more. He'd wait until the dude got to the punchline. So far, what had been said was not radically different than what he's always believed—there was one truth, one power stronger than any other.

He hit play.

CHAPTER TWENTY-ONE

K eri Ann McGraw pulled back her carefully pleated drapes to see who was knocking at her door. Ricky stood on her porch, his unshaven face drooping into a scowl.

But like a loyal hound dog, he carried flowers. Orange and gold, a simple fall bouquet. She'd been after him to move in with her for good since he was always there anyway, but that was where he'd drawn the line. *He never did like this house.* Something she'd have to work on, because no way was she ever going to move. Over the years she'd perfected the place and removed every reminder of her father, from attic to basement. It was comfortable enough; Ricky even said so. But that was not what he'd had a problem with. Ricky let the past haunt him.

After a minute she got up, making sure he heard her grumbling about why he'd bother to knock when he had his own key.

Maybe because his wretched ex Carly was getting out

of her car and walking behind him up the porch steps. It crossed her mind that maybe Carly had broken down and signed the divorce papers. Still, that didn't explain why she was at the front door standing shoulder to shoulder with Ricky. No . . . the only explanation for two of them showing up together like this was that something had come up about Nate.

The last time Keri Ann heard from the kid, he'd been in a lousy mood. He'd just gone through some sort of orientation and he'd changed his mind about wanting to talk to his parents. When she asked why, he said if they really cared so little about him, he was being an idiot to keep reaching out. Keri Ann had been happy to hear this and more of his news, that he'd been put on the short list to go to Ireland. He might have been there now, for all she knew, which would explain why she hadn't heard from him in a while. At this point, it didn't matter. The kid no longer stood between her and Ricky.

More knocking, this time hard and impatient. She messed up her hair a little before opening the door.

"What's the problem, did you lose your key?" Carly stood behind Rick, touching his shoulder. Keri Ann balled her fists, then teetered a little.

Rick caught her by the elbow. "I'm sorry you had to get up, Keri Ann, and I wouldn't have made you, but this is important."

"You could have just phoned." She hobbled back to her couch, slowly lowering her head onto the pillow.

Carly interrupted, "No, Keri Ann. We both need to talk to you."

"About what, pray tell? Those papers, I hope. Carly, you need to stop being so stubborn . . ." She appealed to

Rick, but he was looking at Carly. "This is about Nate, isn't it? You're worried because I'm still the only one he trusts. Well, don't blame me for that. The last time we spoke, he still wanted nothing to do with either of you."

"We find that hard to believe, Keri Ann."

"What do you mean 'we'? Anyway, it's the truth."

A look passed between Rick and Carly. He must have gone behind her back and started seeing her again. But that couldn't be right. Not after Keri Ann had described to him in detail what she'd been doing out on the boat last summer with her old boyfriend.

"Malcolm Worthy has tracked Nate down and thinks he's been recruited by some sort of cult."

Keri Ann roared. "You, of all people, accusing him of joining a cult!" Neither of them got the joke. Instead, they stared at her like a pair of zombies. "OK, I didn't mean to offend you, Rick. Your church is … *was* not a cult. Why don't you sit? You're looking down at me like I'm only a—"

"Child?" Carly finished her sentence before locating a chair and perching on its edge.

"No, an invalid. Which, for now, I am, but not for long." She propped herself upright on the couch. "OK, Ricky, if you promise to make her leave, I'll tell you what I know. Nathan has found himself a decent job." She was pleased to see that for some reason, this tidbit of information made the wrinkle between the wretched ex's eyes sink in even deeper.

She snapped back at Keri Ann way too loudly. "Decent? You call what our son is doing *decent?*"

"And how do you know what he's doing?"

Rick put his hand on Carly, which punished Keri Ann

more than words. "Keri Ann," he said, slow and calm, as if talking to a mental case, "Malcolm Worthy has seen a young man we believe is Nathan on news reports coming out of Ireland."

This time it was Keri Ann who interrupted, "And you're going to take that conspiracy nut's word over mine? Your son has made a great career choice, with a company that pays well, and yes, he did mention it was going to involve a bit of traveling, possibly overseas!"

"So, you knew about this all along and never bothered telling us! And with whatever you did to our phones, he couldn't have called us if he wanted to."

Carly was blowing a gasket. Rick moved his hand from the wretch's knee to her shoulder and they looked each other in the eye. Then Rick took over the conversation. "Whatever confidences you might have shared with our son is not why we're here, Keri Ann. We understand that he doesn't want us involved. I take responsibility for that. Nate could never do anything right in my eyes. I can only imagine what's going through the boy's head right now. The reason we're here is because you love him, too. And if you have any idea how we can find him, we know you wouldn't hold it back. Not if he's in danger."

"You saved him once, Keri Ann," interrupted the wretch.

Keri Ann often wondered how things would have played out if she'd just sailed on by the burning house that day. It might have made getting Ricky back a whole lot simpler. Pulling her quilt up to her chin, she asked, "Even if he has gotten himself in a bit of trouble, what makes you think he wants you bailing him out?"

Rick motioned for Carly to sit, but she shook her

head. He sat on the edge of the chair. "This is the deal, Keri Ann. Malcolm was watching the news last night, something about the English Prime Minister making an important speech in Dublin. Some boys throwing rocks at the building get pulled aside and interviewed. The kids say a bunch of things, all good stuff about freedom— nothing wrong with what they said. But one of them keeps his mouth shut. Malcolm thinks that's strange, so he takes a closer look. He swears it's Nate. He recorded it and we played the thing over and over. It was Nate, alright."

"So what? Acting in—what does he call them—simulations is part of his job. I'd think you'd be happy about him being out on his own, learning about life and doing something he really likes. You always said you wished you'd joined the service when you were his age."

"Keri Ann, it's the look in his eyes that has us worried. Empty, like, I don't know ... like there's nothing going on behind them."

"What Rick means to say is that he's acting like he's been brainwashed, Keri Ann. This isn't the first time we've seen him on TV. Last month he was on the news pretending to be a student at the University of Colorado."

Keri Ann's voice came out more like a whine than she'd hoped. "They're paying him good money for doing something he's always wanted to do."

"Acting. Yes, I know. Maybe it started out that way, but this time he looked so scared ..." Carly was about to lose her cool again but managed to get out one more thing. "We have to get him back."

Keri Ann handed her a box of Kleenex before she touched anything with her snotty hands, all the while looking over her shoulder. Since she'd known her, Carly La Nova had always been one sad thought away from tears. "Rick, you know that Malcolm Worthy is no friend of yours. You want to know what happened to New Wine? They're all meeting over at his house now."

"I know, Keri Ann. I hope to join them, if they'll let me."

The discussion was getting out of hand, so she gave them an ultimatum. "I know a few things that might help. But first, Carly, you need to leave."

The wretch pulled a wad of tissue off her nose mid-blow. "Keri Ann, thank you. We'd be so grateful for any kind of lead."

"Like *now*. What I have to say is only for Ricky."

There. That put her in her place. Her hurt look told Keri Ann she'd hit a bull's-eye.

Carly and Rick did that sappy eye contact thing again, but then Rick pulled keys out of his pocket. "It's OK, Carly. Wait for me in the car."

"But Rick …"

"I won't be long."

His wife gone, Rick pulled up closer to Keri Ann. "Why have you been holding out on me?"

"What on earth do you mean?"

"You knew where he was."

"Not exactly where. He said Ireland—that's a big place."

"Why didn't you have his calls traced?"

"There was no need. He always tells me where he is. And he's only in the same city for a short time. The thing is, he thought you'd be furious if you knew his job involved acting."

"What on earth is he doing in Ireland? He doesn't even have a passport."

"I don't know, Ricky, but you're blowing this thing way out of proportion ..."

"He's not *your* son, Keri Ann."

His last comment really chilled the air. "No, he's not," she said. "Although he might have been, if not for—"

"If not for what, Keri Ann? Your abortion?" His voice a growl, he spit out the question. "How can a woman pronounced by her doctor as nulligravida have ever had an abortion?"

He knew. The secret she'd guarded all these years was now, apparently, common knowledge. She pounded the arm of his chair. "It was supposed to be you and me, Ricky! You know that!"

"No. I don't. Not anymore."

~

Somewhere over the Atlantic Ocean, Nate adjusted his headphones. According to those in charge, whoever they were, this Ireland gig was the last test of his loyalty to the organization. If he nailed it, they promised him he'd be in for keeps. After analyzing his responses to the virtual orientation, Mr. Yellen wasn't convinced of Nate's loyalty, or so he'd been told. How they'd found out he'd been in contact with Keri Ann, Nate couldn't figure, but they had. They knew her name, where she lived, and even that he'd spoken to her about what the company was up to. Before getting on this plane, he'd been warned that he better watch his step. One story he'd heard over and over was that you didn't want to be an ex-employee of Global Connections.

Nate got that he needed to be careful but was less clear about the "ex-employee" part. What could be worse than getting fired from your job and being completely alone and broke in a foreign country?

If he'd had doubts that GC meant business, they died the minute he arrived at the airport. The "yes-men" who'd been telling him how wonderful he was for months had vanished. Instead, he was met by a nonverbal goon who laughed out loud when Nate asked to see their itinerary. All of his questions received the same response. His new associate treated him more like a hostage than a rising star in the crisis actor universe.

The flight being a redeye, both Nate and his handler slept through most of the trip. Nate dreamed about the Thanksgiving dinner they always had at church that he was going to miss for the first time in his life. He yearned for the aroma of roast turkey and apple pie. The clumsy oaf next to him wore enough aftershave to mask the smell of a skunk. All that stink wasn't helping Nate's stomach, which hadn't completely settled since the day last summer when he'd struck out on his own. The good news was that he'd shed the extra ten pounds he'd been carrying. His pants had started drooping on him back in August, and now he was down to a thirty-two waist. But as the stewardess began passing out bags of peanuts, he decided he'd be content wearing thirty-fours forever if it meant eating regular meals.

They landed at Dublin Airport just as the sun rose. Nate found it odd that his smelly new partner, who'd sat next to him for the last six hours without saying a word, became positively chatty while going through customs— "Do I have anything to declare? Not yet, but I will soon enough"—and then spouted off again to the driver of the van Nate was shoved into. "Good morning, my man. Here to hand over the goods right on schedule." Whatever that meant. The driver passed the goon an envelope. Nate assumed it was payment for services rendered, even though all he'd had to do for it was sit. At least somebody was getting paid. The big guy then nodded to the driver, who took off like a racehorse.

Nate wasn't the only passenger in the van but might as well have been since the rest of them whispered to each other in another language. "Hi, I'm Nathan Green," he proclaimed to three rows of blank stares. Nine of them held on to their seats as the driver flew onto the main road at law-breaking speed. Two were girls, and even they looked like they'd escaped from a war zone. If they were fellow actors, he couldn't imagine how they'd made the cut, unless they'd been very well made-up.

For the first time, it dawned on him that maybe he hadn't made the cut, either. Maybe he'd been lied to all along about being on probation. Not one of his performances had been what you'd call stellar. But if that was the deal, why had somebody paid big bucks to fly him all the way to Ireland?

So far, his acting had received mixed reviews at best—one manager saying that he had potential, another that he'd embarrassed the entire team. What this Irish job was all about remained to be seen, but he was planning to give it all he had. If he managed to impress, perhaps he'd finally see some green. If not, he'd be showing up back home for Christmas with empty pockets.

The woman sitting next to the driver smoked one cigarette after another while blathering on in what sometimes sounded like English. As the kilometers went by, Nate made out little snips of the conversation—something about payday coming at last and the boss meeting them later out at the strand. Nate waited for some indication, anything at all about what he was expected to do, but the driver and his female friend seemed to have completely forgotten him. As the open fields turned into suburban roads and finally to city streets, he felt queasier than ever. Motion sickness, cigarette smoke, and complete disorientation were taking their toll. He tapped the lady on the shoulder, and she noticed him for the first time.

"What exactly do they want me to do here?"

"From what I gather, deary, you'll be taking part in a demonstration outside of the Irish parliament building. The prime minister of England will be giving some sort of speech, and he's the bugger you're supposed to be angry at because he was no more than a dirty, lyin' colonialist. Got that?"

"Yes, ma'am, thanks. Will I get a script?"

Her laughter turned into a round of smoker's hacking. "None that I know of, love. But you do know how to swear, right? Plus, we have a few bricks hidden in the bushes."

"Bricks?"

"Sure. To throw."

"At people?"

"Nah, the fat cats will scoot in through the back or maybe some hidden tunnel, no doubt. You're there to make noise. Got it?"

"Will I be interviewed?"

Another phlegmy laugh. "Could be, if you draw enough attention. Like I said, you're there to stick it to the man."

"How about my suitcase?"

"Oh, right. Don't give it a thought, deary. We'll take it on through."

"Through to where?" he said while being pushed out onto a deserted street.

"So long, kid!" She threw her cigarette out the window, missing him by inches.

It was too cold outside for the sweatshirt he was wearing. The last thing he'd bought before making this trip was a new jacket, medium weight, which he was told would be perfect for winter in Ireland, but that was in his suitcase, along with stuff he might need to sell to get back home if things fell apart here. When he'd lay eyes on it again was anyone's guess.

Whoever was in charge here was running things awfully loose. He looked for a familiar face, someone from Simularity or America, even. A few school kids skipped along the sidewalk, scattering like geese when he got too close. He sat on the curb watching little cars zip around what must have been downtown Dublin. But as the late November sun peeked over the building across what the sign said was Kildare Street, protestors began showing up. A few on foot, others by car or bus, two-decker things that he'd seen in movies. When he got a little free time, he'd take a ride in one of those. He'd sit at the very top even though it was almost as cold here today as it must be back home. He wasn't sure which members of the growing crowd were safe to talk to, and even if he found one, what he was permitted to say. No one looked remotely familiar until a girl jumped out of a car.

"Nate! It's you!"

"Hi!"

"You don't remember me, do you? I'm from makeup."

He whispered, "Simularity?"

"Yeah. A few of us came, all wearing something purple—you know, a scarf or hat. Were you briefed?"

"I'd hardly call it that."

"Careful, Nate. You don't want to get a rep as a complainer."

"What's your name today, Makeup Girl?"

"Ahh. You do remember me. How about Shannon?"

"Sounds Irish enough." The crowd booed when a stream of shiny limousines black as panthers filed around the corner.

"The enemy." She raised her fist at the bigwigs and put on a heavy Irish accent. "No scripts today, Nate. And I'd avoid an interview, you know, you bein' a Yank and all. Na'tan, they told me to remind you that you're still on probation. Between you and me, today is not the day you want to screw up."

Nate's muscles tensed. If they needed an Irish accent, why had they sent him? All he wanted was to do a good job, but he couldn't shake the feeling that he was being set up to fail. But he'd need to sort that out later—the media had just pulled up in their own minivan.

CHAPTER TWENTY-TWO

Anya Worthy tiptoed into her husband's study and switched off the radio. Malcolm's head popped up. "Hey, I was listening to that."

"Is that what you call it?"

"So I might have dozed a little. If we lived in a different time zone, I wouldn't need to wait until midnight to hear the best conspiracy talk east of the Mississippi."

"All I can say is that if your friend Dan the Man comes through on this one, I'll stop teasing you."

"I'm glad you woke me. He's just about to open the line for calls. Will you stay here and listen? Please?"

"I don't think so, honey. Baking pies with the girls has worn me out."

Her husband frowned. "I know what you're thinking."

She massaged his shoulders. "That you're a sexy thing?"

"Besides that." He swiveled around and pulled her into his lap.

"I know. You're thinking that if I'm worn out, how must Carly and Rick feel?"

"Something like that. I imagine they're about at the end of their rope."

"But at least these days, it's the same rope."

"Listen. Here he is."

"Setting the standard in AM Talk, Dan the Man Manly, coming to you live from deep down a rabbit hole somewhere underneath Area 51. How are all my conspiracy realists tonight?"

While the talk show host went on his nightly rant about the attempts of the powers that shouldn't be to take over the world, Anya settled in beside her husband who sat at the ready with a pad and pen, hoping for information that might help the Greens.

"Time for you, mighty J Q public, to give voice. What's on your mind on this beautiful November night, the unsullied moon shining bright? This is Dan the Man, you're on the air."

While the first caller rambled on about his theory of an intelligent race of extraterrestrials living under the burning surface of Venus, Malcolm hit the redial. Since Dan was the only late-night host who never screened his calls, it rang and rang until finally, the voice on the other end said, "Dan the Man, you're on the air."

"Dan, this is Malcolm Worthy from Buffalo."

"Ah, an old friend. How are things up in the great white north? How about them Bills?"

"No snow yet, Dan. And you know as well as I do the NFL is rigged. Tonight, I'm calling for a couple whose son has gotten mixed up with a company that may have ties to the CIA. Are you aware of an op called Global Connections?"

Silence on the other end of the line. Finally, Dan replied, "Give me a little more on that one, Malcolm. If they're in bed with the CIA, whatever name they go by doesn't mean much. They can change their calling card in the blink of an eye. It's the operations that usually stay the same."

"Sure. I see what you mean. So this is what I know: The boy—well, young man struck out on his own last July and his parents haven't heard from him since, though he has been in contact with a friend of the family who reports that he took a job doing live-action role-play simulations for a division of this Global Connections company called Simularity. He told this friend that the money was great and that they might fly him overseas to do some acting, all expenses paid."

"Simulations. Hmmm. As you know, I'm of the opinion that many of the events we see on TV are dramatizations—the moon landing and so forth. And that being the case, the powers that shouldn't be find it necessary to control everyone involved, down to the people who clean up the stage. Can't let the cat get out of the bag, know what I mean? Where's the kid now?"

"We have no idea. His parents have called the FBI, but they refuse to touch the case because at eighteen, he's considered an adult, and there are no indications that he's been taken against his will."

"Not surprising. The Bureau has a habit of overlooking the disappearance of young people. For proof, since that's all we deal with here, check out the Franklin scandal. Clearly a case where the feds were told to stand down."

"I'm familiar with Franklin. Boys Town, Nebraska, right?"

"Devilish stuff. What those poor kids went through was so bizarre that no one believed them. If their son has been caught up in a dark op of some sort, forget the feds—the parents are on their own. Do they have any sort of lead?"

"Just one. A few weeks ago, he confided in this friend of the family that he was being sent to work with a crew in Ireland, and tonight I caught some footage of a boy who looks and sounds just like my friend's son protesting in front of the parliament building in Dublin."

"No way of knowing for sure in this case, but I've no doubt the CIA recruits impressionable young people to promote whatever their agenda is at the time. I've had a few call in to the show. No way I can vet them, but their stories sound similar. They get drawn in with offers too good to refuse only to wake up one day realizing that they've become political liabilities and there's no going back."

"Outrageous. I bet the police never even investigated their claims."

"A lot like the Franklin scandal. Who would ever swallow the story that people in high-level positions are capable of using kids and then tossing them out like garbage? But, as we know, some are not only capable of this, they do it all the time. If your friends even suspect that something like this might have happened to their son, I'd follow that trail. Wherever it leads."

"You're saying that they should fly to Ireland."

"I'm saying that if he has been involved in some CIA psyop, there's no time to waste."

~

The protest on Kildare Street died down fast when the TV cameras packed up. This time, Nate knew for sure he'd blown it big time. The reporter's accent had been so thick, Nate had no idea what he was even asking. Why hadn't they interviewed Shannon, the Makeup Girl? This, he told himself, was the last straw. His instincts were right—he'd been set up. For what, he had no idea, but he wasn't going to hang around to find out. He'd track down his suitcase and head directly home.

A white car with the word GARDA on the side slowed to a stop in front of the gate and the crowd scattered. Nate looked around for his colleagues wearing purple—someone, anyone—but they'd all split. One of the cops was on the phone. They both looked at Nate. Hopefully they were part of the simulation and could help him find his suitcase.

Nate tried to smile. "Are you from Simularity?"

"Simu-what?" said the cop.

The driver ended his call and asked Nate his name. Out of the corner of his eye, Nate watched Makeup Girl zip off in one of those double-decker buses. "I'm Nathan Green." She waved to him, but since he was being shoved by a rough pair of hands into the back seat of a car with GARDA written on the side, he couldn't wave back. The man beside him dressed in a police uniform, checkered hat and all, took up most of it. *Probably actors.*

"OK, so do you guys know where they took my suitcase?" Not one of the three men let on that they'd heard him, too busy cussing and smoking. Like everyone else, they were completely ignoring him. Plus, he could barely understand them. They might have been in character, but who would bother to keep working with the cameras off? "Excuse me, are you guys part of the simulation?"

"Well, now, young man, whatever gave you that idea?"

"The company I work for uses a lot of actors, you know, in costumes."

"Do they now?"

The man beside him grabbed him by the neck and pressed a cloth over his face.

When Nate regained consciousness, he was sitting stark naked on the floor of a tiny windowless cubical, barely five-by-five. There was just enough room for a toilet and sink but it'd been stripped of all hardware, anything he might use to unlock the industrial-strength door. The heat coming out of the ancient register was so intense, he could hardly breathe, but the extreme cold that followed was worse. Nate had no idea where he was. He stood and checked the sink and concluded it ran cold water only. He splashed his face.

He'd been kidnapped, imprisoned in a tiny room with a toilet and sink. Time passed. Day or night—who knew when your captors never turned off the overhead lightbulb? He'd considered destroying it, but as if they could read his mind, the voices on the other side of the door warned him if he did, it would remain darker than a tomb. So, he started just unscrewing it a little to catch a nap when he suspected whoever talked to him for hours on end took a coffee break. They caught on to this, too. Whenever he killed the light, they blasted in music from some old horror movie, theremin and all. Nate used to think if he had his choice of torture, sleep deprivation would be the easiest to take. Wrong.

If staying awake was making him crazy, the voices behind the door were doing an even better job. They gave lectures so stupid, they made his father's sermons sound interesting. He could have almost stood them if the speaker had managed to stay on track. But she never did. Over and over he was told he'd been working for a just cause, then the message changed, insisting he'd been corrupted by an evil element in a hopelessly out-of-date system. He'd been accused of having suffered a deprived childhood that had caused him to fight against his true sexual identity. This made him scream till his throat ached, "That's not true! You lie!"

"Then why does it make you so angry, Nate? Is the truth hard to take?"

He'd taught himself not to bite the hook so hard. Trying to have an actual conversation with these voices was like talking to the snake in the Garden of Eden—the game was fixed so that poor guys like him could never win. But whoever was on the other side of the door got back at him when he began refusing to participate. One of them slid his phone under the door. It had been in his suitcase! Now he knew whoever had kidnapped him had to be connected to Simularity.

The screen displayed a long text message supposedly from his mother: *Nathan, we've decided to give up looking for you. Since you never considered us important enough to even put in a phone call, we've concluded that you no longer care. If that's really what you want, son, it's your life. Your father and I believe in free will, so as this is what you have chosen, we release you. We've decided to stop searching for you. From now on, you're on your own.*

He didn't buy for one minute that these were his mother's words. Besides, Keri Ann had promised to tell her and Dad how many times he'd tried to call them.

Though this did make him come to grips with how long it had been since he'd seen his mom, or anyone from his old life. How long had he'd been locked up? Days, maybe weeks. He wasn't sure of anything anymore, except that whoever was behind that door was messing with his mind.

He tried entering his parents' old number into the phone. A stupid idea, but his nerves were shot and he wasn't thinking straight. To his surprise, there was ringing at the other end. Someone answered, a lady with an accent he couldn't make out, telling him he had not been a very good pupil and was likely to fail the course if he didn't start putting more effort into the learning process. She topped it off with a witchy laugh, promising that unless he started cooperating, he'd never see the light of day again since no one knew where he was and after they turned off the water, he'd soon be dead. He smashed the phone against the wall and for good measure drowned it in the sink—cold, because that was all that came out of the stupid faucet.

Time passed.

The next lecture was all about him being gay, and it was the first time he'd given them an enormous, no-holding-back response: "HOW DO YOU KNOW?" He stared down at his body, which, due to eating nothing but the saltine crackers they slid under the door, looked increasingly like the anorexics he'd known in the drama club. He doubted if anyone male or female would ever find him attractive again. How long would it take to recover from this? Was recovery even possible? He traced the outline of his ribs.

Time passed.

The last time the lady spoke to him, she said he'd failed the test. She hadn't brought crackers, but at least she hadn't turned off the light.

Time passed.

He drank from the sink, but how long would he last without food? If he was going to die in this room, there was something he needed to get straight. He'd been brought up to understand that sin separated a person from God. If there had been anything keeping him sane in this miniature concentration camp, it was the idea of going to heaven. As a kid, he'd been good at keeping up-to-date with the Lord. He'd prayed often and always felt forgiven and loved after repenting—that is, until the whole thing about him being gay came up.

What made a person gay? Could he be gay if he'd never even realistically considered having sex with a guy? His policy had always been to let people believe whatever they wanted to because his father was such a homophobe. Nate's wanting to be an actor and having a few gay friends embarrassed his old man. Sure, gays might have made some bad choices, but so did a lot of other people—you know, like the ones who committed adultery and messed around with kids. How about all the people sitting in church who were so fat, they barely fit in the pews?

Nate never bought the idea that all sins were equally bad, but wasn't God the only one qualified to judge stuff like that? Still, people condemned each other all the time. He hated to admit it, but he did too. He judged the people who judged him. *There.* He'd finally gotten that cleared up.

"I have judged people. I'm sorry. Please forgive me.

Whether I'm gay or not and whether that's even a sin, I don't know. I'm just trying to be honest. Please help me get out of here, Lord. I don't deserve a miracle, but I know you can do them." After praying, at least Nate felt freer in his spirit. And it encouraged him that if he still knew the difference between right and wrong, he hadn't lost his mind, not yet.

Since the people behind the door hadn't bothered to turn off the light, he'd spent what could have been hours trying to fit pieces of his busted phone into the door-knob, but none of them went far enough into the tiny pinhole to jimmy the lock. You'd think there would be a little wire inside a phone, come to find out they consisted of two things: a circuit board and a plastic cover, and he couldn't pare either of them down small enough with his hands. He smashed the thing over and over, hoping to come up with something thinner and sharper, but it was useless. He unscrewed the light and whispered to the darkness, "God, am I going to die?"

A voice shouted "No!"

Was he dreaming? In this state, he was never sure. But this voice sure sounded real. Some man had just yelled the word "No!"

He screwed on the light. Coarse laughter came from outside the door. A couple of men in the midst of an argument. God hadn't spoken to him after all. What had he expected? That an angel had come to set him free? His mother believed in stuff like that.

Just thinking of her brought tears to his eyes, but he was careful to swallow his sobs. Maybe this time who-ever was out there would forget to blast in the music. It sounded like they were arguing, which was new. So far, the voices he'd heard had been calm and measured. He put his ear to the door.

"They must have given up on this poor bugger. Taking too long to crack. Bad return on their investment. Buyin' and sellin' kids . . . nasty business. Anyway, this lot don't know what the heck they're doing. Not like the old days. From what I hear, the old guard were experts. They'd do it to their own kids."

"That explains a lot." Nate heard the striking of a match. "But maybe this yank's just too hardheaded."

"Toss me a cig." The smoke they exhaled was almost pleasant to Nate compared to the mildew he'd been breathing. "Poor bloke must be Irish." Their laughter rose and fell. These were not the same psychos who'd been trying to drive Nate crazy—those people never laughed.

Nate recognized the men's accents. They were the cops who picked him up on Kildare Street.

"No doubt. Still, it's a nasty business."

"All I can say is, it's not our problem."

"If the wrong people find out, it will be."

"No. We wipe the place down and be done with it."

"You mean leave him?"

"Chalk it up as experience."

"They won't like it. You know they won't."

Nate's stomach heaved, spilling out nothing but water. They were going to leave him in this little room to rot!

"Jesus!" Nate cried, and again, "Jesus, help me!"

"Shut up, kid! You'll wake the neighbors." They snickered. Wherever Nate was, there were no neighbors. He'd made out the noise of occasional traffic and odd-sounding horns, but the only human sounds were made by his captors.

Nate kicked the door, but all this did was make his toe

throb. A blurry image of the story of Noah came to him while holding on to the sink. *Water ... can be used ... as a weapon.* He turned the faucet on full blast, all the while half singing, half screaming, "I've got a river of life flowing out of me! Makes the lame to walk and the blind to see! Opens prison doors, sets the captives free! I've got a river of life flowing out of me!" He balled his fists and launched into a second round of pummeling the door. Meanwhile, the sink overflowed.

"For the love of God, kid, shut up."

Pleased that the water had made it underneath the door, Nate sang even louder.

"He's floodin' the place!"

"Better do something."

"Sure. Call the guard." More laughter, but the tone had changed. Water seeping through must have made the cops nervous.

"I've about had it with this job, mate. If this is what it takes to get a foot up in the club, well, I'm out. Let them find another stoolie to do their dirty work."

"So what do we do about the kid? I don't fancy the thought of his little white skeleton haunt'n me dreams."

"Spring up, oh well," Nate sang, choking back tears, "within my soul, spring up, oh well . . ."

Their cursing got loud again. *Thank God they haven't left.* Nate screamed, "Thank you, Jesus!"

"Good grief, man, it shouldn't take a rocket scientist to slide the thing under the door." Suddenly, against the trickle of water, the edge of a small blade appeared.

Nate stared at the gift. There were two things to do with a pocketknife—slit his wrists or pick the lock. He fell to his knees.

CHAPTER TWENTY-THREE

I t wasn't easy to get ahold of Louie La Nova, but since the doctors had put her on bedrest, Keri Ann had plenty of time. And when she set her mind to something, she worked it to the end, no matter how bitter that end might be. So far, Old Man La Nova had refused to pick up. She left messages, keeping them purposely vague since she needed him on the line to dish out the scoop in person about the terrible things going on between members of his family.

Her visiting nurse was just leaving when the phone rang. "Hello?"

"Yeah, this is Louie. You been clogging up my machine. What's the matter with you?"

"Mr. La Nova, I didn't mean to—it's just that your daughter and grandson are having some problems and I thought you should know."

"If my Carly has problems, she's a big girl. She'll handle them. What's it to you anyway?"

"I'm not sure you remember me, sir. I'm Keri Ann Mc-Graw, a member of Pastor Green's congregation here in Buffalo."

"Sure, I remember. So what? My Carly told me about you. You're the secretary. You take care of the money. And somehow, there's never enough and no one knows why."

This sent shockwaves through Keri Ann. She took a second to regroup. "Yes, well, it takes a bigger budget than people assume to run a ministry like Pastor Green's. But what I'm calling about has to do with your grandson, Nathan."

"What about Nate? Is he OK? My Carly tells me he decided to move away and look for a job."

"Well, yes and no. You see, he did run away, but it was in anger—mostly at his mother. Did your daughter tell you that she smashed up your boat last summer?"

"She said something about the boat. It's no big deal. I told her to sell it. It's hers. Her sisters don't want it."

"Did she tell you how it got smashed?"

"She took it too close to the rapids trying to get to Navy Island. She knows better than to do something like that. But my Carly, she thinks more with her heart than her ... you know."

"Yes, sir, I do. And that's just what made Nathan mad enough to run away. She wasn't alone on that boat. Her old boyfriend was with her that day."

"Don't tell me that jughead Liam."

"Yes, Liam Dunn. They were on their way to Navy Island together. They were having an affair, Mr. La Nova. I don't know if Carly told you, but she and Rick are separated right now. They've even had divorce papers written up."

"She mentioned separation, not divorce. She was raised to hate divorce—to us, it's a sin. What else do you know?"

"Well, that's why Nate ran away. The reason I'm bothering you like this, sir, is that I care a lot about Nate. Ever since I pulled him out of that fire ..."

"So ... you were the hero."

"I wouldn't say that, sir. Anyone would have done the same thing. The problem is, Nathan has gotten into trouble, but he doesn't want Carly and Rick to know. I'm the only one he trusts these days, and he made me promise not to tell his parents anything we talk about. He doesn't want them to find out where he is or what he's doing. I'm afraid if he thinks I've betrayed him, he might do something stupid."

"What do you mean, stupid?"

"It has to do with the people he's gotten himself involved with. Nate has known for a while that he's not attracted to girls."

"Wait just a minute, young lady. How do you know this about my grandson?"

"Sir, I'm just telling you what Nathan has said to me in confidence. He's been living with another boy and they both take drugs, dangerous ones. Nathan is depressed, and I'm just afraid if we aren't careful, he might ..."

"Take too many drugs and die. Is that what you're saying, Miss McGraw?"

"Yes, sir. That's exactly what I'm saying."

Down the Coast of County Dublin

The blade barely glanced the lock even after Nate had worked at it so long, his arms trembled. He rested his head against the door. The cold felt good on his face. Now that he knew whoever had been trying to confuse his thoughts had given up, he was having more and more of them. He'd been straining his ears for clues as to his location. No way were there people anywhere near the place, although he'd heard plenty of trucks passing, and other kinds of engines. *Not trains—could be boats.* Something like a whistle penetrated the walls now and then. And then there were the birds, the "caw, caw, caw" kind. *Gulls.* Having lived near a river, that was one sound he was sure of. He might be near the sea. Ireland was an island, right?

If, with God's help, he could get this knife far enough into the lock to turn it and he did escape, running outside would be awkward, seeing as he was currently butt naked. He'd need something to cover himself or face scaring away anyone he found to help him. And supposing he did find help, he had no money, passport, or anything to prove his identity. He quickly assessed that what had happened to him amounted to human trafficking.

Whoever was responsible had probably not left his wallet handy, or his shoes, but as his grandfather would say, first things, well, you know. He picked up the knife for round two, jamming it in for all he was worth, and like tipping a puck past a distracted goalie, he scored. The lock clicked, the knob turned, and Nathan Green was once again a free man.

Grand Island, NY

Rick followed his wife out to the end of their dock. After realizing the guilt he'd carried for twenty years had been based on a lie, he'd begged Carly to forgive him.

After weeks of confession, repentance, and forgiveness on both of their parts, they'd been cleaning the house, getting ready to move back in. Serena was watching Benny, and he finally had Carly to himself. She shivered and he put his arm around her.

Carly nestled into his side. "The last time I stood out here, the geese were flying north."

"Look! The water's reflecting the sky. Amazing! I never noticed that before." For some reason, his wife thought this was funny.

"Rick, one thing I still don't get. I knew the reason you lost it on me at camp wasn't just about Nathan."

"You're right. It wasn't."

"Go on."

"After laying it on me that the boys had taken off, she mentioned that it was twenty years ago to the day that she'd aborted our baby."

"You mean the baby that never was."

"Yes. I was a fool, Carly."

~

The prayer meeting at Malcolm and Anya Worthy's home had become so popular that they'd had to rustle up a lot more folding chairs. For the first time since the two men parted ways, Pastor Rick would be attending. Malcolm was nervous. He'd led the group himself for weeks and hoped that Rick wouldn't resent not being the one in charge.

Anya had been after him to relax and trust the Holy Spirit. "Rick has been through a lot. Apparently, the mortgage on the church hadn't been paid since April."

"What's up with that?"

"Nobody knows. Anyway, his accounts are in the red, and Carly's taken a leave of absence from work. I don't know how they're managing."

Malcolm grimaced. He had even worse news for the two of them, but it would have to wait until after the meeting.

After the group settled, Malcolm welcomed Pastor Rick.

"Thanks, Malcolm. I owe you all an apology, but first, I need to apologize publicly to my wife for the cruel way I treated her last summer." When he took her hand and kissed it, a sigh of relief seemed to rise from the gathered saints. "I regret my behavior. Although there were reasons for my anger, there was no excuse for letting it loose at your expense."

The room grew quiet, and Malcolm opened the meeting to prayer requests. Rick raised his hand. "Go ahead, Pastor Rick."

"This will be tough, but I regret to tell you that we've lost the building."

Malcolm held his breath. He and Rick had run the risk of offending people who had only recently begun forgiving one another. How would they take something like this?

"I confess that I was happy to let someone else take responsibility for paying the bills. And for some time now, they haven't been paid, at least not the mortgage. To be clear, I do know where that money went, and I assure you, it wasn't in my pocket."

Malcolm relaxed a bit when Rick's old friends nodded their heads and offered words of genuine empathy. That night, many prayers went up for the restoration of the

New Wine Fellowship, in whatever form it might take.

Carly asked for prayer. "Since we still haven't heard from Nathan, we've decided to go to Ireland to find him." Sister Betty offered the most inspired intersession that Malcolm had heard all year for the Greens' efforts to find their son.

As the last members of the Wednesday night prayer group bid each other goodnight, Malcolm asked Rick to join him in his study. "You need to take a look at this." He pulled an extra chair up to his desk. "Have you ever heard of a government operation called Project Monarch?"

"Does this have something to do with Nate?"

"I hope not, but I found some information that might be relevant. Also, I want you to know that the prayer meeting will be taking up a collection for your airfare."

His former boss bowed his head. "I can't let them do that. I owe them so much already."

"It was their idea. I don't think you can stop them."

Malcolm turned on the computer and navigated to the website while Rick continued. "We've been denied a line of credit by every bank in the city because of the foreclosure. Whatever her faults, up until recently, Keri Ann had been an excellent accountant."

When Malcolm said nothing, Rick went on, "But Carly and I do have a plan. We're going to ask her father for a loan. It was either that or sell the house, and that would leave us with nothing. To be honest, I've been reconsidering the trip. Maybe the boy will come home on his own. All he's doing is traveling around marching in protests, throwing bricks, and lying to reporters. That's bound to get old. And when it does, he'll come back. He never was one to stick to anything for long."

"Look at this, Rick. It's the website of the Council on Foreign Relations. Scroll down, see, way down at the bottom ... here it is. See that?"

"What do you know. It's that company."

"Yes, Global Connections."

"But that's good, right? I mean, if he really is working for a major corporation, that's got to mean it's on the up-and-up."

"I don't know, Rick. So far, what I've come up with on the Council on Foreign Relations isn't good at all. They talk a fine talk, but—and I know this is going to sound extremely conspiratorial—but what they really want to do, I mean in the final analysis, is to take over the world."

"You're right. I don't buy it. And what does this have to do with Nate?"

"Listen to me for one minute. These simulations he's been filming are part of the council's efforts to infiltrate the media. Basically to use TV, the news programs specifically, to get inside people's heads and control the way we think."

"Give me an example."

"The Gulf of Tonkin incident."

"Sure. That's what got us into the war. The Vietcong attacked US submarines in neutral territory."

"So we were told. The only thing is, it never happened. There was no attack. They lied. And to the man, every person in charge of that operation belonged to the CFR."

"The Council on Foreign Relations. Still sounds paranoid, Malcolm. And I still don't get how it concerns my son."

Malcolm massaged his forehead. He reminded himself that to Rick, this information was completely new. He'd need to stick to more familiar ground. "OK, remember me mentioning Project Monarch?"

"Monarch as in a king or butterfly?"

"Good question. Butterfly, although kings have been using similar techniques to control their own families for centuries. The goal is to program individuals to be obedient servants, using a brainwashing technique created by covert ops in the military and secret offshoots of the CIA. The goal is to take a normal person and split their personality into two or three or more different people. The subject switches personalities when triggered by something, a song or phrase."

"If the person is like you said, normal, wouldn't he know this was happening?"

"Not if it's done well. None of the personalities know that the others exist. A good example is the movie *The Manchurian Candidate.*"

"Frank Sinatra gets knocked out and used for experiments."

"If you recall, his sergeant, the man whose brain is most effectively rewired, is programed to shoot the Republican candidate for president."

"But that was just a movie."

"Based on facts."

A knock on the door. "Are you guys wrapping it up in there? Carly's falling asleep on the couch. Rick, you know you're always welcome to stay overnight ..."

"Thanks, Anya. Tell her I'll be right there."

Malcolm turned off his computer. "Listen, man. I can't prove any of this stuff. But I've got a strong hunch that Nathan has somehow gotten involved with some very dangerous people." When his wife closed the door, he added, "Do you have any idea how many kids go missing every year in this country alone?"

"Those faces on the milk cartons?"

"That campaign is misleading. Hundreds of thousands. Most are never found again. And the few that make it back alive tell stories that keep me awake at night."

Along the Coast of County Dublin

Nathan stumbled around in what looked to be a huge open area while his eyes adjusted to the dark. The cubicle he'd lived in for many days was apparently built into the center column of an abandoned factory. Rows of tables where he assumed workers used to sit lined the floor. Boxes of plastic parts were scattered here and there. If this had only been a men's clothing factory! Or a place that made shoes, he thought as he stepped on something sharp. He breathed in a lungful of delightfully dusty air. Whatever lay ahead for his naked skeletal self had to beat being locked up in a porcelain prison and left to die.

Windows! The world outside hadn't ended after all. All around, broken windows let in silvery light, some from streetlamps and some from a moon that appeared to be sinking. He noticed a room behind glass. *An office?* Desks were still cluttered with paper, as if whatever had been going on here ended suddenly. He spotted a coatrack, full of empty hangers. But what was that on the back of a chair? A sweater—hallelujah! Pink and small, but with arms long enough to wrap around his waist. He tied them together to form a bright-colored loincloth. It looked ridiculous, but it was better than nothing. A freight elevator in the center may not have moved since the days of silent movies, so he opted for the stairs. In minutes, he was out on the street.

A lonely strip of factories lined one side of the busted-up cobblestones, and on the other stood a large body of water. *The Atlantic Ocean? The Irish Sea?* A lady waited at a bus stop. Should he ask for help?

Too late. She caught sight of him and ran, her shrieks blending in with the sound of the gulls. He couldn't blame her. If she were his mother, he'd tell her to run from a man wearing a pink loincloth. He needed a plan. *Find the local police?* That might land him in jail again, but at least he might get a phone call.

He heard a familiar whistle. Just as he imagined, it was coming from a boat, small and old like everything else around there. A man on board called to him. "Yo! Young fella."

"Me?"

"The one in the pink kilt. What are ya up to, roamin' the street half naked in the middle of winter?"

The middle of winter—had he been in that room that long?

"I was kidnapped. Can you help me?"

PART THREE

FLOW, RIVER, FLOW

CHAPTER TWENTY-FOUR

C arly peeked into the bedroom she'd shared with Benny since the day they moved in with Serena. He was plunking out a song with a toy piano the Worthy girls had given him. *Amazing.* Those girls were so sweet, taking Benny under their wings like they had. And what a change in her quiet little son! The TV hadn't been on once that day.

Careful not to distract him, Carly slid their suitcases out of the closet. Since he was busy playing, what a normal six-year-old should be doing, she'd leave the bedroom for last. There were personal items she'd bought spread throughout the house. In the bathroom, she nabbed a box of Clairol natural light-brown and a bag of Epsom salts. *Well, maybe Serena could use that.* Being on her feet all day, she enjoyed a hot bath now and then. And of course, the rubber ducky Serena had bought for Benny at the dollar store. *But what about this plaque with the verse from Ecclesiastes, "He has made all things beautiful in His time"?* That was something the two women had bought together. Carly couldn't even remember who had paid.

Next, she moved into the kitchen. When Carly had arrived, just about every spice in Serena's cupboard had been past its expiration date. Her friend wasn't much of a cook. Having dinner on the table when Serena came home from work was one way Carly had been able to show her appreciation, so she'd taken on the project of refreshing the flour, sugar, salt, and oil. They had eaten some good meals together over the last few months, Serena teaching her the one recipe she had down pat— sausage and cabbage stew—and Carly entrusting Serena with her secrets for a perfect apple pie.

It hit her like a smack to the side of the head that Serena, a woman she'd started out hating, had become her best friend. Falling onto a chair, she cried out to the Lord. "I am so grateful to you, Father!"

Benny ran into the room and climbed onto her lap. "What's the matter, Mommy?"

"Nothing, sweetie. Everything's great. Will you help Mommy pray for your brother Nate?"

"Nate ran away."

"You are right. But somebody knows where he is."

"Who?"

"Jesus."

Grand Island, NY

It took a while for Rick to get a call through to Florida, but when he did, he shouted his father-in-law's name. "Hello, Louie?"

"Who is this?"

"Your son-in-law, Rick."

"Son-in-law?"

"Louie, are you there?"

"I'm here. Pastor Rick, do you know what the Lord says about divorce?"

This time the dead air came from Rick's side. Eventually, he responded. "Of course. He's against it."

"One hundred percent. So why are you divorcing my daughter?"

"Who told you that?"

"Your secretary, Miss McGraw. She's worried about Nate. More than I can say for you—not that I'm surprised. I told my Carly to watch out for you. You got married so fast and then, boom, you make your own church. I prayed for you all these years, but maybe God doesn't hear me, or maybe you two are not the good Christians you claim to be. Even my Carly—"

"What else did Keri Ann tell you?"

"That she and that jughead Liam ... I can't say it. All I know is, her mother and I didn't raise her this way. And if she did, commit, you know ... it must have been you who drove her to it."

"Sir, I admit I haven't been the best husband. For years now. But I wouldn't take everything Keri Ann said as completely true."

"So you're not getting a divorce?"

"No."

"Some good news for a change. OK, to what do I owe this ... you know ... ?"

"Why am I calling?"

"Yeah, sure."

"Nathan's got himself in trouble."

"Normal for a kid his age."

"But this may be really bad. We have reason to believe he's been kidnapped. Whatever the case, he needs our help."

"Maybe it's time for the boy to stand up and think for himself. When we were kids, we had to do for ourselves. That's what turns a boy into a man. In your church, you baby the children. If you ask me, this is what happened to Nate ..."

Rick hesitated. He hadn't asked Louie for money yet and was no longer sure he wanted to. *If there was only another way ...*

"Pastor Rick, you still there?"

"I'm here, Louie."

"If you were calling to ask me for money, the answer is no. The time has come for Nathan to pick himself up by his own, you know ..."

"No, I don't, Louie. You tell me."

"To work things out for himself."

~

At the Roswell Park Cancer Institute, the Christmas stockings hung above the receptionist's desk showed that very little care had been taken, although the names of each of Dr. Goldstein's staff were written in big cheerful letters—not at all matching Keri Ann's frame of mind. She'd come for the results of her lab tests. Normally, this would have been done over the phone—and if everything checked out OK, they sometimes didn't even bother to call. That her physical presence has been requested was not a good sign. In fact, the secretary even suggested that she bring someone with her.

She'd called Ricky, but as usual, he didn't pick up. Probably out with Carly now that the divorce had been shelved, at least for the time being.

"Miss McGraw?"

"Yes?"

"The doctor will see you now."

Dockside, Bray Township, County Dublin

Nate stepped onto the tugboat, trusting that the man who smelled fishy was not. "So, what's your story, young fella? Stolen by the fairies?"

"You're half right. I was stolen alright, but the guys who did it looked more like cops."

"A Yank, are ye? Go inside, you'll find something to wear. How can a man even look at a fella dressed ... like that?"

The room the boat's captain directed him to was no more than a closet. "Don't worry, lad. I'll not stand in your way. I don't fancy boys. You're free to go anytime. Remember, you're the one who needs help, not me."

Nate found a shirt and a pair of jeans which might have fit if he hadn't lost so much weight. A glance at the crucifix on the wall nearly made him collapse. "Oh Lord," he moaned, "oh Jesus ..."

"You OK in there, mate? Looks like you could do with some grub. I was just about to fry up a few eggs."

Nate steadied himself. "Yes. I mean, that would be awesome."

"And check the pockets of those pants. There might be a phone number or two." All Nate found were a few damp receipts. "Now, then. You look somewhat better, though I think you should have a seat and a cup a tea before telling your story."

Lackawanna, NY

Rick was supposed to pick up Carly and Ben from Serena's, but he had something to take care of first. Keri Ann's car was gone, but he doubted she'd be out very long. Unless she was not as sick as she'd been claiming. He sat on her porch working on another way to come up with enough money to fly to Ireland. So far, plan B consisted of selling the house on Grand Island. And that would take time, something that, according to Malcolm, they didn't have. Then there was the matter of the house having been a gift to Carly from her father. Louie might never forgive him for letting it go.

Rick agreed with the old man about Nate needing to figure things out on his own. No doubt the boy would have been better at this if Rick had been a better father— helping him more, criticizing him less. It was impossible to know for sure how much trouble his son had gotten himself into; the only thing to do now was find him. Whatever it took.

Keri Ann's car pulled up at the curb. Black makeup ran down her cheeks. He'd never seen her look so sloppy.

She rolled down the window. "It's about time you showed up."

"What's the matter, Keri Ann?"

"First off, you're an idiot. And for the rest, come inside. I don't want the neighbors to hear."

In all the years he'd known her, Rick had never seen Keri Ann throw her coat on the floor. Kicking it out of the way, she headed straight for the couch. When he sat on the step to take off his boots, she called him an idiot for the second time.

"Is everything alright?"

She laughed like someone losing their mind. Maybe a new gimmick to get him to feel sorry for her—the sort of garbage he'd fallen for all his life. Not anymore. He squared his stance. "Keri Ann, have you been spreading rumors about our family to Carly's father?"

She snapped to attention. "What do you mean, rumors?"

"I don't know. I called him this morning to see if he could help us out."

"So, I was right. You've decided to chase after the kid. It's a mistake, Ricky. Just like all those years ago how, you took off when I said I was—"

"Come off it, Keri Ann. That you were what—pregnant?"

"Stop shouting!"

"I believed you, Keri Ann, for years. Not anymore. What did you say to Mr. La Nova?"

She burst into very convincing tears. "That Nate doesn't want any of you interfering in his life."

"That's what you said to Louie?"

"Why not? It's true!" She let out a rattling noise that, to Rick, sounded like the groan of a demon. "Do you want some more truth, buddy?" She propped herself up on her elbows. "I got my test results back today. They had me drive down there in person to hear the great news."

"And ... ?"

"The cancer's back. This time in my bones."

He fell onto a chair like a man punched in the gut. "What does that mean?"

"I'll spell it out for you, Ricky. I'm going to die—soon—and there's not a blessed thing I can do."

Rick pressed a hand to his chest. "On the level?"

She shrieked like a ghost. "They give me six months to a year."

"I'm so sorry."

"Oh yeah? Me too."

"What can I do?"

He jumped when she let loose another witchy laugh. "Ricky Green, I've been waiting for you to ask me that for twenty years." More strange sounds flew out of her smudged-up mouth. He leaned close and put one hand on her back. Her body shook.

"Cry, Keri Ann, let it out. All of it! God is here. He's listening. You're safe. Its time."

Rick listened to his oldest friend weep and sob and open her hurting soul to the Lord, but when she began confessing a list of lies and half-truths she'd told throughout the years, he was shaken to his core. She claimed her goal had always been to bring him back to her.

Other sins spilled out in the flow, like how she'd started stealing from the church just to spite him when he did or said anything that ticked her off, and how she'd stopped paying the mortgage when it looked like his marriage was falling apart, squirrelling the money into a private account that they could use to run away together. Rick begged her to stop, but she gasped out one more thing, a warning that the company that had hired Nate had no corporate identity—she'd checked. "On the books it's a nongovernment agency, but any business that covers its profits so completely must be up to no good."

"Why didn't you tell us? You were risking his life!"

Ignoring him and spewing emotion so intense that

she retched as if to vomit, she lashed out one last time. "Ricky, I told your son that you didn't want to talk to him, that you were glad he ran away, and you were too busy with your own problems to be bothered with him. He's always missed you, whining like a baby about needing his mommy. Every time he calls, he makes me swear to give you the full report. I say, 'Sure, Nate, I'll get right to it.' But don't you see? You Greens all getting along swell again would have spoiled everything!"

"I can't believe you'd do that to us, Keri Ann ..."

She grabbed his hand, squeezing it so hard, his fingers throbbed. "You know what your problem is, Ricky? You believe everything. Always have. Some fool down in Ohio says it's God's will to marry Carly, so you jump to it. Another says, 'Time to start a church,' so you do. Never stop to ask questions—not you, not if some guy holding a Bible says this or that it's God's will. You make me sick."

"So all this time, you've been pretending to be serving the Lord?"

She retched again. "My God, Ricky. You're so naïve. Get me my purse." He brought it and she pulled out a pack of Cools.

"When did you start smoking again?"

"When I knew you were never going to leave your so-called wife." She coughed.

"There is no such thing as a so-called wife. When I married Carly, she was God's will for my life. But after she screwed up with Liam, well, things got confusing."

"Sure did." She threw a match at an ashtray and missed. "I used to believe in stuff like doing God's will. Then I got a new idea—start doing my will for a change." She coughed, hard.

Ricky looked too shocked to speak, so she rammed one more thing into his open ears. "Don't ask me why, but all I ever wanted in this life was you. I thought if I was patient and just let things play out ..."

"You could, what, ruin my marriage? Turn my son against me?"

She'd gone too far. Enough truth for now, anyway. He stood and she reached for him, but he backed away. "For what it's worth, I'm sorry things have ended up like this."

"Yeah. Me too."

He hid his eyes. "Is that all you have to say, Keri Ann?"

She grasped for words. "Only that when I called Mr. La Nova, I told him Nate was living with another boy and that he was taking drugs and so depressed that if we didn't respect his wishes, he might commit suicide."

"That explains it."

"I take it you asked him for money, and he said no way."

"Yes. And he was our last hope."

She squashed out her cigarette. "OK. I'll fix it."

"And tell him the truth?"

"Yes. But now you need to go."

"Let me pray for you."

"No. Just go."

CHAPTER TWENTY-FIVE

After a bowl of soup and a scone, the most delicious food Nate had ever eaten, he related bits and pieces of his story to the sailor, who'd introduced himself as Declan Moran.

"Let me get this straight. You ran away because people in the church were calling you a poof?"

"When you put it that way, it sounds lame, but yeah, I guess so."

"Are you ... ?"

"You mean am I gay? Good question. I don't know."

Declan Moran found this hysterical. When he'd recovered enough to speak, he told Nate his own story, the tale of a merchant marine in all its grit and sin, and then circled back to Nate's problem. "You say you don't know who you are. One thing I've learned from crossing oceans in the company of men. We're all prodigal sons." He pointed to the wall. "See that, mate?"

Nate looked at the crucifix. "Yes."

"He died for every black-hearted one of us."

"What are you saying?"

"Something I heard down at the mission, 'For all have sinned and fallen short of His glory.'"

Nate pushed away from the table. "So you'd say that the gay lifestyle is a sin."

"I'd say people justify all sorts of sinful lifestyles." He pointed again to the cross. "If someone really wants to know if what they're up to is wrong, what they need to do is ask Him." He pointed once again to the crucifix. "If they're serious, He'll tell them. Look at me—I've been there. I'm far from the man I should be, but at least I'm no longer foolin' meself."

~

Nate arrived at the address the fisherman gave him, a three-floor walk-up in Dublin, on a street called The Bachelors' Walk with a note in his pocket and instructions to give to a girl named Roisin, which the fisherman pronounced Ro-sheen, with his kind regards.

Scenes from the past came and went now that he no longer suffered from hypothermia, had eaten a few good meals, and had slept a real night's sleep in a warm bed. The fisherman decided rather than turning Nathan over to the local police, he'd drop him off with a group of missionaries who'd occasionally helped him find his way home in the aftermath of a night on the town. "Don't get me wrong, lad, there are many good cops, but you know what they say about one bad apple."

As the grandson of Louie La Nova, Nate had been groomed in the art of completing unfinished sentences. "Sure. It only takes one to ruin your day."

"Something like that, mate." Driving the straight shot of road from the coastal town of Bray to Dublin City proper in a truck smelling like fish, he dropped Nate off a block away from the mission. "Good luck to ye, Natan Green."

Nate read the message.

Please don't be alarmed at the scrawny young man at your doorstep. I've reason to believe he's the latest failed experiment of our local branch of the so-called enlightened ones down in Bray. I don't doubt the lad's story since he was half out of his mind with hunger and cold when I found him. Too addled in the head to come up with such an elaborate lie. If you have any questions, don't hesitate to call.

Sincerely,

D. M.

The lady who welcomed him read the postscript out loud. "Declan Moran. Oh, that rascal. Come on in—who are you, now?"

"Nathan Green." A dog sniffed his borrowed shoes.

"Enough, Mufasa. This one's friend, not foe." The German shepherd took another whiff of Nathan and sneezed twice before backing off. "Well, Nate, you timed it right. We're just sitting down for tea. But first, let's see if we can find you a pair of trousers that don't require a lasso to keep'm up."

Nathan thanked God that he'd landed in a house full of the Holy Spirit. The people around the table were Christian missionaries, and most look to have been at it for ages, except for Roisin who, with her fairy princess hair and slender figure, he easily picked out of the group.

"Declan Moran sends his kind regards, Roisin."

"Ah, yes. Mr. Moran, to be sure, a hardened criminal." The rest of them chuckled. Nate found it easy to imagine Declan falling in love with this girl.

The woman-in-charge added, "Mr. Moran is a wee bit rough around the edges, but he has a good heart. We're glad he brought you here."

A man in a parson's suit carried in a plate of cookies. "It's the goal of our mission to help those in need, no matter what shape we find them in." The gathering laughed as this, too, but Nate spoke up.

"If it weren't for Declan, I might have been thrown in jail for indecent exposure."

That brought a blush to the cheeks of the already rosy Roisin.

"Well," said the woman, "I'll be takin our guest downstairs for a new wardrobe so he's presentable for the meetin' tonight."

The new clothes Nate selected from the pile of donations, though still too big, were at least clean, and he was amazed at how much he was looking forward to this meeting.

The little chapel next door was ancient, like so many things in this city. A tall, narrow building on a cobblestone street next to the River Liffey, which smelled more like coffee grounds than a river. Polluted or not, he was grateful to be breathing free air again. He had so much to thank God for, and the first song the missionaries sang that night was "Great Is Thy Faithfulness." In the past he'd often pretended to sing, having inherited his mother's tin ear. But tonight, he let it fly.

His eyes had been closed so far, but when they opened for the first time, he noticed another pair, bright and blue, looking his way from across the aisle—those of Roisin.

When they finished singing, a preacher gave a word about reaching the lost of the city, especially the university students on holiday who'd be flocking up and down among the pubs on Grafton Street tomorrow looking for fulfilment that only Jesus could provide. Nathan couldn't have agreed with him more, though he was having a hard time focusing. He was still working out what Declan had said about sin—*If you really wanted to know whether you're in the wrong, ask Jesus. If you're serious, He'll tell you.* And that night at the mission church, the scenes playing out in his head showed how angry he was at his father.

Eventually, only Nathan, the woman-in-charge—whose name was Tillie—and the man in black who he assumed was her husband remained in the little chapel. "Nate, after a bit of discussion, Tillie and I have decided to let you stay at the mission as long as you have need."

"Before I do anything, ma'am, I need to get a hold of my parents."

"There's the phone, lad. Go to it."

Nate estimated that back in Buffalo it was about four or five in the afternoon, a decent time to call. He'd tried this so often, he should have given up, but never in his life had he been filled with such faith. He was eventually put through to who he hoped were his grandparents, the only number he was sure of anymore. He was encouraged to hear ringing at the other end. His grandfather answered.

~

Rick bought tickets for the earliest direct flight to Dublin, a nerve-wracking experience since this transatlantic journey would be the first time he'd ever even been on a plane. After having been set straight on the facts of the matter, Louie wired him and Carly enough money for airfare and a weeklong stay if necessary. They believed that wouldn't be the case, but Dublin was a large metropolitan area, and they had no guarantee their son was even still in it. Nearly a month had gone by since Malcolm had spotted him on the news.

A man from the home meeting suggested that they start at the American Embassy. This sounded reasonable to Rick. He'd thought to bring Nate's birth certificate and photo ID. Carly told him she was proud of the way he'd taken charge of the trip. So often in their marriage, she or Keri Ann been left to work out such details.

As the wheels of the jet lifted off the runway, she asked him, "Did you remember to take Benny's piano over to the Worthys'?"

"Check. The girls have enough of Benny's toys over there to keep him busy."

"At least he's playing with them now." She rested her head against his shoulder. "I hope Benny staying there doesn't ruin Christmas for the Worthys."

"The word I got was that it was going to *make* their Christmas. They consider him part of the family."

The pilot introduced himself over the intercom and let them know they could now unfasten their seat belts. He reported that there'd be a bit of turbulence up ahead, but nothing to be concerned with, and that they'd be arriving at Dublin International at approximately ten a.m. Irish time.

"Rick, look at the ocean."

"I'd rather not."

"You're shaking!"

"Carly, we're sliding over the home of Leviathan in a little piece of steel."

"It's taking a lot of faith for you to believe this plane won't crash."

"More than whether or not we'll find Nate. More than you and me being able to forgive each other."

"More than having the courage to start over?"

"More than that. I believe in those things. This hunk of steel? Not so much."

The stewardess offered them snacks and drinks. Rick declined, but Carly took them up on a bottle of water. "It's not that bad. People do this every day."

"Easy for you to say. Your family flew to Florida every year."

"What I mean is, people rely on God to hold the whole world up every day." She sipped her water. "I have a story from the past that I never told you."

Since it might take his mind off the fact that they were hurling through space in little more than a tin can, he said, "OK, go for it."

"As a little girl, I somehow got the idea that God had one special person for everyone in the whole world to marry. It bothered me that it was entirely possible I'd never find the one he'd made just for me. I mean, how would you know for sure?"

"Good question." A picture of Keri Ann popped into his mind.

"But what if you missed the guy? Theoretically, you could walk right by each other, and if one of you wasn't paying attention, you'd both be out of luck."

"Where'd you hear that?"

"I don't know, probably from one of the nuns. But now I know marriage has everything to do with faith."

"I've been thinking about something along those lines myself. You already know how things were between Keri Ann and me before we met."

"That you thought about getting married."

"More than that. We figured—maybe because of the way our fathers treated us as kids—that we were meant for each other. For my part, I believed she was the only one in the world who would ever understand me. It was like that for her, too."

"Rick, you don't ... I know it's hard for you to talk about."

"That's no excuse. Now here's a story I've never told you. Last summer, when Malcolm and I weren't exactly seeing eye-to-eye, he said something that flipped me out. Something along the lines of 'Once you marry a woman, she becomes God's will for your life.' He was right. You, me, Nate, and Benny were meant to be. If not, we wouldn't be sitting here right now."

Carly hugged his arm, and Rick forgot about the dark ocean beneath.

~

The shuttle driving them to the city was filled with Americans in a holiday mood. Quite a contrast to what she and Rick were feeling, though they tried to be polite.

"Is this your first trip to the Emerald Isle?" a woman maybe ten years older than Carly couldn't hold back her enthusiasm.

"Yes." Carly looked out the window, hoping this was where the conversation would end.

"We come every year—for Christmas. It's our way of avoiding the hustle and bustle back home. Where are you staying?"

She wanted to say, 'Maybe on a park bench.' Truth be told, they hadn't thought that far ahead. Ideally, they'd find Nate right away and head back without needing to pay for a hotel. "We're not sure."

"You mean you have no reservations?"

Rick intervened, "We're visiting relatives."

"Ah! Lucky you! We wish we had somebody like that. The dollar is strong over here, but it all adds up."

Fortunately, they wouldn't need to keep up the chit-chat much longer; they were already entering the out-skirts of the city. In a few minutes, the driver delivered them at the gates of the embassy. Carly smoothed out the wrinkles in her coat and pulled her overnight bag from under the seat. "Thanks so much," she said as Rick handed the driver a tip. She was amazed at how confident he looked, even though she guessed that he was even more panicked than she was.

They were told that they'd need to make an appointment to see the ambassador, and a meeting might not be possible for several days or even weeks depending on his schedule. When Rick explained why they were in Dublin, he was advised to go straight to the Garda, the Irish word for "police." Rick got directions to the nearest station. "Is it within walking distance?"

"Depends on what you mean. A few blocks south of here. Or you could take a taxi."

"We'll walk."

After four longish blocks, Carly was wishing she'd worn sneakers. The city was sure hopping. In a way, Dublin's mix of the old and the new and the fact that few of the buildings were more than four or five stories high reminded her of Buffalo, the one she'd lived in or across from most of her life. Finally, they found something that looked like a police station, white with blue and yellow just like the cars scooting around the streets. They entered, and once again Rick took charge, telling the lady at the desk that they'd like to report a missing person.

Surprised at his accent, she stuck a form under the window. "First, you must fill out a report."

This took all of five minutes, and after a while, a man in uniform walked them beyond the desk to a large room filled with cubicles. "Mr. and Mrs., um ... Green, I see here that you're not entirely sure your son is still in the city, only that he was spotted here over a month ago at a protest in front of the parliament building."

"Yes, that's right."

"Does he know anyone here that he might be staying with?"

"Not that we're aware of."

"He's, let's see, eighteen years of age, no longer a minor. To get Garda involved, you'll need evidence of a suspected crime. Do you have any?"

"No. But I do know the company he was working with isn't completely legit."

"And what company would that be, Mr. Green?"

"Simularity."

He raised and lowered his caterpillar eyebrows, the first sign that anything they'd said so far had made an impression. "Do you have any picture ID?"

"Yes, sir. Here's our Nate."

The officer showed Nate's graduation photo to another man, and they disappeared for a while. Carly put her hand on her husband's knee. "You're doing a great job, honey."

This reassured him, but when the detective returned, any hope the Garda would be able to help them dissolved.

"I can post a copy of this, if you'd like, but given the circumstances, the protocol is to bring the matter up with the American ambassador."

The winter sun slanted down on her husband's profile as they rested at a coffee bar on Grafton Street. It had been ages since she'd looked at Rick this closely. Deep wrinkles lined his forehead, and his sideburns had become more salt than pepper. She loved him so much, she felt a pain in her chest.

"What now?"

"I don't know, Rick."

Young Dubliners, student types, came and went. Nate would have blended right in here. "Did you notice the cop's expression change when you said Simularity?"

"Yeah. Like he'd heard the word before."

A young woman holding a pair of to-go cups turned to face her. Something about her—the hair, dark and wavy like a fairy princess, or maybe the bright blue of her eyes—sparked in Carly a sense of urgency. "Rick, there's something else I never told you because I figured you'd laugh."

"I'm listening," he said, though she could tell he was more concerned with the change he'd been given by the barista.

"Once in a while, I get a strong feeling that something big is going to happen."

"You mean like a premonition?"

"Or the Holy Spirit. A couple times I even saw something. I can't prove it, but I think I've seen at least one angel in my time."

"So, what's your angel saying now?"

"To go for a walk."

~

That close to Christmas, the Faith and Hope missionaries stuck close to home base, handing out tracts to students on holiday. At first they were hesitant to let Nate join the group, even though the night before he'd shared his updated testimony, which included how his prayers to be rescued from what might have been a gruesome death had been answered and how he'd felt the joy of the Lord more intensely than he'd ever dreamed he would at the worship service. They finally relented on the condition that he let Roisin, a seasoned evangelist, do all the talking.

After a dozen or so blow-offs, polite and otherwise, from people hanging around in Stephen's Green Park, they wandered up to a coffee shop on Grafton where Roisin said she often stopped. "How do you take yours?"

"I'm OK, thanks." He didn't want to come off like a sponge. If he'd had his wallet, he would've ordered them both a full breakfast, complete with an umbrella-covered glass of OJ for the lady.

"Listen, Nate, I watched you guzzle down two cups yesterday. What do you take?"

"Double double."

"Alrighty, then. Are you coming in?"

"No, I'll wait outside."

~

Carly tried to follow the girl with the fairy princess hair, but by the time she and Rick left the café, the street was crowded with people and she'd disappeared. Rick was content to let her take the lead, so she chose a direction they hadn't yet tried. The air took on a heavy scent, and Carly suspected they were heading to the river that she'd seen on the map. Running alongside it was a cobblestone street with a charming name, The Bachelors' Walk. "I think this is the Liffey."

"Not much of a river. Stinks, too."

"Yes, but look—over there." Down the way, a neon cross stood over the door of a storefront church. They were too far away to see more, but they picked up their pace when they could make out the sign: Faith and Hope Mission. "At least we might find some friends."

When Rick knocked on the door, a dog inside barked. They waited. The dog didn't sound happy. Rick rang the bell, and they waited some more. On the way there, her shoes pinching, Carly felt sure they were heading in the right direction, but no one appeared to be home.

"No one home," said Rick.

"Maybe we should pray."

"Carly, I haven't stopped. I'm relying on Jesus here, completely, for the first time in a long time."

After that humbling admission, he launched into a prayer for guidance. Carly thought she knew everything about this man, his pride, his stubbornness, his gullibility. But if he'd asked for help from the right people once in the last few months, he'd done so a hundred times. And he'd listened to her premonition without laughing, which, given their history, was more of a miracle than seeing an angel!

The dog's bark turned into a whine. "Amen," said Rick. "But so much for finding friends."

Carly sat on the stoop and Rick squeezed in next to her. "This building reminds me of the little West Side church Keri Ann and I went to for Bible Club about a million years ago. Just think of how many saints have walked up and down these steps throughout the years."

"Saints and sinners."

Elbows on his knees, Rick closed his eyes and prayed a second time. "Oh, Lord, I'm so sorry I've failed my son. So many times he came to me for help, and what did I do? I pushed him away—'Nate, you talk too much,' 'Drama club is for sissies,' 'Why don't you wise up and ...'" His voice broke. " ... 'and be like me.'"

Carly put her arm around him. Inside, the dog scratched at the door. "It's OK, Rick. Our son is out there. God didn't bring us this far to go home empty-handed. Let's just keep moving. An object in motion is easier to direct than one ... you know." They headed for the park.

~

It was slow-going on the mission field, with everyone focused on getting the best deals at the shops, so Roisin suggested they call it a day. Back at Faith and Hope, Mufasa looked very anxious to go for a walk. "Listen, Nate, I better take him now. Otherwise I'll not want to go out again."

"I'll come with."

"You don't need to. Why don't you take a break? You're still recovering. Give yourself time."

Nate was weak from inactivity. His legs and back, heart, and lungs all cried out from strain, but she was so beautiful. "No. Please. I want to."

"OK, Yank, whatever you say. Let's go."

~

Rick and Carly crossed the O'Connell Street Bridge, wondering what on earth could have caused the water underneath to smell so foul. Carly said, "Years of pollution."

"Remember when the Niagara used to stink so bad?"

"They really cleaned it up."

"No more 'Armpit of the East.'"

They walked awhile in silence. Rick took his wife's hand. "They honestly did clean it, didn't they? And Lake Erie, too." He balled his hands into fists. "Carly, we're going to find Nathan."

~

Roisin pulled the leash. "Easy, boy. I don't know what's gotten into him today."

"Maybe it's the falafel stand." The dog lead them toward an outdoor vendor in the middle of Stephen's Green Park.

"Mufasa, heel!" Too late—he took off, the leash flying behind him. Roisin followed, Nate trailing behind. The dog came to a full stop at a picnic table occupied by an older couple who turned around, the man stooping to scratch behind Mufasa's ears.

"Dad?" cried Nate. "Mom, is that you?"

"Son! Oh, Nate!"

CHAPTER TWENTY-SIX

Alone as usual on Christmas Eve, Keri Ann McGraw stared out her front window. The guy across the street was hanging blue lights around his porch. Late, but normal in the neighborhood she'd lived in for forty years. People here never changed. Life went by and they let it; what will be will be. But letting things happen by chance was one thing no one would ever accuse her of, even though her most important project, marrying Ricky Green, had been a failure. She'd just run out of time.

She stretched her body to full length, toes touching the end of the couch. Funny—for a while when the cancer was secretly growing, she'd never felt much pain. If she had known, she'd have asked them to take it out right away. One more way that God had failed her.

Another thing she couldn't be accused of was never having prayed. She'd prayed, alright, night and day for years. First for her mother, then for the pregnancy that never came about, then for Ricky and her. And what good did it do? The game was over, and she had lost.

What depressed her most was not being sure how her last days would look. One more thing she would be forced to leave to chance.

Her neighbor powered up his lights, which, to Keri Ann's annoyance, didn't merely brighten the darkness; they switched from blue and white to purple and pink, dazzling and blinking and driving her nuts. She yanked the curtain shut and in the process knocked over an open bottle of pills. "Darn." Bending over to pick them up was a challenge, but leaving the mess on the floor was more than she could stand. Moving into position inch by inch, she grabbed the bottle, a half-full prescription of sleeping pills, held it for a minute, then set it upright on the table.

Rick and Carly had just returned from a successful trip to Ireland, having found Nathan by what they claimed was a miracle. Apparently, some people's prayers did get answered. Rick's plan to divorce Carly was now ancient history. He'd at least been civil to Keri Ann the last time they'd spoken, and he'd acted genuinely sad that the cancer had spread.

Of course, that was after she'd done him the courtesy of coming clean with everything she'd known about Nate, even agreeing to call the old man back to confess that she'd been less than honest about the Greens and that he should help them out if he wanted to. She'd felt good about clearing the slate. But now, they could all go to hell as far as she was concerned. Since they'd found Nathan the Greens were one big happy family, seeing any of them again would mean having all that happiness pushed right up in her face.

She glanced around the living room, looking for the ghosts from her past that liked to materialize when she fell into this mood. The voice of her father telling her she'd always be a loser, or her poor mother crying at what he did to her children in the middle of the night. But the ghosts were quiet. Maybe now that she was going to die, they'd given up trying to torture her. Even the taunts of her brothers, who'd mocked her for not running away like they had, were silent at last. Or maybe she'd finally learned how to make them shut up. That was at least one battle she'd won.

She scooped up the sleeping pills remaining on the floor, brushed each one off, and lined them in neat rows on the coffee table. A dozen obedient soldiers. Pouring herself a glass of water, she swallowed every one of them.

~

That December 25, Carly couldn't remember a Christmas as full of love. All four Greens, the Worthys, Serena, and her former husband who was now back in the picture due to another miracle of forgiveness, sat around the Worthys' dining room table. Carly was bursting with praises to God.

Anya lit a pair of candles, and little Benny adjusted the cardboard centerpiece that he and the girls had made so it didn't get singed. Malcolm said the blessing over the food that all three women had brought together. Anya was responsible for the clove-studded ham and sweet potatoes, Serena for the canned cranberries, and Carly had managed to whip up a pan of her mother's famous tiramisu in record time.

"Oh, Lord, we marvel at the way you bring order out of chaos, light out of darkness, and forgiveness out of strife. We thank you from the bottom of our hearts for healing the wounds in all of our relationships, and most of all that you've brought home young Nathan."

At the mention of his brother's name, little Benny said, "Amen!" Everyone at the table laughed except Malcolm. "Excuse me, dear ones. I'm not finished."

"Preach it, brother," said Rick.

"And Lord, we also remember one person we all know who's not with us today."

Carly tensed. She assumed he was referring to Keri Ann, who'd been invited but had chosen instead to wallow in whatever comfort she got from holing up in that old house of hers. Malcolm continued, "Our sister Keri Ann McGraw, who you love as much as you do us and who's bearing a particularly heavy burden at this time. Please show her mercy, Lord. Help us not to keep a record of wrongs but to forgive like you do. We pray all these things in the name of Jesus, amen."

The glow of peace Carly had imagined hovering over their Christmas feast began to dim. She had not forgiven Keri Ann. God knows she'd tried. She'd asked forgiveness for any stubborn pride that was holding her back; she'd even fasted and prayed, hoping to flush out any sin she might not have seen. On the flight back from Ireland she'd had plenty of time to write in her journal, to read her Bible, but still has not been able to let go of her resentment toward the woman who'd caused her family so much grief.

Even knowing that poor Keri Ann had been told she might only have one year left to live made no difference.

Carly would be ashamed to admit that the news of her former rival's early demise had been a relief—it meant she no longer needed to worry about her desire for Rick interfering in their lives again. The only downside to Keri Ann dying so young was that it might make her, as someone who didn't deserve the honor, come off like some sort of martyr.

"Carly, yoo-hoo, can you pass the ham?" Serving plates were piling up in front of Carly, but suddenly she'd lost her appetite.

When the Worthys' phone rang in-between dinner and dessert, Carly expected it to be her father calling from Florida. She glanced at the clock. *Just a little after four, kind of early for him.* Plus, he'd called already to wish everyone merry Christmas. Malcolm answered. "Keri Ann?"

Stunned, Carly strained to hear what Malcolm was saying, but he handed the receiver to Anya, telling her he'd better take this one in his office.

In the meantime, only the sounds of coffee being poured and forks hitting plates could be heard in the dining room, except for Benny, who needed to be restrained from picking up the receiver again to talk to Keri Ann.

When Malcolm finally returned to the table, he asked Anya to make up a to-go plate and Rick to put on his coat because they had a Christmas errand to run.

Carly joined Anya in the kitchen. "What's this is all about?"

Overhearing the question, Malcolm took her aside. "Keri Ann took half a bottle of sleeping pills last night before, enough to kill a horse, but somehow—either because they were defective or she's experienced a miracle—she woke up about fifteen minutes ago, feeling better than she has in weeks."

Anya handed her husband a bag filled with Tupper-ware containers. "Fifteen minutes ago is almost exactly when you prayed for her."

"Indeed. She said something about having had the most amazing dream and wants us to take her over to Grand Island, to the dock in your backyard."

"Why there?" Carly washed gravy off her hands.

"You got me, sis. But I've never heard her sound so ... full of life. Thanks for the food. If it looks like we'll be a while, I'll make sure to let you—"

Carly cut him off, "Hey, Malcolm, I'd like to join you."

Malcolm looked at Rick, who shrugged his shoulders. "Why not? Let's go."

It being Christmas Day, there was no traffic to speak of and it still hadn't snowed, so the three of them got to Keri Ann's in no time. This didn't give Carly much of a chance to nail down a plan. All she knew is that if this was an opportunity to unload some guilt, she was going to give it her best. Every offence, big and little, that she'd felt toward this unfortunate person flooded her mind, too many of them to confess. And there was Keri Ann now, thin and fragile, standing on her porch in that old green parka she'd been wearing since forever.

"Merry Christmas, you guys! What's this, dinner? How thoughtful." Keri Ann took the bag of food and stashed it inside the screen door. "Whatever it is will keep. And if somebody takes it, I guess they needed it more than me. We need to get to the river before dark."

Wow, that was really something. She'd never known Keri Ann to leave anything to chance. When they were all tucked into Malcolm's car, Carly asked, "So, Keri Ann, the guys tell me you had an interesting dream."

"More like a revelation. We were having a baptism service, you know, like in the old days."

Carly remembered their last baptism distinctly. It had been the day she realized she couldn't take the isolation, the jealousy—the day it all had become too much. And then she'd seen the man in the boat.

"And there I was, hoping nobody noticed that after all those years as church secretary, I'd never given a public testimony myself. In the dream, I argued with God about this, saying that my sins were too disgusting for anyone to hear except maybe Ricky, because he knew me when I committed them—but God just smiled. Then a verse came to mind. 'All things work together for good for those who love the Lord'—it's something an old lady I knew used to say. And when I woke up, the sun was pouring in, so I knew I must have been out a long time. There was the empty bottle of pills reminding me of what I'd set out to do. You guys, I took twenty-three of them, enough to slay Goliath."

"What were they, Keri Ann?"

"Trazodone, I think. Yes, Trazadone for sleep."

Carly calculated the appropriate dosage in her head and concluded that twenty-three tabs of Trazodone could easily kill a giant. As they crossed the Grand Island Bridge, Carly noted the lack of ice in the river. *Not un-usual.* Lake ice rarely started flowing until later in spring when it clogged up the flow, swirling and drifting on its way to the falls. Today the water was clear and calm, a gentle mist hovering over the surface. Was Keri Ann bringing them there to have Rick and Malcolm baptize her? The way she felt right now, like a monster for hating on this poor woman, Carly was going to have to go right down in the freezing water with her.

When they pulled in the driveway, Carly thought to stop in the house and maybe put on some coffee to warm them up, but Keri Ann was having none of that, instead running out back to the dock. "OK, you guys, I know it sounds crazy, but I want you to dunk me."

Rick spoke up, "Do you really think that's necessary? It's below freezing."

"Listen, I should be dead right now. I'm not worried about the cold. But first, I've got a few things to say."

They huddled together at the foot of the dock as Keri Ann sometimes whispered and sometimes shouted her testimony, starting at the beginning with her anger at God for not healing her mother and for giving her a father who violated her and her brothers and left them to grow up feeling worthless and dirty. She took a deep breath and went on to acknowledge that she'd lied to Rick about being pregnant to try to get him to marry her. As she launched into her jealousy of Carly, her voice failed, and she cried silently for a minute or so.

Carly tried putting her arm around her, but she gently pushed it away, forefinger in the air. "No, I need to finish. I am sorry for lying to your son and letting him join up with those terrible people and trying to turn him against you. I was jealous of you, Carly, and I always have been."

The two women looked at each other, at a loss for words. Keri Ann broke the silence. "But God showed me something else last night. I remember Carly's crazy talk about the secret things lying at the bottom of the river, shipwrecks, skeletons, and such. And I thought, 'Who

294

really does know what's down there anyway?' We can't see what goes on under the surface, so we never really think about it. Anyway, last night I saw everything bad I'd ever done like junk piled up in the river. I hated myself for it until God fished every one of them out, let them dry, and burned them up. Then I felt so free, my feet left the ground and I started floating up like a bird, like those geese." She pointed at the sky and paused to blow her nose. "That's how I feel right now, Carly. Like I could fly."

No longer able to stop her, Keri Ann let Carly hug and squeeze her tight. Across the river the sun had just set, its last rays lining the clouds with orange and pink, the last few sparkles of light dancing on the water. The men looked on, quiet for a change, as Carly began her own confession. "Keri Ann, I know I made it worse by refusing to forgive you. I couldn't let go of my anger, or I wouldn't let go. I'm so sorry, Keri Ann. I forgive you for everything. Can you forgive me?"

"Yes! Yes! I do. Look, what's that out at the end of the dock?"

Carly looked up. "A gull."

"No, it's a dove."

~

One year later, finding enough pictures of Keri Ann to fill an easel was not hard for Carly. Her former rival had saved every photo she'd ever owned in neat boxes, complete with labels and dates. Those with Keri Ann and her mother were the best preserved, and the long gap between the brownish snapshots from the early years and pictures of Keri Ann after the passing of her father was notable. Most of them were from her days with the church, cooking, cleaning, and helping with the Sunday school. More happy times than Carly would have guessed.

Rick had been concerned that not many people would show up, which might have been the case if she'd died last Christmas like she'd originally planned. But during the year following her amazing rebirth, Keri Ann made many new friends as well as carving out peaceful spaces with old ones. Rick was even able to locate one of her brothers who'd stayed away for decades out of guilt and shame. He and Keri Ann had managed to reconcile, another beauty from ashes story, and he'd even started coming to Malcolm and Rick's home group, which was now meeting at a local theater instead of in Malcolm's living room.

Dozens of people Carly had never even seen before who claimed to be old friends from this or that support group took up seats in the back. Apparently, her former rival had lived a life totally unknown to Carly. She'd have thought Keri Ann would have her own memorial service planned to the T, but that was another miracle. After her repentance on the beach, her drive to control everything and everyone around her fell away like a cocoon off a butterfly. She even let her house get messy enough for Serena and Carly to have to come over once in a while to spruce it up.

While mingling with the guests, Carly proclaimed to whoever would listen that only God could bring four women from such different places—herself, Keri Ann, Serena, and Anya—together. It had taken many difficult years, but Carly finally gotten the friends she'd always desired.

A familiar voice caused her to turn and look. "Pop! You made it!"

"Of course I made it. What, did you think I was going to miss sending Miss McGraw off to the great ... how does that song go, 'The Great By-and-By'?"

Since her parents had moved back to Grand Island, her father had made a sincere effort to finish his sentences. "Sure, Pop, but this is a Protestant church."

"Oh ye of little faith!"

When Carly's father heard that Dunn Construction was up for sale, he'd decided to buy it. He'd made a success of one company—why not make it, you know, two? He'd also managed to recruit his son-in-law, Rick, with his undeniable leadership skills to build back the morale of the remaining staff. Along with helping Malcolm pastor their growing flock, Rick kept the men in line and secured jobs for the company. Louie had also tried to enlist Carly to work in the office, but she was enjoying her part-time job training employees at local group homes. He'd also failed to interest Nathan, who'd just finished his first semester at Bible college, where he was studying ways to use drama to spread the gospel.

"Where's my manager?"

"Up front, Pop. Looks like he's getting ready to start."

"Where's Nate?"

"At the water cooler talking to a pretty girl, Roisin. Have you met her yet, Pop? She's here on sabbatical visiting Nate."

"Not yet, but I don't want to interrupt."

"Yes, I know. We'll see. Where's Benny?"

Carly pointed to the front of the room. "Is that him up at the piano?" The Worthy girls were standing over him as he practiced a tune on the keyboard. "Sounds like the kid has an ear for music."

As her husband and his co-pastor approached the podium, the gathering took their seats. Malcolm was the first up to speak. "I want to thank all of you who came out today, especially with it being so close to Christmas, to celebrate the life of our sister Keri Ann McGraw. My relationship with Keri Ann doesn't go back that far, certainly not as far as most of you in this room. I was, however, fortunate enough to have known her during a quite astounding transformation in her life.

"Last Christmas, right about this time in the afternoon, she called me at my home to confess that she'd taken an enormous number of sleeping pills, trying to end her own life rather than wait for God's timing in the matter." This caused several members of the crowd to stir.

Malcolm cleared his throat and continued. "One thing I knew—that *everyone* knew about her was her reluctance to let others take charge over her affairs, even God. But her voice during that phone conversation had been full of joy, even wonder. She'd obviously experienced something remarkable, clearly a rebirth. You see, she tried to cause her own death but hadn't been able to—she'd been spared.

"Those of you sitting here who have not yet experienced such a profound realization of the power of God should take note. It changed her life. Hours after waking up from what she claimed was the best sleep she'd had in years, she repented of some deeply rooted sins. She said God had told her these sins were like ugly old things at the bottom of the river that He'd fished out and burned. That day she was born again, physically and spiritually. Some of you might say, 'No, she's over there

298

lying in a casket, soon to be six feet underground!' And I would counter that Keri Ann McGraw is no longer in that body. She's got a new one."

Many in the group shouted "Amen!" while Malcolm opened his Bible. "We shall be changed, from mortal to immortality, in the twinkling of an eye." He closed the book and added, "This is our promise, our inheritance as believers in Jesus Christ." More amens. He moved aside, letting Rick take over.

"Thank you, brother. As you said, most of us in this room have known Keri Ann McGraw for a long time. For me, it was all my life. We grew up next door to each other, and my earliest memories include her. We were best friends. Usually, boys choose other boys to hang around with, but the bond between Keri Ann and I had to do with something deep. See, both of our families were abusive, and even worse than that—criminal."

Rick paused to steady his voice. "Neither of our fathers knew how to treat their wives or children. You could say it was because their own fathers hadn't been exactly wonderful. Whatever the case, we put up with things at home that no child should have to. It's tough to really understand this unless you've been through it yourself, but as kids, Keri Ann and I helped each other hold it together."

Once again, he stopped, this time unable to control his emotions. When he covered his face, not holding back his sobs, Anya began playing one of the home meeting's favorite songs.

Then an extraordinary thing happened. Their son Benny, barely seven years old, got up in front of the crowd and began to sing:

There is a river that flows from deep within,
There is a fountain that frees the soul from sin.
Come to this water, there is a vast supply,
There is a river that never shall run dry.

The whole place stood up, Carly with tears streaming down her face. Saints and sinners alike joined her little boy, repeating the chorus. Carly's heart was so full, she would have easily let go of life as she'd known it on this earth and flown away right behind Keri Ann. She was ready.

Every prayer she'd ever prayed for her husband and sons had been answered. She'd been blessed beyond measure with Serena and Anya, sitting beside her. But a glimmer somewhere above the podium, where her son led the group in one last round of the song like a holy presence—one more angel, perhaps—created a sense in Carly that she was not done yet.

It was a season to embrace the now, to be filled with the Holy Spirit. Not to grow weary in well-doing or waste time listening to lying spirits, but to love God and all those he'd given her with her whole heart and soul. Lifting her hands, she praised the author of love.

End